Adam captured Susan's face in his hands, tilting it upward to meet his gaze. "I won't let anyone harm you."

Susan's breath locked in her lungs. She'd never looked into eyes that held such an intense promise of protection. "You do look like the kind of man who could take care of a woman."

Adam smiled. "To protect and serve, that's what I've been trained to do," he drawled.

Susan saw his mouth coming closer. The heat of his hands was sending a warmth through her, and the stirrings he'd woken before were growing stronger. Twinges of desire prickled within her.

And then, suddenly, she was thinking of another man who had aroused those same urges. He, too, had vowed to protect and care for her.

Terror surged through her, an old, familiar terror, and she jerked away from Adam's grasp....

Dear Reader,

The kids are on their way back to school, and that means more time for this month's fabulous Intimate Moments novels. Leading the way is Beverly Barton, with *Lone Wolf's Lady,* sporting our WAY OUT WEST flash. This is a steamy story about Luke McClendon's desire to seduce Deanna Atchley and then abandon her, as he believes she abandoned him years ago. But you know what they say about best-laid plans....

You also won't want to miss Merline Lovelace's *If a Man Answers.* A handsome neighbor, a misdialed phone call...an unlikely path to romance, but you'll love going along for the ride. Then check out Linda Randall Wisdom's *A Stranger Is Watching,* before welcoming Elizabeth August to the line. *Girls' Night Out* is also one of our MEN IN BLUE titles, with an irresistible cop as the hero. Our WHOSE CHILD? flash adorns Terese Ramin's wonderful *Mary's Child.* Then finish up the month with Kylie Brant's *Undercover Lover,* about best friends becoming something more.

And when you've finished, mark your calendar for next month, when we'll be offering you six more examples of the most exciting romances around—only in Silhouette Intimate Moments.

Yours,

Leslie J. Wainger
Executive Senior Editor

Please address questions and book requests to:
Silhouette Reader Service
U.S.: 3010 Walden Ave., P.O. Box 1325, Buffalo, NY 14269
Canadian: P.O. Box 609, Fort Erie, Ont. L2A 5X3

GIRLS' NIGHT OUT

ELIZABETH AUGUST

Published by Silhouette Books

America's Publisher of Contemporary Romance

SILHOUETTE BOOKS

ISBN 0-373-07880-3

GIRLS' NIGHT OUT

Copyright © 1998 by Elizabeth August

All rights reserved. Except for use in any review, the reproduction
or utilization of this work in whole or in part in any form by any
electronic, mechanical or other means, now known or hereafter
invented, including xerography, photocopying and recording, or in
any information storage or retrieval system, is forbidden without
the written permission of the editorial office, Silhouette Books,
300 East 42nd Street, New York, NY 10017 U.S.A.

All characters in this book have no existence outside the imagination of
the author and have no relation whatsoever to anyone bearing the same
name or names. They are not even distantly inspired by any individual
known or unknown to the author, and all incidents are pure invention.

This edition published by arrangement with Harlequin Books S.A.

® and TM are trademarks of Harlequin Books S.A., used under license.
Trademarks indicated with ® are registered in the United States Patent
and Trademark Office, the Canadian Trade Marks Office and in other
countries.

Printed in U.S.A.

ELIZABETH AUGUST

lives in western North Carolina with her husband, Doug, and her three boys, Douglas, Benjamin and Matthew. She's always wanted to write and began writing romances soon after Matthew was born.

Elizabeth does counted cross-stitching to keep from eating at night. It doesn't always work. "I love to bowl, but I'm not very good. I keep my team's handicap high. I like hiking in the Shenandoahs, as long as we start up the mountain so the return trip is down rather than vice versa." She loves to go to Cape Hatteras to watch the sun rise over the ocean. Elizabeth August has also published under the pseudonym Betsy Page.

Chapter 1

Susan Hallston sat on a step about halfway up the flight of stairs leading to the second floor of the old, well-maintained, white frame, two-story house. Her arms were wrapped around her legs so that she was in as tight a physical bundle as possible. She couldn't believe this was happening. Tears trickled down her shock-paled cheeks.

Trying to erase the images in her mind, she focused her attention on the two policemen below. The one in uniform, trim, in his late thirties with a thick head of brown hair, was Jack Connelly. The other, dressed in civilian clothing, didn't look familiar. That was unusual in as small a town as Bandits' Gorge, North Carolina, population barely six thousand. Nearly everyone looked familiar. Even if you didn't know them by name, you'd seen them in the grocery store, post office or local diner.

The stranger was in his thirties, she guessed. And definitely fit...broad shoulders, flat abdomen...a man who could hold his own in a physical confrontation. This thought caused an uneasy tremor, and she turned her full attention to his face. He wasn't handsome. There was a harshness to his features, giving them sharp definition.

Upon his arrival, he had gone directly into the living room. A few moments ago he'd emerged and was now speaking to Jack in hushed tones. For the first time, she realized he was carrying a camera. Immediately the lawmen were forgotten as the image of her neighbor, Linda, lying lifeless on the couch filled her mind. Susan began to tremble and a fresh stream of tears rolled down her cheeks. Attempting to regain control, she tightened her hold around her legs.

"Miss Hallston, Officer Connelly tells me that you live next door and that you're the one who discovered the body."

Susan's attention jerked back to the officers. "Yes."

"I know you've already been over this with Officer Connelly, but I need to be certain I've got all the facts straight."

"Yes, of course." She was surprised by how calm she sounded, then realized that part of this was due to the stranger. His voice had a soothing effect. There was just the right blend of sympathy and authority.

"Mrs. Claire Kinter, the victim's mother-in-law, was with Miss Hallston when the body was found," Jack Connelly interjected, from his post by the entrance to the living room. "But she was real shaken. I let Carol Hawkins take her over to her place. Miss Hallston insisted on staying. She said she didn't feel right about leaving Linda Kinter among strangers. I tried to explain…"

"It's all right." The man in plain clothes cut Jack short. A tiny twitch in his cheek told Susan he hadn't liked being interrupted. Immediately the soothing effect he'd had on her vanished and her inner shield came up. Jack had only been trying to be helpful. Clearly, the plainclothesman was on a power trip and experience had bred in her a strong dislike of men on power trips.

"Why don't you wait on the porch for the medical examiner? Make sure no one else enters the premises," he said to Jack, his tone polite but with the authority that made this an order.

Jack nodded and obeyed.

The officer then turned his attention back to Susan. He mounted a couple of the steps, shortening the distance between them. "I'm Detective Riley...Adam Riley."

Recognition sparked. The local newspaper, published twice weekly, had run a story on him. He'd come here after being on the New York City police force for several years. The news story had mentioned something about him being wounded and almost dying. He'd been quoted as saying he'd come here looking for a quieter, more peaceful existence.

Adam Riley took a pen from his jacket pocket, along with a small notebook. "Your name is Susan Hallston...you spell that H-a-l-l-s-t-o-n?"

"Yes." His tone was again soothing, coaxing her to trust him, but this time she wasn't fooled. He was playing a game with her. For the moment he was the good guy. But she was well aware that "good guys" could turn into "bad guys" in a wink.

Adam wasn't certain what he'd done to cause her to suddenly become defensive, but he had. He read it in her body language. She'd stiffened ever so slightly and a distrust had come into her eyes. Or maybe she had something to hide and what he saw was due to fear. Deciding not to let her know he'd noticed any change in her demeanor, he asked in the same I-want-to-be-your-friend tone he'd been using, "And your address?"

"It's 25 Willow Road." Susan motioned with her head to the left. "The house next door on the north side."

Next to the name and address, Adam jotted down a quick description. This was a skill he'd learned early in his career. It kept him from getting faces and names mixed up when an investigation began to have numerous witnesses. "Hair—brown, short. Eyes—brown. Face—pleasant, girl-next-door type. Age—late twenties. Expression—stricken at first. Became defensive or scared when questioning began." Then he said, "I realize this is difficult for you but I need to know how you came to find the body."

Susan concentrated on the events of the morning. "Claire called me around eight-thirty."

"Mrs. Claire Kinter, the mother-in-law?" Adam interrupted to clarify.

Susan was surprised that he'd remembered who Claire was. She'd been certain he was on too much of a power trip to have paid attention to what Jack had said. "Yes," she confirmed. "She called and said Linda..."

"The woman in the living room?"

That he hadn't said "*body* in the living room" caused Susan to not dislike him quite so much. At least, he was showing Linda some respect. She nodded. "Linda was supposed to pick up Claire for church at a quarter after eight. Claire had allowed her ten minutes to be late, then called here. When there wasn't an answer, Claire called me. She thought Linda might be at my place. When she wasn't, Claire got upset."

"Isn't getting upset just because someone is ten minutes late a little extreme? Mrs. Kinter could have been at another neighbor's house or running late and still in the shower. Or did she have a medical condition that would cause her mother-in-law to be fearful something had happened to her?"

"No. No medical problems. At least none any of us knew about." Susan drew a shaky breath. "But there must have been something we didn't know."

It was obvious to Adam that Miss Hallston didn't want to consider all the possibilities. He didn't have that luxury. "Did she have emotional problems?"

For a long moment, Susan stared at him as the implication behind his question sunk in. Her jaw firmed. She refused to believe Linda would have taken her own life. "No, she didn't have 'emotional problems.' She was upset yesterday but not to the extent you're implying."

"Her mother-in-law was obviously worried," Adam reminded her.

"Not that she'd take her own life," Susan insisted. "Claire was afraid Linda might have left."

"Left? Left as in being so unhappy with her mother-in-law, she went to church without her?"

"Left town." The detective's suggestion of suicide was making Susan uneasy. She told herself it was absurd, still it nagged at the back of her mind.

"Left town without telling anyone?" Sounded very much like a possible suicide, Adam silently concluded. "She must have been extremely upset for her mother-in-law to consider that possibility."

"I would have sworn she was handling everything all right. She was angry but not distraught." Guilt flowed through Susan. Could she have been wrong about Linda's mental condition?

"I'll need to know what she was upset about."

Unable to bring herself to blurt out her friend's secrets to a stranger, Susan said stiffly, "Something had happened to cause her to be angry with her husband. Claire thought Linda might have left town to give herself time to think." Tears glistened in her eyes. "Neither of us thought she was so despondent she would…" Her chin stiffened. "I refuse to believe she would…" Her voice trailed off, unable to speak the words. "It has to have been a stroke or an aneurysm. I've heard you can have an aneurysm and never know it, and then one day it just bursts and that's it," she blurted, her eyes pleading with him for confirmation that this was so.

"That can happen," Adam conceded, hoping that was what had happened. But for the moment, he had to cover all the bases. And cases involving marital problems were his least favorite. They got messy and a lot of people got hurt. On the other hand, they were usually relatively easy to solve. Statistics showed that if the victim hadn't died of natural causes or suicide, it was, most likely, the spouse who had done the deed. "Where is the husband?"

"He's on a fishing trip with a couple of the other men from the neighborhood." The thought of telling Ken about his wife's demise caused a bout of threatened nausea.

"When did they leave?"

"Friday afternoon." Susan's jaw tightened in her attempt to remain in control. "They'll be returning this afternoon. Ken's going to take this very badly. He was crazy about Linda."

"But he did something that upset his wife so badly, his mother thought she might have left town?"

"No marriage is perfect," Susan replied.

Adam experienced impatience at her resistance to telling him about whatever had happened between the husband and wife. However, he understood her attempt to respect her friend's privacy. And he didn't want to alienate her. He wanted her cooperation. Eventually he would find out what the marital difficulties were. For now, he would concentrate on the discovery of the body. "I'm really sorry I have to put you through this," he said sincerely.

Susan breathed deeply, hoping the added oxygen would help. It did a little. "Better me than Claire," she said, recalling how hysterical Claire had become.

"You were telling me how you and Mrs. Kinter came to find the body."

Susan tried to remember where she'd been in her sequence of events. "I told you she called me when she couldn't reach Linda?"

"Mrs. Kinter called here and got no answer so she called you," he repeated from his notes.

Susan nodded. "I told her I was certain Linda was simply running late and was probably in the shower and didn't hear the phone. But Claire is excitable and when she gets that way, it's hard to calm her down. She was frantic about what she was going to tell Ken if we did discover that Linda had left town.''

''And so she came over here to check on her daughter-in-law?''

Susan shook her head. ''Claire has arthritis and some days it's worse than others. Stress has a bad effect on it. Since Friday night, it's been really acting up. Her ankles are swollen and her hands and wrists as well. Plus, she's not a small woman. This morning she was barely able to get herself dressed and downstairs. She'd been counting on Linda to help her out to the car. She asked me to come over here and check.''

Adam frowned. Inconsistencies made him uneasy. ''I thought Jack said Mrs. Kinter was here with you when you found the body.''

''I came over and knocked on the door. When there wasn't an answer, I looked in the garage window. That's when I saw Linda's car and got worried myself. There was always the possibility she had slipped and fallen and injured herself too badly to get to a phone. Claire had come out to her front porch.'' Susan gestured with her head to her right. ''She lives next door in that direction. When I told her the car was still in the garage, but that I hadn't gotten an answer when I'd knocked, she insisted I use her spare key to Ken and Linda's house and go inside.''

''So, you entered alone?''

''Yes.'' Susan trembled.

Afraid she might faint, Adam came up another couple of steps to shorten the distance between them more. ''Can you describe what you did upon entering?''

''I called out from the open doorway. There was no answer so I stepped inside. Everything looked normal.'' A more violent tremble shook her. ''Then I glanced into the living room. I saw an arm dangling off the couch. I assumed it was Linda's. I crossed to the couch. She looked like she was sleeping, but I knew something was wrong.'' Susan hugged her knees until it felt as if the circulation was going to be cut off as she recalled looking down at her friend still clothed in the slacks and shirt she'd been wearing the day before, her face a pasty gray, her long naturally blond hair arranged around her head like a halo. "I reached down and touched her, shook her shoulder a little and said her name. She was cold. That's when Claire screamed. She'd managed to hobble over and follow me inside. I hadn't even noticed. I'd been so shocked to discover Linda…like that.''

"Other than shaking Linda Kinter, did either of you move the body or touch anything?''

Susan thought for a moment, then said, "No. Claire looked as if she was going to faint. My concern for her brought me out of my shock. I got her to a chair in the hall and dialed 911 from the telephone in the kitchen. Jack…Officer Connelly arrived almost immediately. The ambulance arrived very soon after that. But the paramedics didn't stay. I heard Jack telling them he didn't want them disturbing anything and one of them saying that she'd obviously been dead awhile so there was no use in them hanging around.''

"Did you or Mrs. Kinter return to the living room?''

Susan shook her head in the negative. "Officer Connelly said he didn't think we should. Claire was crying and getting more and more hysterical. That's when I called Carol to come get her." Her gaze again went to the entrance to the living room. "I didn't want to leave Linda alone. It didn't seem right. Officer Connelly said I'd be out of the way here on the stairs.''

Jack Connelly suddenly stuck his head in the door. "The medical examiner is here,'' he announced, then stepped aside to allow Dr. Miller—tall, lean, gray haired, in his seventies—to enter. Susan experienced a sense of relief. Dr. Miller, she knew, would treat Linda's body with respect. He'd been practicing medicine in Bandits' Gorge since before she'd been born. He had, in fact, delivered her and was her family doctor. He was also Linda's doctor.

"Susan, are you all right?" he asked seeing her and heading in her direction.

"I don't know," she answered honestly. "I can't believe this is happening."

The doctor cast Adam a disapproving glance.

"I have a job to do," the detective returned curtly.

Doctor Miller's scowl deepened. "There was no reason for you to keep her closeted in here. You could have at least taken her outside in the fresh air and sunshine to question her."

Susan was still not ready to like Detective Riley but she didn't want him getting into trouble because of her. "I wanted to stay. I didn't want Linda left to strangers."

The doctor cast Adam a look of apology, then his voice and features softening noticeably, he turned back to Susan. "I'll take care of her now."

A fresh wave of guilt that she hadn't been here when Linda needed help caused Susan to hesitate.

The strain on her face told Adam she couldn't take much more. "Mrs. Kinter will be taken care of now. It's time for you to go home." It was an order. Afraid she might fall or even faint when she rose, he held his hand out to her.

Susan ignored him.

When she continued to remain immobile, Dr. Miller said with fatherly coaxing, "Linda has already gone on to a better place. Only her shell remains. You go home. It's time for me to perform my final duties."

As he started into the living room, Adam's gaze swung to him. "I'll need to gather evidence and take more pictures before you go in there."

Dr. Miller stopped dead in his tracks and turned back, a stunned expression on his face. "Jack said she was dead. He didn't say you suspected she'd been murdered."

"I'm not sure what happened here," Adam replied. "But unless you can tell me differently, she looks as if she were too healthy to have died from natural causes, which means I have to treat this death as questionable."

"She kept herself in very good shape," the doctor confirmed.

Susan considered insisting on staying. Linda was a modest person. She wouldn't have liked these men gawking at her. Not even the doctor. Even more, she hated having her picture taken unless she was looking her best. But then Linda wasn't going to care anymore about anything, Susan reminded herself. Suddenly the need for fresh air grew too strong to resist. She started to rise, realized her legs were more unsteady than she'd thought and accepted the policeman's aid. She didn't like needing a man's support but she also didn't like the idea of falling down the stairs.

The contact seemed to burn. Startled, she reasoned her shock-cooled skin was causing her to overreact.

Adam had been concentrating on the doctor, but as Susan's hand grasped his, a current of energy shot up his arm, jerking his attention back to her. He'd never experienced so intense a reaction to a mere touch. Helping her to her feet, he had to fight the urge to slip his arm around her waist, not because he thought she needed the added support but because he wanted to increase his hold on her. So maybe my swearing off women has been going on too long, he mocked himself. He wasn't ready to trust one, but a date now and then was clearly becoming necessary.

Susan released her hold on him the moment she was on solid ground; still the heat lingered.

"Would you like me to walk you home?" the doctor offered.

"No. I'll be fine." She cast a final glance toward the

living room. It was going to take time to get over this. Suddenly she couldn't stand being inside any longer. In the next instant she was out in the sunlight.

Standing on the long, wide, roofed porch, her hands resting on the wooden railing, she let her gaze travel up and then down the quiet, tree-lined street. All of the homes were older structures built in the thirties. They were mostly large and two-storied like Linda's, with roofed porches. Some were smaller, but all had well-kept yards, many with flower gardens lining the walks and fronting the porches. The sun was bright. There were only a few white fluffy clouds in the sky. The sweet scent of lilac was in the air. This was not a day on which to die.

Desperate for any diversion that would erase the image of Linda's lifeless body, she remembered the test papers she'd been grading when Claire called. Her students would be expecting them back tomorrow. A part of her argued that it was callous of her to think about getting back to her daily activities when Linda lay dead. Another part—the part that wanted to escape from the horror of the image that haunted her—reminded her that the summer session was short. If she got behind in her grading, she would never catch up.

Her legs carried her in a stiffly robotic gait to her own porch. But, once there, she couldn't make herself go inside. The test papers forgotten, she sank onto the porch swing. Linda was only twenty-seven, a year younger than herself. It didn't seem right that she could be dead. Clutching one of the throw pillows in her arms, she began to swing slowly. She knew from a first-aid class she'd once taken that shock victims sometimes rocked back and forth. Now she understood why. There was something very comforting in the movement.

"What's going on?"

Susan looked up to discover Barbara Reynolds mounting the short flight of steps to join her.

The thirty-two-year old, slightly plump brunette, frowned with concern. "Are you all right? You look awful."

"Linda's dead." The stunned look on Barbara's face made Susan wish she'd been a little more subtle but she was not in the mood for subtleties.

"Dead! How?"

Susan shrugged. "I don't know how. She looked like she'd simply laid down to take a nap and died in her sleep."

Barbara sank into the nearby rocking chair. "Do you think this has anything to do with Friday night? You know...stress? Maybe finding out the truth about Ken's past was too much and she had a heart attack or a stroke?"

"I don't know. I've heard of women her age having strokes. Or it could even have been an aneurysm." Susan assured herself it had to be one of those two things or some other physical defect. She couldn't face the other possibility the detective had suggested. It carried too much guilt.

The July sun was getting higher in the sky and, although it was still morning, the day was already hot. Barbara raked her fingers through her thick mass of short curly hair, sweeping the sweat-dampened locks away from her face. Abruptly an uneasiness spread over her features as if a new and worrisome thought had just occurred to her. "Who's going to tell Ken?"

"The police or Claire."

Barbara frowned at her. "The police are too impersonal and, if I know Claire, she's a basket case. She never handles traumas well." Her gaze leveled on Susan. "I think you should be the one. You've known him all your life." Rising, she glanced at the house Susan had so recently left. "Life is peculiar. Linda was always looking down her nose at me because she didn't think I exercised enough, and I'll admit I eat a few more sweets than I should. But you only live once. And look at which one of us is still walking around.'' Barbara gave a small snort as if to say ''Well, I won that round,'' then left.

Susan watched the brunette go down the street past the two Kinter houses, then around the corner. Barbara's less than sympathetic attitude had rankled her, but she'd been too numbed by strain to respond. Besides, Barbara's behavior wasn't all that unexpected. Susan had always sensed an underlying competition between Barbara and Linda. There had never been anything overt. Publicly, they were both civil to each other. However, behind Barbara's back Linda had made some unkind remarks regarding the brunette's weight. Susan had never understood this tinge of animosity between the two neighbors. Both were normally very tolerant of others.

''She's right. You're the one who's going to have to tell Ken.''

Susan let out a small shriek of surprise as her front screen door was flung open and Carol Hawkins stepped out onto the porch.

''I didn't mean to frighten you,'' Carol apologized briskly. ''I've got Claire resting in my guest room. Thought I should come by and see what's going on.''

Watching the fifty-four-year-old divorcée ease her tall, lanky frame into the rocking chair Barbara had so recently occupied, Susan drew a calming breath. She knew how Carol had gotten into her house. Carol's property backed onto hers. The woman, showing her usual disregard for the privacy of those she considered friends, had simply entered through the unlocked back door. When she'd discovered Susan wasn't home, she'd come through the house and out the front. ''I don't see why I've been elected to tell Ken.''

Carol frowned. ''I certainly can't. Besides, you two grew up together. You were even childhood sweethearts.''

Susan issued an impatient sigh. ''I thought I put that rumor to rest years ago,'' she grumbled. ''We were *never* childhood sweethearts.''

Carol screwed her features into a self-effacing grimace. "I really should stop bringing up the past. It only serves to irritate people and cause trouble."

"I'll second that," Susan replied caustically.

Carol's expression turned to one of self-righteous indignation. "But husbands shouldn't keep secrets from their wives. Eventually everything comes to light." A malevolent gleam entered her eyes. "And then they should have to pay till they're bled dry."

Grateful for anything to think about other than what was happening next door, Susan asked, "And how is your ex?"

Carol grinned dryly. "Working his butt off to pay my alimony and keep his new young wife satisfied." Her expression turned bitter. "I could have sworn every romantic bone in that man's body died when he turned forty. All he ever talked about was work. Now I know why... Little Miss Redhead with the swivel hips. I was home cooking, cleaning and raising his kids, and he was doing a nightly rumba on the office sofa with his secretary."

Actually, Harold Hawkins' extracurricular activities had taken place in a mountain cabin he'd purchased in his secretary's name. Susan knew this because Carol had showed her and half the neighborhood the pictures the private detective had taken of Harold and Tammy there. Some had been embarrassingly explicit. After seeing Harold in the all together, Susan had a hard time wondering how Tammy could be attracted to the man. But then, he had acquired a great deal of wealth during the past years. As president of the bank, he'd been first in line to buy up defaulted mortgages on property at a bargain price. And his investments had paid off.

Carol abruptly laughed. "I'll never forget the look on his face when my lawyer handed him the list of all assets he thought I didn't know about. Did he think I was completely stupid? I knew the combination to that safe in his study. I guess he just didn't think I had the brains to go through all those papers and figure out what they meant. Or, maybe he thought he'd gotten them out of the house before I thought about doing that.'' She smiled triumphantly. ''Men always underestimate women. They...'' Carol's voice faded as her attention was captured by the activity next door.

Susan followed the direction of Carol's gaze to see Detective Riley and Jack Connelly descending from the porch carrying a long dark bag. Dr. Miller preceded the lawmen to his station wagon and opened up the back.

Not wanting to watch but unable to pull her gaze away, Susan sat numbly as the men loaded the bag into the back of the vehicle.

''I can't believe they carried her out in a bag!'' Carol fumed. ''You'd think they'd do something more dignified like use a gurney with a sheet draped over the body. It's a good thing Claire or Ken isn't here to see this.''

Susan had been thinking the same thing.

In the next instant, Carol shrugged off her anger. ''But I suppose it really doesn't matter to Linda.'' She turned back to Susan. ''Do they know yet how she died? Claire said she looked as if she'd simply fallen asleep and hadn't woke up.''

Thinking of Linda in that bag had caused another wave of nausea. Swallowing it back, Susan said, ''No. Not yet.''

For a moment Carol was silent, then scowling disparagingly, she said bluntly, ''Surely she wasn't the type to take her own life.''

''Why would you even think that?'' Susan demanded, the idea of suicide again causing an uneasy curl of guilt to weave through her.

''I don't really,'' Carol said. ''Actually now that I've said it aloud, it sounds totally absurd.''

''Yes, it does,'' Susan returned curtly. ''It has to have been an aneurysm or a stroke or something like that. She was angry...furious, but she wasn't distraught.''

Carol again glanced toward the doctor's car and frowned cynically. "I can't believe she'd get herself so worked up. It isn't as if she had to face what either you or I faced." Interest suddenly sparked in her eyes. "Looks like we're going to have company."

Susan saw Detective Riley approaching and said a silent prayer that he'd have some answers for them.

Mounting the porch steps, Adam extended a hand toward Carol and introduced himself. "I'm Adam Riley."

"Carol Hawkins." She introduced herself as she accepted the handshake.

Her hold, Adam observed was firm as was the set of her jaw. Strong woman, he noted, and defiant. "Mrs. Kinter is at your house?"

"Yes. She's resting right now." Carol's gaze traveled appraisingly over him.

Embarrassed by Carol's scrutiny of the policeman, Susan promised herself that at the next opportunity, she was going to have a serious talk with the woman. Ever since her divorce, Carol had developed a habit of eyeing men in the same way lechers eyed pretty women. She did it to make them squirm. "Just giving them a little of their own medicine," she'd told Susan. But this time she'd gone too far. Linda was dead and Carol was treating the detective as if he were fresh meat ready for the slaughter.

"I told her I'd come over here and find out what was going on." Carol's gaze, which had traveled swiftly down his athletic frame then worked its way slowly upward, had now reached his face. "How did Linda die?"

Adam felt as if he'd been sized up for market. Normally that would have angered him, but Carol Hawkins was so flagrantly obvious, he found her behavior almost comical, almost. "We won't know that until after the autopsy. Do either of you know if she had been taking any medication?"

"She wouldn't even take an aspirin." Carol spoke up

immediately. "She was one of those health nuts. If she had a headache, she practiced yoga or some other relaxing technique to stop it. For muscle aches, she simply exercised more." She frowned with distaste. "No pain, no gain. That was her motto. If you ask me, that shows definite masochistic tendencies." Abruptly she flushed. "That was just a joke. But I suppose it wasn't very appropriate considering the circumstances."

At least she realized she'd crossed the line that time, Susan thought.

"You didn't like Mrs. Kinter?" Adam asked.

"I didn't dislike her," Carol replied. "But she did get on my nerves the way she catered to Ken. She worshiped the ground he walked on. I tried to warn her that it was stupid to become so thoroughly enamored of a man. She accused me of being bitter and callous because of my divorce. I told her that she should learn from what happens to others." Carol's expression softened. "But I am truly sorry she's dead."

Carol Hawkins was an angry woman, Adam noted.

Susan found herself studying the detective. In the sunlight, she could see his features more plainly and while his voice still carried the same friendly, coaxing quality, she noticed that there was nothing warm and cozy about his eyes. They were cool and shuttered. "Wouldn't Dr. Miller know if she had been taking any medication?" she asked. "He was her doctor."

Adam turned to her. Her color had returned but the strain lines in her face remained. "Some people take pills that aren't always prescribed."

Understanding flashed across Carol's features. "What you really want to know is, did she use drugs," she blurted, then laughed. "No way. Not Miss I'd-Never-Mess-With-My-Body. A little wine was the only liquor she ever touched, and she only did that because of some studies she read that said people lived longer and had less

stomach cancer…or maybe it was some other cancer…"
She shrugged. "I'm not real big on details where medical
discoveries are concerned. They're constantly popping up
and then being discredited. I figure that when your time
comes, it comes. Anyway, she'd read somewhere that a
little red wine in moderation was supposed to be good for
you."

Adam took a moment to jot down some notes. It was a
ploy he used to give himself thinking room when trying
to decide how to proceed. The Hawkins woman was getting on his nerves. A woman, in what should have been
the prime of her life, was dead and this neighbor was
shooting barbs at her corpse. Besides, he preferred questioning people on a one-to-one basis. It helped him sort
out the facts from the rumors. He looked up, his expression
official but polite. "I was wondering if I could speak to
Miss Hallston alone?"

"You've got a nice way of saying get lost." Carol
smiled flirtatiously. "If I were twenty years younger I'd
enjoy having you hanging around our neighborhood for a
while. As it is, I'm not a young chicken any longer. Susan,
however, is and—" Carol's gaze again raked over the policeman "—I hope she appreciates the view."

Through the years, Susan had learned never to be surprised by what came out of the woman's mouth. But before
Carol discovered her husband's infidelity, at least in the
presence of strangers, she'd behaved with decorum. Now,
however, whatever she thought was in danger of spilling
out at any time. Nonetheless, Susan was still shocked.
"Carol, really," she snapped reprimandingly.

Carol cast her a righteous glance. "Policemen like honesty. Now I need to get back and check on Claire." Be-
stowing a final speculative smile on Adam, she said, "It's
been nice meeting you, Detective." Then her gaze shifted
back to Susan and her voice took on authority. "And you
will have to be the one to tell Ken." Reaching for the

doorknob, she added, "I'll just run back through your house."

Adam was acutely aware of the quiet here in Bandits' Gorge. In the big city, there was so much noise, it covered conversations. Here, however, if someone wanted to eavesdrop, anything said on an open porch could be heard easily from several steps away. "Perhaps we could go inside?"

Susan had been frowning at Carol's departing back. Didn't the woman have any sense of decency? "Carol used to show better taste before her divorce," she muttered, rising from the swing.

Adam experienced a sting of insult. Startled by the sharpness of his reaction to her words, for one brief instant cynical defiance showed in his eyes.

Realizing he'd misinterpreted her words, Susan flushed. "I didn't mean that the way it came out. Carol's right. You're interesting looking. Certainly more so than most of the men around here." Silently, she groaned. She'd said way too much. He could think she was flirting and she wasn't. "I just meant that this isn't the appropriate time for looking." Feeling as if she'd put a second foot in her mouth rather than extricating the first, she clamped her lips together, rose and preceded the officer into the house.

Behind her, Adam found himself smiling crookedly. She was cute when she got flustered.

Susan nodded toward the living room. "Make yourself comfortable." Her mouth felt like cotton. She needed something to drink and a moment alone to collect her thoughts. She was beginning to emulate Carol…letting words flow out of her mouth without thinking first. Continuing to the kitchen she asked over her shoulder, "Would you like some iced tea?"

"Yes, thanks." Adam ignored her directions to wait in the living room. Following her, he made a quick survey of the surroundings. What he saw of the house was neatly kept, clean. The furniture was old but in good repair. "Do you mind?'' he asked, not waiting for an answer but taking a chair at the kitchen table. He wanted to make this interview seem as informal as possible. The more at ease people were, the more they talked. And in most people's minds, kitchens made interviews seem much less intimidating than living rooms.

"No, not at all.'' She had to admit she preferred this room to the living room. She felt her grandmother's presence more strongly here than anywhere else in the house, and right now she needed that bit of comfort. The detective's questions about Linda taking drugs had shaken her. "Did you find something in Linda's house that makes you think she might have had some drugs around?'' she asked bluntly.

Adam wasn't ready to reveal all he'd found at the Kinter house. "I have to cover all the bases.''

Susan chose to believe that meant he hadn't; that he was simply being thorough. Finding out that Linda had been secretly taking drugs and had overdosed was more than she could handle at the moment. For the umpteenth time she pictured her friend as she'd been the last time she'd seen her alive. Linda had not been despondent. "Dr. Miller couldn't even give you a hint about what might have happened?''

Adam saw the strain on her face increasing and knew she was fighting to hold on to the belief that her friend had died from natural causes. However, the prescription bottle he'd found in the kitchen suggested otherwise. Still, until he had proof, he would give Linda Kinter the benefit of the doubt. He also found himself disliking the thought of distressing Susan any further but he had questions that had to answered. "Mrs. Hawkins mentioned that Mrs. Kinter was not a heavy drinker, but there was an empty wine bottle on the coffee table and only one glass.''

"Maybe she'd been drinking out of the bottle for some time and just finished it off last night,'' Susan suggested.

Considering the day Linda had had, she could easily understand how Linda might have drunk the whole bottle in one sitting, but she wasn't ready to tell the policeman that.

"Maybe," he conceded. "There was also an open container of homemade fudge on the coffee table. I've heard that some women turn to chocolate when they're depressed."

He was again asking her about Linda's state of mind. Her jaw firmed. "And some women simply like the taste. Besides, isn't chocolate supposed to cause a person to feel better…stimulate the endorphins or something like that?"

Time to stop playing softball, Adam told himself. "You mentioned that there was a problem between Mrs. Kinter and her husband. When I went through the house, I found that a drawer in the desk, in what I assume was Mr. Kinter's study, had been pried open. The contents were scattered around on the floor."

Susan breathed a tired sigh. No sense in playing this cat-and-mouse game any longer. She sank down onto the chair across from him. "Linda pried open the drawer. Ken doesn't know anything about this yet." Resting her chin in her hands, she faced him glumly. "I have come to the conclusion that girls' nights out should be outlawed. Without men or children around, some women drink too much and tell secrets that shouldn't be told. Of course, normally anything Carol knows eventually sees daylight no matter whether she's been drinking or not."

"You're referring to Mrs. Hawkins?" Adam clarified.

Susan nodded, wishing she could turn back the clock. "It was Friday night. Barbara Reynolds had suggested that since The Backyard Society was entirely husbandless…"

"The Backyard Society?"

"Myself, Ken and Linda Kinter, Claire Kinter, Ray and Pauline Carter, Ted and Barbara Reynolds and Carol Hawkins. We've been neighbors a long time and have sort of christened ourselves The Backyard Society because our backyards all face each other.''

"I'll need the addresses of the others.''

"To be honest, I'm not certain what their addresses are. You know Ken and Linda live in the house next door.'' She paled. Linda didn't ''live'' there anymore. She pushed that thought from her head. ''Then there's Claire's house. That's the last one facing Willow. The Carters' house is next. It fronts on Oak. Then comes the Reynolds' house. It faces Spruce Street. Carol Hawkins' house is right behind mine. The two houses between Carol's and the Reynolds' belong to the Olivers and the McFays.''

"The Olivers and McFays aren't part of your little social circle?''

"No. We've invited them to barbecues but they generally don't come. The Olivers are a young couple, both lawyers. They just moved in a couple of years ago. Deborah, the wife, is from around here. Her parents own a farm just outside of town and her brother and sister both still live here. Between their careers and her family, she and Trevor are kept too busy to have time for us. The McFays have lived here for—'' Susan paused to calculate ''—eight years, I think. Both also have a lot of family living in town and spend their time socializing with them and friends from the country club. They're avid golfers.''

The members of the tight little social group played through her mind. ''I guess the rest of us have sort of clung together because we really don't have any relatives close by. We're sort of surrogate family.'' She stopped and corrected herself. ''That isn't entirely true. Ray Carter's parents live in town but he doesn't get along with them. They've never liked his wife, Pauline.'' Abruptly, she clamped her mouth shut. She was rattling on, some would even call it gossiping. This wasn't like her.

"I need to get this straight.'' Adam looked down at his

notes. "It's Ken Kinter, Ray Carter and Ted Reynolds who are on the fishing trip?"

"Yes," Susan replied.

"And it was their wives plus you and Carol Hawkins and Claire Kinter who went out to dinner Friday night?"

"That's right."

"And it was while you were all out that Carol Hawkins revealed some secret that caused Mrs. Kinter to pry open the desk drawer?"

Susan shook her head as her mind went back to Friday night. "Not at the restaurant. It was afterward when we were at the Reynolds' house. Barbara likes to tie one on occasionally and she'd stocked up on beer and wine. After a while the subject of children came up. Barbara knew she was getting drunk and she started complaining about how difficult Saturday was going to be. She said something to the effect that she knew she was going to have a hangover and taking care of two kids wasn't going to be any fun. Linda got angry and said Barbara should feel lucky to have children. Barbara said she did...most of the time. Then she made some crack about people who don't have kids shouldn't criticize those who do."

Susan fought back a fresh wave of nausea. "Barbara's remark was a really low blow. We all knew Linda wanted to have children badly. But she hadn't been able to get pregnant. I wanted to change the subject but I didn't have a chance. Before I could say anything, Linda announced she'd contacted a fertility specialist. She said she hadn't told Ken yet. She didn't think he'd like the idea of going. That was when Carol opened her mouth. 'Ken doesn't need to go,' she said. 'He's already proved his bullets are loaded.'"

Susan massaged her temples and wished she'd clamped a hand over Carol's mouth. "After Carol's declaration, you could have heard a pin drop. Then Linda asked Carol what she meant. Both Claire and I were scowling at Carol, daring her to say anything. It was a stupid reaction but we were a little drunk. Anyway, it put Carol on the defensive. That's always dangerous. There's no telling what she'll say or how undiplomatically she'll say it. She just blurted out that Ken had been married before and there had been a child."

"Linda Kinter had no idea her husband had been married before?"

"No. I doubt more than a handful of people even remember it ever happened. The marriage didn't take place here in Bandits' Gorge, and Ken and his wife never lived here. In fact, as far as I can recall, they only came to visit once. They weren't married very long. Maybe a year. Maybe less. The only reason I even remembered the marriage is because I've known Ken all my life. This house belonged to my grandmother and he was born and raised in the house his mother lives in. When his son was born, Claire went to Raleigh to help and brought back pictures. But after the marriage ended, she never spoke of it or her grandson again. I know Ken ordered her not to. We all figured the divorce must have been pretty awful. Anyway, out of respect for his feelings, those of us who knew never mentioned it, either."

"Until Friday night."

Susan nodded. "Carol has lived here since before Ken was born. And she never forgets anything. Sometimes it gets buried at the back of her mind but eventually it pops to the forefront. The problem is knowing when that's going to happen and hoping that she'll be discreet." Susan frowned. "Since her divorce, *Carol* and *discretion* are two words that don't usually occur in the same sentence, but I was shocked that she told Linda about Ken's former marriage. I'm sure Claire had specifically asked her not to. They've always been good friends and Carol usually respects Claire's requests."

"You said you also knew about the marriage. Had

Claire Kinter asked you to remain silent on the subject as well?''

"It was Ken who asked my grandmother and me to keep his secret. We both warned him that he should tell Linda but he said that his first marriage was a part of his life he wanted to put behind him. Neither of us felt it was our business to tell her. Besides, we all thought he wasn't having anything to do with his ex-wife or their child. That was part of the divorce agreement.''

"He had no visitation rights?''

She could see he was thinking that the court must have judged Ken to be a terrible person to have denied him fatherly privileges. ''It wasn't the way it sounds. From what I recall of the one time I saw Ken and his wife...Ruth...yes, that was her name. Anyway, from what I recall of seeing them together, I would swear he adored her. And from Claire's description of his actions at the time of the birth, he loved his son as well. Claire said he absolutely hovered over Ruth and the child, driving the nurses crazy and after they got home, he would sit and rock the baby for hours.''

Susan's expression darkened. ''It was his father-in-law who was the cause of all the trouble...that, and the fact that Ruth was used to being pampered. Her father is extraordinarily wealthy. He was certain Ken was marrying his daughter for her money and forbid her to go through with the wedding. But she was already pregnant, and I honestly thought she was as in love with Ken as he was with her. Anyway, as soon as the marriage vows were exchanged, her father disowned her. However, as it turned out, she didn't like living poor. Ken was still in college at the time and although his parents helped as much as they could, the couple had very little. Very soon after the baby was born, she struck a deal with her father. She would divorce Ken and she and the baby would move back into her father's home. Ken was not to see either her or the child again. Ken wanted what was best for his son. He knew he couldn't provide him with all the advantages the wife's father could.''

Adam recalled the photographs that had been among the letters and other papers scattered on the study floor. ''It would appear that neither he nor his ex-wife lived up to this agreement.''

''Apparently not.'' In her mind's eye, Susan saw Linda, her eyes red from crying, coming into Susan's kitchen the day before and throwing the pictures of Ken, a rather plain-looking woman she recognized as his former spouse and a child in various stages of growth, over her kitchen table. In a couple of the photos, Ken, the woman and child were obviously on a picnic near a lake. In another they were at a zoo. In another they were in the mountains. Claire was even in some of them, looking the part of the proud grand-parent. ''In a way, it was a relief to know Ken was keeping in contact with his son. It always bothered me that he could just walk away from his child even if it was for the boy's sake.'' Susan fought back a flood of angry tears. ''But Linda should never have been allowed to find out like she did.'' Her chin trembled. ''It was probably the shock that caused her to have a stroke or the aneurysm to burst,'' she added, determined to cling to the belief that Linda had died of natural causes.

Suicide was beginning to look more and more like the answer, Adam thought but kept this to himself. ''How long were Ken and Linda Kinter married?''

Susan forced herself to concentrate harder. ''They were married the year before my grandmother died. That would make it a little more than six years.''

''You said Mrs. Kinter pried open the drawer. How can you be so certain she was the one?''

''She brought some of the letters and the photos over here for me to look at.''

''When was that?''

"Around ten yesterday morning. I was trying to grade papers." Susan stopped herself from adding that the hangover from the night before had been causing her head to pound and the words on the test papers to blur. "She came barging through the front door. That wasn't like her. She always knocked and waited to be invited in. She said she hadn't been able to sleep, then she'd remembered the locked drawer in Ken's study. She'd pried it open and found the letters and pictures. She dropped them in front of me and said, 'Now I know what Ken was really doing on those business trips he used to take to Maine.'"

"How would you describe her reaction to this discovery?"

"She felt betrayed."

"Was she depressed?"

Susan refused to follow where he was leading. "She was angry...a little at those of us who hadn't told her the truth before, but mostly at Ken. If you'd seen the fury in her eyes, you'd know. I remember thinking that I'd hate to be in Ken's shoes when he got home." Her jaw tightened. "She didn't take her own life. Her death has to have been from some natural cause. I'm sure her blood pressure was off the scale."

"Maybe," Adam conceded noncommittally, suicide remaining at the top of his list. Hating the pain he saw in her eyes, he reached across the table and touched her arm in a comradely gesture. "It'll be all right. No matter what happened, you can't blame yourself."

"I should have insisted she stay with me for the night," Susan said stiffly, fighting to keep her tears in check.

"You are not to blame for what happened," he repeated.

She looked into the brown depths of his eyes. They held a warmth that seemed to draw her in. Memories she'd pushed to the dark recesses of her mind suddenly flashed to the forefront and she jerked free of his gaze and his touch. "I'm really tired. If you're finished with your questions, I'd like to rest."

Her sudden withdrawal startled Adam. It was as if he'd sparked fear in her. More likely, she's appalled that I'd come on to her at a time like this, he mused dryly. It did seem callous on his part. Even he was shocked. He'd felt sympathy for witnesses before but he'd never wanted to take them in his arms to comfort them and that was exactly what he wanted to do with Miss Susan Hallston. Better get out of here before I make a complete fool of myself, he decided. "Thanks for the drink," he said and left.

Pushing the images of the past from her mind, Susan watched him leave. She knew he thought Linda had taken her own life. The thought brought a renewed rush of guilt. If that was the case, she should have seen it coming and stopped her. She dropped her head into her hands as tears trickled down her cheeks. None of this seemed real but she knew if she pinched herself, she'd feel it.

Chapter 2

Pauline Carter crossed her long shapely legs and maneuvered a strand of sweat-dampened auburn hair back behind her ear with a bloodred acrylic-nail-tipped finger. "They should be home soon," she said, breaking the silence hanging over the gathering of women seated in lawn chairs under the elm tree in her front yard.

Susan had been staring down the street in the direction from which the fishermen would come. The heat seemed more oppressive than usual. She blinked and shifted her gaze to the left. The Carter house was on the corner. From where she sat, Susan could see up the street in the direction of her and the Kinters' homes. Detective Riley's car was again parked in front of Linda and Ken's place. She'd seen him go inside a while back and wondered what he was doing there. He'd had Officer Connelly seal the house after the body was removed so that no one could enter. Now he was back.

Just knowing he was so close, had an unnerving effect on her. After he'd left her house, his image had remained sharp and clear…the cut of his jaw, the shape of his mouth, his penetrating brown eyes. She'd even recalled a small scar that ran through his right eyebrow. It had been a long time since a man had made such a strong impression on her. A cold sweat had broken out on her brow as old memories had suddenly impinged. Better safe than sorry, she'd told herself and pushed the detective from her mind. Now he was on it again, his brown eyes taunting her to take a chance. A cold chill ran through her. She wasn't ready yet.

"Susan, you're going to have to tell Ken." This time it was Carol Hawkins who spoke.

Susan jerked her attention back to the group of women. They were all looking at her expectantly.

"I just can't tell him," Claire said.

Although not quite sixty, Claire's arthritis normally made her look much older than her true age. And, today with the strain of Linda's death weighing on her, her stocky five foot, eight inch frame seemed to be even more bent than usual. Knowing that this was going to be enough of an ordeal for her without her having to tell her son about his wife's death and realizing that no one else in the group would accept the grim task, Susan said resignedly, "All right, I'll tell him."

"And I think I should make myself scarce," Carol added. "He's probably going to be angry with me. I wouldn't want him saying things to my face that he'll regret later and I won't be able to forgive."

"It might be best if you weren't here," Claire agreed and glances exchanged among the others seconded this.

Carol rose. Defiance showed on her face as her gaze traveled over the group. "Men and their secrets. Ken should have told her," she snapped, then stalked off in the direction of her house.

"Everyone has their secrets. Both men and women." Pauline frowned down at her carefully manicured nails, then looked up and grinned wryly. "And I don't plan to ever let Carol learn any of mine."

Barbara scowled. "This isn't a joking matter. Ken's going to be very upset."

Pauline's gaze swung to her. "Who said I was joking?"

"I can't believe Linda is dead," Claire murmured for the hundredth time, tears again threatening to flow.

A bird's chirp caused Susan to glance upward. Out of the corner of her eye she glimpsed Angel Carter, Pauline's sixteen-year-old daughter, at an upstairs window. The high school junior was a beautiful girl by anyone's standards. From her father's side of the family she'd inherited an early maturing, curvaceous figure. Her green eyes, good complexion and long, thick, wavy auburn hair she'd gotten from her mother. The mother's and daughter's facial features were also similar except that Angel's were more finely sculptured adding a delicacy to her appearance. But that delicacy was a trick of nature, a natural facade. Angel, Susan knew, had a will of steel.

She didn't particularly like Angel. The teenager was sly and spoiled. Susan frowned at herself. She was being overly critical. Yes, Angel was spoiled but that wasn't her fault. Her father and mother doted on her. They bragged about her constantly and bought her whatever they could afford of the things she wanted. But they didn't let her run wild. Her father was a firm believer in curfews.

As for the slyness, most likely it wasn't really slyness but a standoffishness born from the usual distrust of adults all teenagers seemed to go through. Feeling guilty about the unkind thoughts she'd had about the girl, Susan smiled up at her. After all, a death so close to home had to be a traumatic experience for a child that age.

Angel smiled back lopsidedly giving the impression she thought the women below were silly things to be held in contempt. Then suddenly she was gone.

Susan's smile curved to a frown as she continued to watch the vacant window. She'd tried to be friendly. Of course the fact that she'd given the girl a C in history last year could cause Angel to hold a grudge. But as it was,

Angel was lucky to have gotten that grade. Her classroom participation had been nil and her attitude aggravating. The points for the C had been difficult to scrape together but Susan hadn't wanted to have to put up with her for another year. It wasn't that Angel wasn't smart. She was, in fact, extremely intelligent according to her IQ test. She simply chose not to strain herself.

"They're back," Barbara blurted, then covered her mouth as if she'd spoken too loud.

Susan looked down the street to see Ray Carter's Jeep Grand Cherokee, pulling his long bass boat, coming their way. Parking in front of the house, he waved and yelled with a laugh, "Now this is the way it should be, the women all waiting anxiously for their husbands to return."

From the back seat, Ken called out, "I hope you're hungry. We're going to have one heck of a fish fry tonight."

Claire burst into tears and Susan groaned. This was going to be even more difficult than she'd imagined. As she rose to approach Ken, she caught a glimpse of Adam Riley watching from a short distance away. His presence, she realized, had a steadying influence on her.

Reaching Ken as he and the other men climbed out of the vehicle, she took his hand in hers. "I've got some bad news," she said, thinking that was probably the biggest understatement she'd ever made. Slowly, choosing her words as carefully as possible, she told him that Linda was dead.

For a long moment, he just stood regarding her in a stony silence, then a pain-filled groan of agony escaped him. "No," he said, shaking his head, refusing to believe her.

"I'm so sorry." Suddenly worried by the paleness of his complexion, she gently but firmly guided him to the grouping of lawn chairs. She fought back a flood of tears.

Sinking into one of the chairs, he buried his face in his hands and cried.

Ray Carter and Ted Reynolds had followed. When Ken

began to sob, they mumbled a few conciliatory words, then edged away and began unloading the camping gear and stowing the boat. Typical behavior, Susan noted. Most men, she'd observed, didn't like to be around anyone who was crying, especially one of their own.

"I'm sorry to intrude."

Susan looked over her shoulder to see that Adam Riley had approached the cluster of women who now circled Ken, attempting by their silent presence to console him. The policeman didn't look any more comfortable than the two fishermen who had quickly deserted the group.

"I'm Detective Adam Riley," Adam introduced himself. Kinter was blond and blue eyed with a strong chin and jawline. He stood six feet plus an inch or two in height, with a lithe build and was handsome by most women's standards. But was he worth dying for? Adam wondered.

Ken lifted his head from his hands. He tried to speak but the words caught in his throat and he looked as if he were going to be sick.

Adam hated this part of the job. "I'm sorry but we're going to have to keep your house sealed for a day or so, just until we get an official cause of death."

Confusion showed on Ken's face. "Susan said Linda died from a stroke or an aneurysm."

"Those are possibilities," Adam replied.

"What else could it have been?" Ken's gaze suddenly focused on Adam's badge. It was as if only then did the fact that Adam was a policeman sink in. Shock replaced his confusion. "And why are the police involved?" His gaze swept the women and came to rest accusingly on Susan. "There's something you haven't told me."

Susan noted that the men at the boat had stopped and were listening. "I've told you what I know for fact," she replied, stiffly.

"She was perfectly healthy when I left," he insisted.

"She had a shock." Claire, standing by her son, put a

comforting hand on his shoulder. "She found out about Ruth and Jason."

Ken's complexion turned gray. "She found out? How?"

Claire's chin trembled. "Carol just blurted it out."

Fresh tears rolled down Ken's cheeks. "I should have told her." Suddenly, as if all the pieces had just fit together, his gaze jerked back to Adam. "You think she committed suicide." Guilt spread over his features. "Oh, my God. If that's the case, I'll never forgive myself."

Susan glanced to the others. A subtle look exchanged between Pauline and Barbara told her that they'd been considering this a strong possibility. She turned to Claire. The way the woman's gaze flickered and shifted downward indicated that Claire agreed with them.

Adam noticed the others' reactions as well. His gaze turned back to Susan. The strain lines in her face were deeper than before. More to ease her pain than the husband's, he said, "There was no note. Until we have an autopsy report, there's no reason to jump to any conclusions."

Ken looked like a man who'd been punched in the stomach. "If she did take her own life, I have only myself to blame," he declared and started crying once again.

"I think you should take him over to your place, Claire," Barbara suggested.

Claire nodded. "Yes, come along. Help your old crippled mother home." Her gaze shifted to Adam. "He'll need a few things. Can we go into his house to pack a small suitcase?"

"Sure." The apology on Adam's face deepened. "But I'll have to tag along, and you won't be able to go into the living room."

Ken shook his head. "I can't…"

"Susan?" Claire's voice held a plea.

Why me? Susan moaned silently, the thought of reentering Linda's home causing her stomach to churn once again. But she couldn't refuse Claire's request. "Yes, of course, I'll take care of it," she agreed resignedly.

Adam preceded her to the house, unfastening one end of the yellow-and-black tape hanging between the posts at the top of the porch steps, to allow her to pass. At the door she paused to wait for him to unlock the security box Jack Connelly had installed. When he opened the door and stepped aside, for a moment she balked, then forced herself to enter.

One of the smaller bedrooms had been converted into a walk-in closet for the master bedroom. Susan found a suitcase in there, brought it out into the bedroom, set it on the bed and headed to the dresser. Adam Riley's gaze was like a physical touch…a comfortable hand on her shoulder, helping to see her through this ordeal. She was amazed that this near total stranger's presence could bring her such comfort. I'm just grateful not to be in here alone, she reasoned.

The first drawer she opened housed bras and panties. Abruptly she closed it and moved to the opposite side of the bureau.

"Mr. Kinter appears to have been very fond of his wife," Adam said, breaking the silence between them. It was a mundane thing to say, but he'd felt the need to say something.

Susan was carrying some briefs and undershirts to the suitcase. Pausing, she turned to the detective. "He loved her very much. In fact, he doted on her."

Adam recalled the photos from the study. If this was a suicide, he wanted Susan to understand that she wasn't the one at fault. "Sometimes outward appearances hide the truth. No one can be certain what goes on behind closed doors."

"You're right, but not in this case."

Arguing with her wasn't going to help, Adam decided. Besides, she could be right. The husband's reaction certainly seemed genuine.

For the next few minutes the only sounds in the house were those made by Susan packing. As she moved around the room, reminders of Linda taunted her. She tried not to look at the photos on the bureau, but her willpower wasn't that strong. Linda's gold-framed smiling image caught and held her attention. "She didn't take her own life!" The words exploded from her.

Seeing her suddenly begin to tremble, Adam breached the distance between them in two long strides. "Whatever happened, it wasn't your doing," he soothed, wrapping his arms protectively around her.

Tears of guilt began to flow. She fought them. "I refuse to believe she was that despondent and I didn't see it. I would never have left her alone if I'd thought for one moment, she might do something rash. She was angry. Angry! Not suicidal!" Giving up the struggle to hold back her sobs, she buried her face in his shoulder and wept.

Just below crying men, who were at the top of his list of things Adam hated most about his job, came crying women. But in this case, he was glad it was his arms holding Susan Hallston.

As her bout of grief began to ebb, Susan became aware of the strong shoulder on which she was leaning and the warm embrace that was providing comfort and support. Then suddenly it was only Adam's strength that filled her senses and terror swept through her. Pushing free, she took a step back putting distance between them. "I—I'm fine now," she stammered, holding her hands up in front of her warning him not to approach.

Adam frowned at the fear he saw on her face. "I'm perfectly safe to be around. I've never taken advantage of a woman in my life."

Her first reaction was to believe him, but faith in a man had nearly cost her her life once. She wouldn't be that stupid again. "I just want to get out of here." Quickly, she gathered the other items she thought Ken might need.

Adam was puzzled. He could understand her thinking

he'd been a little too forward, but he didn't understand her fear. She's probably just overreacting because of the strain of her friend's death, he decided. Seeing her snap the suitcase shut, he lifted it from the bed.

Wanting only to get out of this house, Susan strode out of the room. But as she passed Ken's study, she could not keep herself from glancing inside. The empty drawer was lying on its side on the floor. The contents were gone and she guessed they'd been bagged and were now in the policeman's car. "Secrets," she muttered, "can be very dangerous things."

An hour later, as Adam Riley pulled up in front of Dr. Miller's place, he recalled the expression on the practitioner's face when the old man had first entered the Kinter living room. Adam was used to medical examiners being impersonal toward the bodies they collected. There was nothing impersonal in the way Dr. Miller had reacted to Linda Kinter's death. There had been honest grief in the man's eyes.

Following the doctor's instructions, he walked around to the rear of the small clinic attached to the residence and entered through the back door. "Where are you, Doc?" he called out.

"Down the hall. Last door on your right," an elderly voice responded.

Adam found the doctor in an unexpectedly elaborate laboratory.

"I've been running some tests on Linda's blood," Dr. Miller said, placing a test tube in a holder then glancing at the open notebook beside him. "Her blood alcohol level was fairly high. The wine would have enhanced the effect of the narcotic. Looks like it was a combination of morphine and the wine that caused her death."

"There would have been enough of the drug in that bottle I found in the kitchen to kill her?"

The doctor nodded. "Like I told you this morning, that

prescription was a highly concentrated solution of morphine prescribed for patients in the final stages of cancer or other painful diseases. It wouldn't take much.''

''The pharmacy tag on the bottle indicated it had been prescribed for an Edward Barkley several months ago. Do you know him?''

''I knew him.''

Adam caught the past tense in the doctor's reply. ''Knew?''

''He died soon after that prescription was filled.''

''Was he related to Mrs. Kinter?''

Dr. Miller stripped off the rubber gloves he was wearing and tossed them into the trash can. ''Nope.''

Adam frowned at him. ''Have you got any idea how she got hold of his medicine?''

The expression on the physician's faced darkened. ''I know where the chain started, but I can't tell you how the stuff ended up in Linda's hands. Edward Barkley was a patient at the Shady Rest Nursing Home. Shortly after his death, one of the nurses was discovered to have been stealing drugs.'' Seating himself on a stool, the doctor continued, ''When a patient dies, their remaining medications are supposed to be recorded, then disposed of. We're a small community here. People trust one another. When a narcotic is being disposed of, the person disposing of it is supposed to be observed by someone else who signs a paper saying the deed was done properly. But the nursing home is run on a tight budget. They don't have extra hands. They'd gotten into the habit of allowing whoever had the time to take care of disposing of the drugs to do so, then someone would sign the slip whether they'd watched or not.

''After a while it had gotten to be accepted that Zelda Jones would take care of clearing the pharmacy. Zelda grew up here in Bandits' Gorge. People knew her. They trusted her. Then Sandra Cortland started to work there. She got upset by the laxness with which the rules were being observed. She started keeping an eye on the drugs and began to suspect that Zelda wasn't disposing of them like she claimed. Zelda must have realized the authorities were on to her. By the time they got to her place with a search warrant, she'd skipped town. Maybe she kept her clients or maybe someone else was holding her stash and has been selling it slowly.''

Adam frowned at the corpse. "The neighbors all swore Linda Kinter would never take drugs. Guess nobody really knows anyone else.''

"If she wasn't laying here in my morgue, I wouldn't believe she would, either. I could barely get her to take antibiotics. But then people are very good at hiding their vices.'' The doctor raked a hand agitatedly through his hair. "I'm going to send tissue and blood samples to the state lab for confirmation. But I'll do the autopsy myself.''

Adam's gaze again swept the room. "Pretty elaborate setup you have here.''

"About fifteen years ago a murderer got off scot-free because of sloppy work done at the state lab. The victim was the daughter of a close friend. I promised myself that no one was going to get away with murder in Bandits' Gorge again. I learned what I needed to know to do my own forensic work and now I only use the state lab for verification. Besides, you can learn a lot to help the living by discovering what killed the dead.''

"I suppose.'' Adam's gaze again came to rest on the covered body on the metal dissecting table.

Following his line of vision, the doctor sighed. "I still can't believe she's lying there. But then we all have our dark side and she did have a vulnerability about her. Most people do. The problem is knowing how deeply it runs and how freely it will bleed once it's tapped. In hindsight, I can't say she struck me as being so strong she would never have considered suicide as a possible solution to her problems.''

"Friday night she found out that her husband had been married before and had a child."

The doctor looked suddenly very tired and sad. "Then I'm responsible for what happened. I was the one who told Ken he had to tell her."

"You knew about his past?"

"He and his mother are both patients of mine. I delivered him."

"And you knew he hadn't told his wife?"

The doctor nodded. "She wanted very badly to have a baby. She'd talked to me about going to a specialist to have both herself and Ken tested. If she'd known about his son, she wouldn't have been concerned that he was sterile. I called him and spoke to him. I told him, he had to be honest with her."

"It wasn't Ken who told his wife. She found out from a neighbor. Seems while the men were fishing some of the women got together, got drunk and the secret about his wife and child slipped out."

The doctor continued to eye the corpse sadly. "I should have had her and Ken in my office and forced the issue in my presence. That way I could have observed her reaction and been in a position to help her through the trauma."

Adam pictured the pale blond woman beneath the white sheeting. All the evidence pointed to suicide. But Adam was beginning to get an uneasy feeling about it. Susan Hallston had insisted that Linda Kinter was angry, not despondent. But what really nagged at him was that there hadn't been a note. Most suicides liked to leave a final farewell message. "This case looks pretty open-and-shut. But I'd feel a lot better if there'd been a note. I've looked all over the house. There wasn't even evidence that she'd started one."

"Could be that she was so despondent, she didn't realize what she was doing," the doctor suggested. "This solution is more potent than most of the drugs she would have been able to get her hands on. My conscience would feel a lot better if I could believe this was an accident rather than a premeditated action. And that would explain the absence of a note."

Adam was used to reading people and right now he was certain there was something the doctor wasn't telling him. "I could swear you're holding out on me."

"There are some things I'm bound by the Hippocratic oath not to discuss. However, I can't help wondering if she discovered something else that might have added to her depression. If I were you, I'd have a long talk with Ken."

Adam knew when he was being tossed a bone. "I intend to."

The doctor's gaze again turned to the shrouded body. "And unless my autopsy turns up something unexpected or you can give me any reason to state it differently, I'm going to list the death as an accidental overdose. Makes it easier on the family."

Leaving the doctor's office, Adam was certain the old man was convinced Linda Kinter had committed suicide. He was equally certain the doctor knew of another reason she might have done so and it also had something to do with the husband. When he found out what that was he could wrap this case up.

Two hours later Adam was slouched in one of the two chairs facing the couch where Linda Kinter had died.

It had been early evening when he'd left the doctor's place. He'd considered going over to Claire Kinter's and talking to her son but, recalling the stricken expression on Ken Kinter's face, he'd decided to give the man until the next morning. So, he'd grabbed some Chinese takeout and gone home.

Home was a room in a boardinghouse on Mulberry Street. The bathroom was down the hall. He shared it with the two other tenants on the second floor of the huge old rambling residence. He'd have liked more privacy but the breakfasts provided by Mable Mallery, the proprietress, were tasty. They definitely qualified as Southern cooking. The woman considered butter and sugar two of the basic staples of life. Until he decided if he wanted to put down roots here, the place would do.

He'd been sitting in his room, eating his dinner and channel surfing when Linda Kinter's face came back to haunt him. Almost immediately, it had been replaced by Susan Hallston's, and he'd found himself wishing they'd met under more pleasant circumstances. From deep within came the urge to erase the strain from her face. But that wasn't going to happen until this case was closed, Linda Kinter laid to rest, and her friends and family had time to get over the shock.

His sweet-and-sour pork had lost its appeal. The next thing he knew, he was on his way back to the house on Willow Street.

This afternoon he'd gone through the residence carefully, taking fingerprints off the drawer left lying on the floor of the study, collecting the letters and the photos. He'd bagged everything on the coffee table in front of the couch from the empty wine bottle and the glass she'd drank from to the open canister of homemade fudge. Now he had just completed a second, even more thorough search.

Something about this death just didn't feel right. "Nothing about a suicide feels right," he grumbled to himself.

Again he wished there'd been a note, or, at least, a small stash of drugs somewhere. All he'd found was some headache tablets.

The opening of the front door and footsteps in the hall brought him to his feet.

Ken Kinter froze in the doorway of the living room, his gaze locked on the couch. "That's where she...?" His words seemed to stick in his throat making it impossible for him to finish the question.

Adam frowned. "You shouldn't be in here, Mr. Kinter. Officially this house is still sealed."

Ken's attention jerked to the policeman. "Do you know yet what caused her death?"

No sense in hedging Adam decided. Besides, he wanted to see the husband's reaction. "She overdosed on morphine mixed with alcohol."

"No." The word came out in a moan. "She wouldn't do that. She knew I loved her." Recrimination etched itself into Ken Kinter's features. "I should have told her."

"Why didn't you?" Adam asked.

"On the surface my wife appeared to be reasonably secure. But it was a facade. Inside she was very insecure. Her parents had both died when she was in her late teens. She'd been tossed back and forth between her mother's sisters, neither wanting to take on the full burden of raising her. When I first met her she made a crack about never dating divorced men. She said they'd failed in one marriage and would probably fail in another. She said she wanted someone she knew she could rely on. From the first moment I saw her, I was crazy about her. I figured after I convinced her to fall in love with me, I'd tell her the truth. But there just never seemed to be the right time."

Adam recalled Beth Johnson from his sophomore year in high school. He'd have said almost anything to get a date with her. In fact, he had. He'd told her he could get his father's car. When he'd showed up in his old pickup truck, she'd slammed the door in his face. He jerked his mind back to the present. Would he have skirted the truth the way the husband had? He looked at the pretty, smiling blond woman in the gold frame on the mantel. Maybe. "Was your wife prone to moods of depression?"

"She had her ups and downs." Ken shifted uneasily. "I figured they were normal for women. I joked a couple of times about her maybe taking Prozac. But that was just a joke."

The husband was giving him what he needed to seal this case. "So, your wife did have bouts of depression?"

"Women have their moods," Ken hedged.

"Did you ever suspect your wife might be using drugs?"

"No." Ken rubbed his face hard like a man hoping this was a nightmare and he could wake himself up. There was a haunted expression in his eyes when he again looked at Adam. "I thought I knew her. I guess maybe I didn't pay as much attention to her as I should have. I tried to be a good husband."

Adam couldn't help feeling sorry for the guy.

Ken Kinter looked sick. "She wanted a child real bad. I figure finding out I already had one was more of a blow than finding out about my ex-wife."

Adam recalled the doctor's parting words. "Is there something more she might have discovered about you that could have caused her to cross the line?"

Ken paled even more. "Like what?"

"Dr. Miller suggested I talk to you. I'm trying to understand why your wife would have taken her life."

As if his legs were suddenly having a difficult time supporting his weight, Kinter leaned against the wall. "I'm sure she didn't find out."

"Find out what?" Adam prodded.

"About my vasectomy. My first wife had a dangerous pregnancy. I was terrified that she might die. If she had, I would never have been able to live with the guilt. So, even before our son was born, I had a vasectomy to ensure I never got her pregnant again."

Adam tried to recall if he'd ever seen the kind of scar left by that kind of operation. "And, Linda, your second wife, never noticed?"

"There's not much to notice. Besides, she wasn't the sexually exploratory type."

Linda Kinter had mood swings. Finding out about the vasectomy in addition to the former wife and kid could have easily sent her over the edge. The husband was definitely tying up the loose ends. Adam just had one final question. "Did your wife know Zelda Jones?"

"The name sounds familiar."

"She worked as a nurse at the Shady Rest Retirement Home," Adam elaborated.

Ken nodded. "I remember now. She's the woman who was caught stealing medications."

"Yes. Did your wife know her?"

Ken looked uneasy. "I suppose she could have. Until my mother's arthritis got really bad last winter, she used to do volunteer work there. She talked Linda into donating some time as well. But my wife quit after only a short while. There was a patient she got attached to, an elderly man, Edward something or another, I can't remember the name. He was in an advanced stage of cancer. When he died, the death depressed her so badly I encouraged her to quit and she did."

Mentally Adam closed his book on this case. He'd tied the source of the drugs to the victim. He also had a picture of a woman who, while maintaining a stable facade for her neighbors, was prone to depression. "As soon as the doctor finishes his autopsy, I'll be submitting my report. You should be able to move back into your home real soon."

Ken shuddered. "I don't know if I can ever think of this place as home again." Abruptly he left.

Adam's mind returned to the sweet-and-sour pork he'd left uneaten. After again securing the house, he headed back to his car.

"Detective Riley," a female voice called out to him.

He looked up the street to see Susan Hallston descending her porch steps. As she strode toward him the swing of her hips caught his eye and his apartment suddenly seemed like a very lonely place. "Evening, Miss Hallston."

Approaching, Susan saw the masculine gleam of ap-

proval in his eye. It sparked a flattered feminine response.
Then she recalled the strength of his arms and fear curled
through her. Her instinct for self-preservation caused her
manner to become cool. "Has Dr. Miller determined how
Linda died?"

She was clearly still angered by his forwardness this
afternoon, he mused. Her attitude rankled him. He'd been
trying to help. Then he caught the glint of guilt in her eyes
and his irritation faded. She'd had a tough day. He wished
he could tell her the death had been due to natural causes.
He couldn't, but the doc had given him a way to soften
the blow. "It was probably an accidental overdose."

Susan thought she was prepared for whatever he said.
She wasn't. "Overdose?" she asked shakily. "What?"

Figuring she would learn the truth from the Kinters anyway, he elaborated. "She had some morphine and mixed
it with wine."

The color drained from Susan's face. "Where would she
get morphine?"

"Most likely from Zelda Jones or someone who dealt
with her." Seeing the confusion on her face, he added,
"Zelda was suspected of stealing medications from the
Shady Rest Nursing Home."

Susan forced herself to concentrate. "I vaguely remember some rumors about something like that. I suppose it's
possible. Linda did volunteer out there for a while."
Abruptly she shook her head. "Linda wasn't the type to
deal in stolen drugs. I can't believe it. It has to be a mistake."

Adam saw her guilt intensifying and his desire to ease
it increased. "Things happen. People behave in ways we
least expect."

Susan's jaw tensed and she fought to control the hot
tears at the back of her eyes. "Dying just because Ken
wasn't totally honest with her is absurd."

"People do stupid things without thinking of the con-
sequences." Mentally, Adam ticked off several cases but

chose not to give her any examples. She didn't look as if she could handle them.

"I can't believe Linda would behave that stupidly. I was sure she was more angry than distraught." Her gaze shifted to the house where the death had occurred. "But then I would have sworn she'd never have taken any drugs, either. I thought I knew her. I guess I didn't."

"No one can know for certain what's going on in another person's mind."

"I suppose," Susan conceded. "Thank you," she added stiffly and headed back to her porch.

"Believe me, I know what I'm talking about," Adam muttered under his breath, continuing on to his car. He also made a mental note to ask her out on a date when this business was over.

Chapter 3

"Interesting coincidence."

Adam looked up from the report he was writing to see Judd Claymont standing in front of his desk. Judd had been on the force for more than twenty years, starting as a rookie patrolman and working his way to detective. A native of Bandits' Gorge, he knew a lot about what went on behind closed doors in this town. And right now Adam had a feeling the man knew something he hadn't been told about this case. "Coincidence?"

Judd lowered his long, lanky frame into one of the two wooden captain's chairs in front of Adam's desk. "Nine years ago, Ken Kinter discovered the dead body of Susan Hallston's husband. Now she up and finds the body of his dead wife."

Adam's neck muscle, the one that always tensed when a case took an unexpected turn he didn't like, knotted. "Susan Hallston buried a husband? Jack Connelly told me she was a 'Miss.'"

"I suppose legally she is. Her married name was Bartram. Changed it back right after the funeral."

Adam massaged his neck, trying to work the knot out. It remained. "An unhappy marriage?"

"One of the most. Seems Lyle Bartram thought the right to beat his wife was part of the marriage pact. About six months into the marriage he beat her bad enough she ended up in the hospital. I had her convinced to file charges against him, then she backed out. A month or so later she was walking around town with a broken arm...crossed the street so she didn't have to speak to me. I knew he'd done it."

Picturing Susan Hallston as a battered wife, Adam experienced a rage of protectiveness and wished he'd had a chance to take a swing at the husband...give the man a little of his own medicine. "How did Kinter get involved?"

"She and Kinter have known each other all their lives. There were those in town who thought the two of them would marry."

The protective urge vanished and the knot that had begun to loosen tightened painfully. "You're telling me that at one time there was a romantic involvement between Susan Hallston and Ken Kinter?"

"Can't say I ever saw it firsthand, but I recall hearing that a few people were surprised when it wasn't her and Kinter walking down that aisle."

"How did Kinter react to her husband's behavior?"

"Didn't like it one little bit. Came to see me and demanded to know why I didn't do something. I told him my hands were tied as long as she refused to file charges. He stormed out of here mad as a hornet.

"About a month later I got a call to come out to the Bartram place. It was around ten at night. Kinter was there. He said Susan had showed up at her grandmother's place hysterical and with a broken ankle. She'd said that this time, instead of just beating her, Lyle had grabbed up a knife and threatened to kill her. She'd run upstairs. He'd thought he had her trapped and had come more slowly. But she'd climbed out a window, dropped to the ground, breaking her ankle in the process, then hobbled the five miles to her grandmother's place, keeping away from the road for fear Bartram would catch her. Hattie wasn't home. Turned out she was playing bridge at a friend's house.

"Kinter had found Susan lying in front of Hattie's door sobbing. He'd taken her to Dr. Miller's place and then gone to confront Bartram. He told me he intended to tell Bartram to stay away from Susan, then he was going to get her things and move her into her grandmother's house. But when he got to the Bartram place there wasn't any answer. He had Susan's keys and decided to go in and get her things and confront her husband another time. Inside, he discovered Bartram lying dead, facedown at the foot of the stairs. Looked as if the man had tripped and fallen on his knife. The blade had gone right through the heart."

"So, what did the investigation turn up?"

"It was my case. I listed it as an accident." Judd's expression hardened. "Truth is, maybe I didn't look as close as I should've. I don't think Doc Miller did, either. Lyle Bartram deserved his fate. But Linda Kinter's another matter. I'd sure hate to think she got helped along the path to the pearly gates and whoever did it is going to get away scot-free."

The man had given him a motive for murder. With Linda Kinter out of the way, Susan Hallston might think she had a chance with the husband. And, he knew from experience some women would do anything to get the man they wanted. The fact that there had been no note seemed suddenly more important. "I intend to do a very thorough investigation," Adam assured him.

Judd nodded. His point made, he eased himself out of the chair and left.

Adam stared at his computer screen. Love triangles. He hated them. What he hated even more was the thought that he might have allowed himself to be duped by Susan Hallston. He was sure he'd learned his lesson where women were concerned…never trust one you don't know and never trust those you do know until you're certain you know everything.

Leaning back, he closed his eyes. Her image filled his mind. She'd looked so stricken sitting on those stairs. But then, Charlie's wife had wept buckets at his funeral. Pretty, sweet Lisa, he mused. When his partner, Charlie, married her, he'd thought they were the perfect couple. Admittedly they had their fights but he'd never expected his investigation to reveal that Lisa had killed Charlie for insurance money.

He recalled the fear directed at him he'd seen in Miss Hallston's eyes on several occasions. It could have been due to her history of having been married to an abusive husband. Some women never got over that and stayed wary of men all their lives. Or she could have something to hide.

The knot in his neck felt like a rock. He massaged it harder. If there was foul play, he reminded himself, nine times out of ten the spouse was the guilty party. Maybe the marriage hadn't been as idyllic as everyone thought.

"Or maybe I'm letting past experience influence me too much," he grumbled. He had no evidence of murder. In fact, everything he'd learned so far pointed to suicide or an accidental overdose. The latter explained away the lack of a note as well.

Reaching for the phone, he dialed the state lab and asked them to put a rush on the fingerprints on the bottle of wine, the glass and the morphine bottle. The response was that they had a backlog of cases and when his stuff came in, it'd have to take its place in line.

Cursing under his breath, he called Dr. Miller to tell him he was on his way over.

"I didn't find anything I didn't expect to find," Dr. Miller informed Adam, handing him a copy of the autopsy report. "There was no sign that she was a heavy user of drugs, but that doesn't mean she didn't indulge once in a while. Also, she did want to have a child. That might have induced her to clean out her system. And if that was the case, it would easily explain that particular prescription bottle she had. She might have purchased it from Zelda, decided to clean up her system rather than use it but couldn't bear to part with it. After all, if she was using drugs, they were her crutch. It would have been hard to completely toss it away."

"True," Adam admitted.

"There were also no signs of a struggle or of anything being forced down her," the doctor continued. "And since there was no note, it's my guess, she simply took a little too much without realizing it. She was pretty upset. However, I believe in being totally thorough. I don't have the equipment to analyze the stomach contents so I sent them on to the state lab and I sent along samples of blood and tissue for a second opinion."

"And we'll probably hear back in about six months," Adam muttered, recalling his conversation with the people there.

"I've got a friend there. We should know a lot sooner than that," Dr. Miller assured him. "I know what a strain this can be on a family so I called in a favor."

"Can you see what he can do about getting a report on the fingerprints?" Adam requested.

"I asked him to get as much information back to us as quickly as possible," the doctor replied.

Adam glanced at the report but at the moment, Linda Kinter wasn't topmost in his mind. Charlie's grieving widow was. Only now her face had become that of Susan Hallston's. Admittedly, Susan Hallston's situation was different, but the husband had ended up dead and Adam wanted to know if the doctor shared Judd's suspicions.

"Judd Claymont was telling me this morning about Susan Hallston's husband."

The doctor shook his head sadly. "A bad seed. A real bad seed. Shame no one knew until after the fact."

"I got the impression Judd thought the man's death might not have happened exactly the way it's written up in the report," Adam persisted.

The doctor met his gaze. "I've been Susan's doctor all her life. She made a bad choice for a husband. I figured she'd been punished enough."

"So you think he might not have been alive when she left the house that night?"

Miller shrugged. "Even if she had something directly to do with his death, it would have been self-defense. Could be she shoved him down the stairs. You can't blame a person for fighting for their life. He'd beaten her badly several times. When Ken brought her into my office that night she was hysterical and in shock from the pain of going all that distance on a broken ankle. She was just nineteen and I recall thinking that if something wasn't done, she wouldn't see her twentieth birthday. If Bartram had shown up on my doorstep that night, I might have done something rash myself."

Again Adam experienced a surge of protectiveness toward the brown-eyed woman. "What about her family? Didn't they try to help her?"

"Her father had taken a job in Alaska when she was in high school. She hadn't wanted to leave her friends. Her mother had been worried about leaving the grandmother here on her own so everyone had been happy when her father agreed to let Susan stay and move in with Hattie. When she got engaged to Lyle, her parents were a little disappointed she wasn't going on to college but they sanctioned the wedding. On the surface, Lyle looked like good people. He came from a God-fearing home. His father is hardworking, raises cattle and farms on a large spread outside of town. His mother is a schoolteacher. When he started beating Susan, she kept it a secret for as long as possible. When she landed in the hospital, she begged her grandmother not to tell her parents and Hattie agreed to respect her wishes. I think both she and her grandmother were afraid her daddy might come down here, kill Lyle and end up in jail. Anyway, I do know her parents never knew what was going on.''

Another possibility had occurred to Adam. "What about Kinter? I understand he was pretty hot under the collar about what was going on. Maybe when he got there, Bartram was still alive, they had a row and he killed him."

"There wasn't any evidence that Kinter was involved. His clothes didn't show any signs that he'd been in a struggle, there was no blood on him from Bartram's wound, and the only fingerprints on the knife belonged to Bartram."

"What about evidence that Miss Hallston was involved?" Adam persisted.

The doctor's gaze hardened. "She looked like she'd been through hell. And, yes, there was blood and, no, I didn't do a comparison. Like I said, if she had struggled with him and he'd died in the struggle, it would have been self-defense. I didn't see any reason to put her through the ordeal of a trial."

Adam pictured a youthful Susan Hallston, bruised, bloodied and hysterical. "I probably would have reasoned it out the same way," he admitted. "But it could have set a bad precedent."

The doctor raised a questioning eyebrow.

"If a person gets away with having killed someone once, they might think they can get away with it again."

Miller scowled at him. "You honestly think Susan might have had something to do with Linda's death? That's absurd. Why in the world would you even consider that possibility. What motive…"

That the doctor had stopped in midsentence, told Adam the man had thought of one.

Miller suddenly shook his head. "No. I'll admit there has always been a feeling among some that Susan was sweet on Ken Kinter, but she'd never kill to get the man."

The man spoke with authority and Adam wanted to believe him but he wouldn't be duped a second time. "Are you absolutely certain of that?" he challenged.

For a long moment the doctor studied him in curt silence, then said, "If what you're suggesting is true, Susan would have had to have planned the murder in advance, purchasing the drug, then biding her time, waiting for the right moment. No. I can't believe that of her. It's too cold and calculating."

Adam recalled how shocked he'd been when the evidence had begun to point to Charlie's widow. "Women can be surprisingly deceptive." Heading out the door, he added over his shoulder, "Let me know when you get those analyses back."

Back in his car, Adam drove to Susan Hallston's house. Until he knew for certain which direction this case was going to take, he would treat it like a questionable death which meant finding out as much about the victim's movements as possible. He also made a mental note to check on any insurance policies Linda Kinter might have had.

A self-mocking grin tilted one corner of his mouth. He was looking for motives for the husband. In fact, he was hoping that if there was foul play, the husband was the guilty party. The grin became even more lopsided. After months of being wary of all women, here he was attracted to one who, if the case did turn into a murder investigation, would be one of his chief suspects. Even more, although both Judd and the doctor were convinced it was self-defense, it was obvious they both believed she had something to do with her husband's death.

"Obviously, I didn't learn much from my brush with death," he muttered under his breath.

A few minutes later he'd parked in front of Susan Hallston's house and was starting up her walk when a female voice said from behind him, "She's at the high school. She's teaching history in summer school."

He turned to discover a strikingly pretty auburn-haired teenager approaching. "Do you know when Miss Hallston will be back?"

The girl came to a halt a couple of feet away and studied him with a speculative glimmer in her eyes. "Nope."

Children, it had been Adam's experience, saw a great deal more than people thought, and this girl looked as if she kept her eyes open. "Do you live around here?"

She nodded toward the end of the street. "The house on the corner."

"The Carters are your parents?"

She nodded. "I'm Angel Carter and you're the policeman who's investigating Mrs. Kinter's death. I saw you yesterday."

"Did you know Mrs. Kinter?"

"I know both Mrs. Kinters."

She was playing word games with him. He knew the type. She thought she was smarter than him. "Did you see or speak to Mrs. Linda Kinter on Saturday?"

"I saw her but I didn't speak to her. My mother had told me what happened on Friday night. Stressed-out adults get on my nerves so I stayed out of her way."

In spite of her above-it-all attitude, Adam got the distinct impression Angel Carter had sought him out. "Is there something you know that you think I should know?" he asked bluntly.

"Old lady Kinter told my mother that Mrs. Kinter died from an overdose of drugs and alcohol?" Angel paused, clearly waiting for a response.

"Looks that way," Adam replied.

"My mother's been ranting all morning about how weak and stupid Mrs. Kinter was to kill herself over an ex-wife and kid." A malicious glimmer came into the teenager's eyes. "But maybe it wasn't just finding out about her husband's former wife that sent her over the edge. Maybe she also discovered she should have been keeping an eye on him closer to home.''

The girl's insinuation was clear. ''You're saying he was having an affair with one of the women in the neighborhood?''

An expression of innocence spread over the teenager's features. ''That'd be gossiping and I'm not a gossip. You're the detective. Detect.'' Sending her hair swinging with a flip of her head, she strode down the street.

Watching her, Adam frowned. Did Angel Carter really know something or was she merely making up a story to confuse the issue and make herself seem more important?

The soft curves of Susan Hallston's figure played through Adam's mind and he pictured her with Kinter. The image caused a surge of self-directed anger. ''Do I have to be kicked by a mule a second time to learn a lesson?'' he grumbled at himself.

With purpose in his step, he headed to Claire Kinter's place. It was time to have another interview with the husband. After that, he'd interview the neighbors. By the time he was finished, he'd know all there was to know about the Kinters and Susan Hallston.

Claire Kinter answered his knock. ''Have you come to tell us my son can go back into his home?'' she asked hopefully. ''He has papers and things he needs.''

''I'm going to have to keep the place sealed a little longer.'' Adam had meant to sound apologetic but the statement came out tersely. He couldn't stop thinking about Susan Hallston's possible involvement and how he'd actually considered asking her out on a date.

Claire's hand went up to her mouth. ''Oh, dear.''

''What's going on?'' Ken Kinter came out of the kitchen looking pale and drawn. ''I've just been on the phone with Dr. Miller. I wanted to make funeral arrangements but he says he's not certain when the body will be released.''

Adam ignored the man's question. Taking out his notebook, he said, "I need to ask the both of you a few questions."

Claire stared at him in bewilderment. "I don't understand."

"My wife took her life either by accident or intent," Ken growled. "I'm barred from my home. I can't bury her. And you're back to ask more questions that will, no doubt, cause all of us to feel even guiltier. Do you have any idea how much pain you're inflicting, Detective?"

The man did look as if he were honestly suffering, but Angel's hint that he'd been having an affair was still ringing in Adam's ears. "I'm sorry, Mr. Kinter, but there is information I need before I can finalize my report."

Claire laid a soothing hand on her son's arm. "Detective Riley is only doing his job." She motioned with her cane. "We can go into the living room and sit."

Ken's expression remained hostile as he nodded his agreement.

In the living room, he helped his mother ease into a high-backed wing chair, then seated himself nearby on the sofa.

Adam took a chair at the end of the coffee table that allowed him a clear view of both of them. "I want to trace Mrs. Kinter's movements beginning with Saturday morning."

"I can't tell you about my wife's movements on Saturday. I wasn't here. I understand she spent most of the day with Susan," Ken said stiffly.

So the late Mrs. Kinter had spent her final day with Miss Hallston. Adam turned his attention to Claire Kinter. "Did you see or talk to your daughter-in-law on Saturday?"

"I called her around nine. I could tell she was upset but she was insistent that she didn't want company. I tried to reassure her that Ken loved her deeply." Claire looked toward her son and sighed. "You should have told her about Ruth and Jason."

"I've already agreed to that," he snapped. His chin

trembled as he added, "It would probably have cost me my marriage but at least Linda would still be alive."

"I shouldn't have said that," Claire apologized quickly, looking to him for forgiveness. "I'm still in shock."

Ken mumbled something about them all being in shock.

Adam had to admit the man's grief seemed truly genuine. He returned his attention to Claire. "Did you speak to or see your daughter-in-law after the nine o'clock phone conversation?"

Claire nodded. "I was sitting on my porch a little later when I saw her going over to Susan's place. She was carrying something. Susan told me later it was some of the photos Linda had found in Ken's study."

"About how long was she at Miss Hallston's?"

"I'm not really sure. I went inside shortly after that to watch a game show on television. Then I had some lunch and took a nap. When I went back outside I saw Susan coming out of Linda's house. I waved her over and asked how Linda was doing. Susan told me that Linda was upset but she thought she was calming down. She said that she and Linda were going to go out to dinner and a movie."

"So, you didn't actually speak to your daughter-in-law again?"

"Yes, I did. I wanted to reassure myself that she was feeling better." Claire reached over and patted her son's hand. "And I wanted to put in a good word for Ken. I used the excuse of checking on the time she would be picking me up for church the next morning and went over to see her fairly soon after Susan went home. Linda was getting ready to shower and change for her evening out."

"And how did she appear?"

"Controlled, I guess would be the best way to describe it. Sort of wooden as if she were holding everything in. I tried to get her to talk to me but she refused. She said she would talk to Ken."

Claire patted her son's hand again. "I was certain she would forgive him. She was crazy about him."

"Do you know if your daughter-in-law spoke to or saw anyone other than Susan Hallston on Saturday?"

Claire thought for a moment, then shook her head. "No, not to my knowledge. Like I said before, she really wasn't in the mood for company."

Adam turned to the husband. "Did you have any contact at all with your wife after Friday night?"

"You know he was off fishing," Claire said, her tone indicating she thought the policeman was addled for asking this. "You were here when he got back."

"There are such things as telephones," Adam returned.

"Yes, there are." Ken Kinter's voice was gruff with emotion. "But Ted, Ray and I had vowed to leave civilization behind for a couple of days. We pitched our tent along the river and never made any attempt to communicate with anyone." His eyes became teary. "If I had called her this would never have happened. I'd have come home and straightened this whole mess out. I loved my wife, Detective."

Adam again found himself thinking that the man sounded sincere, but he wasn't ready to discount Angel Carter's insinuation. He rose, approached Claire's chair and offered her his hand for assistance. "I hope you won't be offended, but I need to speak to your son alone."

Claire glanced worriedly toward Ken. For a moment, Adam had the feeling she was going to protest being excluded, then she smiled weakly at him. "Yes, of course." Accepting his offer of aid, she rose. "I was going to make some tuna salad for lunch. Would you like to join us, Detective?"

"No, but thanks," Adam replied. He waited until she'd left the room, then reseating himself, gave Ken Kinter his full attention. "Did you ever cheat on your wife?"

"No, of course not."

Adam caught the momentary downward shift of Kinter's eyes and was certain the man was lying. "It'd be best if you told me the truth."

"We all have moments of weakness, Detective. I loved my wife. That's all you need to know," Ken stated curtly.

The firm set of his jaw told Adam that pursuing this line of questioning would get him nowhere, at least not right now. "Was your wife insured, Mr. Kinter?"

Anger at the insinuation in this question brought a bright red flush to Ken's face. "No, Detective, she was not."

"Do you have any idea where your wife got the morphine she ingested?"

Kinter glared at him. "You were asking about Zelda Jones. I assume that's where she got it. I know nothing about drug dealers, Detective." Kinter raked a hand through his hair. "I still can't believe this is happening. I loved my wife. I wasn't a perfect husband, but I never did anything to intentionally hurt Linda." Tears began to roll down Kinter's cheeks and anger spread over his face. "My wife killed herself and it was my fault. Dealing with that is hard enough without your questions. I'd like you to leave."

Adam considered again trying to find out who Kinter had been involved with, but knew that would only make the man more defensive. Deciding that the diplomatic thing to do would be to respect the man's request, he rose. "Thank you for your time, Mr. Kinter." Not wanting Kinter to think he'd been cowed, he added, "I may have more questions later."

"I have answered all the questions I'm going to answer," Ken growled back. "This is a nightmare. Can't you let it end?"

"As soon as I'm satisfied I have all the facts," Adam replied.

"You know all you need to know." Ken started to rise, then sank back on the sofa as if the strength had been sapped from him. "You'll have to see yourself out."

The man did look like he was going through a living hell, Adam thought as he exited the house. Of course it could be an act. Maybe Kinter had decided he wanted to attempt to get back with his former wife and be a full-time dad to his son. If that was the case, he could have hired someone to kill his wife. Divorce would have been simpler, but maybe he didn't want to pay alimony. On the other hand, a hired killer could prove to be very expensive. There was always the possibility of blackmail. And there was the problem of finding one. And once found, the logistics of carrying out the act wouldn't have been easy. In this neighborhood, a stranger hanging around would have stuck out like a sore thumb. Also, if a hired killer had done the job, he would most likely have made it look like a robbery gone bad or an accident. Staging a believable suicide was difficult. It took a lot of planning. And how would a hired killer know Carol Hawkins was going to spill the beans and cause Linda Kinter to be in a depressed mood? No, the hired killer angle was fraught with flaws.

Even more to the point, from all accounts so far, Linda had not been in the mood for company, and he doubted she would have invited a stranger into her house. All the evidence indicated that if she had had company, she had been comfortable with whoever was there. She'd sat and drank wine and ate the fudge without any struggle.

Still, he was certain Kinter hadn't been honest with him about the affair. However, just because Kinter had been unfaithful didn't mean he didn't love his wife. He'd implied it had been a moment of weakness. That happened. Adam didn't approve. He was old-fashioned in that respect. But he wasn't judgmental enough to label Kinter a bad person.

"Everyone has their weakness," he muttered, again finding himself thinking about Susan Hallston. He couldn't get the woman off his mind and she was causing a real mix of emotions. If Charlie was alive, he'd be kidding Adam, saying Adam was finally experiencing the kind of animal magnetism that had brought Charlie and Lisa together. "And look where that got you, Charlie," Adam said under his breath, looking skyward.

The Carter house was Adam's next destination. Maybe Angel would prove to be more cooperative this time.

But Angel wasn't at home. However, both Ted and Pauline Carter were. When questioned about the Kinters' marriage, they both told him what he'd been hearing from everyone except Angel...Ken was a devoted husband and Linda was an adoring wife.

Asked if she'd seen or spoken to Linda Kinter on Saturday, Pauline said she hadn't. "I slept until noon. When I got up, I was worried about Linda so I called her house but all I got was the answering machine," she elaborated. "I left a message asking Linda if she was feeling all right and telling her to call me when she got home. But as soon as I hung up, I got worried. Linda had been very upset. I decided I should go over there...just in case she was home and wasn't answering her phone. It's never healthy for a person to sit and brood alone."

Indicating she was going to relay a confidence, she leaned forward, closing the distance between her and the policeman and lowered her voice. "I suppose I knew intuitively that Linda wasn't as strong as some of us."

"So, you went over to the Kinter house?" Adam asked, guiding the conversation back to Pauline Carter's movements on Saturday.

Straightening, she returned her voice to its normal level. "No. I'd called Angel and her friend, Melissa Colby, in for lunch. When I told them I was going to leave them to fend for themselves and go next door to check on Linda, Angel told me she'd seen her going over to Susan's house earlier. Linda's always considered Susan a closer friend than me so I figured she was in good hands." Pauline breathed an exaggerated sigh. "I wish now I'd acted on my intuition. I'm a little more mature than Susan. Maybe I could have said something that would have helped Linda cope better."

"So, you never actually even saw Linda Kinter on Saturday?" Adam said.

"No. After lunch, I took the girls shopping in Ashville. We were there all afternoon. Then we dropped Melissa off at her home and Angel and I had a mother-daughter night out. We went to dinner and a movie. When we got home, I went directly to bed. I still had a lingering headache from the hangover I got on Friday night."

"Did you notice any activity at the Kinter house when you returned home?" Adam asked.

"No." She frowned at him as if confused by the question. Then her gaze narrowed and disbelief mingled with morbid interest in her eyes. "Are you suggesting that Linda's death wasn't self-inflicted?"

"I'm merely trying to determine her movements during the last hours of her life," he replied noncommittally. He noticed the speculative glimmer in Mrs. Carter's eyes remained. It increased when he asked her husband about the fishing trip.

Ray Carter practically snarled at him. "If you think Ken Kinter came home and killed his wife, you're all wet," he said. "The man was with us all the time. Besides, he adored Linda. He'd have walked through the fires of hell for her."

Adam thanked them for their help and left. The Reynolds' house was his next stop.

The husband wasn't home.

"I know Ken must be devastated. He was devoted to his wife," Barbara said as she poured lemonade for herself and Adam.

Her daughter, a slimmer, ten-year-old version of the mother, was sitting at the kitchen table watching Adam with a worried expression. "Mom was always talking about what a health nut Mrs. Kinter was. Seems kind of weird that she'd die so young."

"She just didn't pay enough attention to the directions on the medicine she was taking," Barbara said hurriedly.

"And she mixed it with alcohol. You know how I always warn you to be careful. This will teach you to listen."

The girl grimaced impatiently. "I don't drink."

"I know, dear." Barbara looked frazzled and Adam guessed she'd been fielding questions by the worried youngster all day.

"Get real!"

Adam looked toward the door to see who had spoken.

A boy somewhere around twelve years of age, was standing there scowling at the girl as if he suspected her brain cells weren't all clicking in unison. "Mrs. Kinter killed herself."

The girl looked stricken. She turned to her mother. "She did? Is that what happened?"

Barbara glared at the boy. "We don't know for sure that's what happened and until we do, we are going to assume it was an accident. Now, since you don't seem to have anything better to do than to spread rumors, you can go up to your room and clean it. I'll be up to check."

The boy tossed her a grudging scowl. "Everyone knows. I heard Angel talking," he grumbled as he stalked off.

"Why don't you go outside for a while or go watch some television," Barbara coaxed the girl.

Giving her mother a look that said she knew she was being thrown out, the girl sulked out the back door. Through the window, Adam saw her flop on a lounge chair and sit staring toward the Kinter house.

"I apologize for my children," Barbara said, handing Adam his lemonade and motioning for him to take a seat at the kitchen table. "Linda's death has them both a bit shaken. They simply react differently."

Adam nodded. Beside his description of the slightly plump, brown-haired, brown-eyed, cute-faced woman he added "domestic nature." The way she interacted with her children reminded him of his mother. Ann Riley had devoted her life to her home and family. And Barbara Reynolds struck him as being of the same caliber. Her lemonade was even freshly squeezed.

Taking a seat across from him, Barbara shook her head slowly. "If Linda did take her own life, she was a fool. Ken's first wife is ancient history. He loved Linda." She leaned closer. "You know what I think?" She paused for a moment. "I heard it was morphine that did her in?"

"So it appears."

"Well, that's a painkiller. She was always so proud of her athletic ability. She worked out a lot and I think she was in more pain than she was willing to admit to. I know when I tried taking one of those classes, I pinched a nerve and ended up flat on my back for three weeks. Anyway, I think she kept the drug around to ease whatever pains she had and make it look as if her exercising didn't hurt one little bit."

A very dangerous measure if that had been Linda's ploy, Adam thought. "I was wondering if you spoke to her or saw her on Saturday?"

Barbara shook her head. "I feel a little guilty but then she and I weren't really good friends." She flushed. "Not that I didn't like her. We just didn't pal around on a one-to-one basis." The flush faded and her chin firmed. "Besides, I really didn't have any spare time on Saturday. I'd promised Jane I'd take her clothes shopping that morning. John had my afternoon booked so for us to have any time to look around, we had to be at the mall in Ashville when it opened. I dropped John off at a friend's house. Shopped with my daughter. Picked up John on the way home. Fed the kids lunch. Dropped Jane off at a friend's house and spent the rest of the afternoon watching John play baseball. By the time he was finished and I picked up Jane, my head was pounding. We got fast food, came home, I took a shower and went to bed."

She shook her head. "Then John got sick and I was up off and on all night with him." She scowled. "I'm sure it was sunstroke. Those kids shouldn't be out there running around in the hot sun."

"Next time I'll be sure to drink plenty of water," John said, returning to the kitchen in time to hear his mother lamenting his illness. He tossed Adam a grimace. "She insisted on sleeping on the other twin bed in my room and she snores."

Barbara flushed. "I do not."

"Do, too," the boy replied and hurried outside so that he could have the last word.

Adam thanked Barbara for her cooperation and left.

The Olivers weren't at home.

Mrs. McFay admitted to barely knowing her longtime neighbors. Like Susan Hallston had told him, the woman had her and her husband's families in addition to her children to occupy her time. She also hadn't seen or heard anything that had gone on over at the Kinter house on Saturday.

Carol Hawkins was next. She didn't have anything to add. At Claire's suggestion and that of Susan, she'd avoided Linda. "They were afraid I might say something else to upset her," she admitted frankly.

"And did you know of anything else that might have made her more upset?" Adam asked, again recalling Angel's insinuation about the husband's infidelity.

Carol thought for a moment, then shook her head. "Nothing." Her gaze leveled on the policeman. "Ken adored his wife. Linda was an idiot for letting the news about his first marriage shake her so badly." Her jaw firmed and a defensiveness entered her voice. "I'm sure her death was an accident."

Thanking her for her time, Adam left. His stomach growled and he glanced at his watch. It was lunchtime.

Chapter 4

Susan walked slowly home. She was glad she'd agreed to teach the summer session. The diversion had been a relief. Last night she'd had nightmares about finding Linda's body. This morning they'd continued to remain sharp in her mind until her class had demanded her full attention.

But as soon as the final bell had rung and the students had fled the room, the images had returned. Hoping the sweet scent of lilac on the summer breeze would lighten her mood, she took a deep breath and tried to concentrate on the flowers and the sun. The images remained.

A bike passed her on the street. She recognized the rider as Melissa Colby. Melissa, a somewhat plain girl, with nondescript brown hair, a little on the chubby side and shy, was one of the few summer school students who was there because she wanted to be. She was taking a computer course she couldn't fit into her regular schedule. Other than being as smart as or, perhaps, even smarter than Angel,

Melissa was, in nearly every other way, the opposite. Yet, the two were best friends.

"If I were Melissa's parents I'd encourage her to find a new friend," Susan murmured. But she doubted Melissa would listen to them. The girl was a middle child. Her parents both worked and whether it was fair or not, she felt neglected and the least loved of the three children. Susan had gleaned this information from Pauline Carter. The problem, as Susan saw it, was that Melissa was much too pliable. She could easily visualize Angel leading the other girl down paths that could prove harmful.

"I suppose teaching a room full of students who'd rather be outside enjoying their summer can drive a person to talk to themselves," a now familiar male voice commented from behind her.

She glanced over her shoulder to discover Adam Riley rounding the corner from Spruce Street. Every time she saw him, he seemed to get better looking, she thought, a womanly appreciation sparking to life within her. Immediately her guard came up. She wasn't ready to have those kind of reactions to a man again. "Afternoon, Detective."

Adam caught the glint of fear in her eyes. Again he wondered if it was a reaction due to her husband's treatment of her or did she have something to hide? Was she the object of Kinter's "moment of weakness?" Something that felt very much like a curl of jealousy wove through him. "I've been talking to Mrs. Kinter's neighbors. There are a few questions I need to ask you."

"I've told you everything I know." A lock of his hair had fallen onto his forehead and she had the most tremendous urge to comb it back with her fingers. Panic spread through her. Since the night her husband died, she'd been immune to men. Now suddenly every feminine instinct in her was sparking to life. Finding it much too disconcerting to stand there looking at him, she began to walk once again.

Adam fell into step beside her. "I've been trying to

piece together Mrs. Kinter's activities on Saturday. From
what I've learned, you spent most of the day with her.
What did you do?''

Organizing her thoughts with him beside her wasn't
easy. He made her feel giddy, like a schoolgirl being
walked home by a boy for the first time. *Think of Linda.*
This order brought an immediate end to the giddiness as
the image of death she'd been working so hard to push to
the dark recesses of her mind came vividly back to the
forefront. ''She came over to show me the letters and photos she'd found. I listened to her tirades about Ken and I
commiserated with her. He should have told her the truth.''

''That seems to be the general consensus.'' His attention
suddenly caught by a slow trickle of sweat winding its way
down her neck, Adam wondered if it would taste salty.
Keep your mind on business, he growled at himself.

''When she calmed down, I fed her lunch. Neither of us
ate much. We talked until she was able to get her anger
under control. About midway through the afternoon, she
said she felt tired and wanted to lie down. She looked
exhausted. I was worried about her so I walked her home.
Almost as soon as we were inside her house, she got rest-
less. She said the walls felt as if they were closing in on
her. I suggested we go out to a movie and dinner. I thought
it would take her mind off everything that had happened,
at least for a while. She agreed. We went to a movie and
then to Granny's.'' They had reached her front door. Looking toward the house next door, a fresh wave of guilt
washed through her. ''When we parted company, I was
certain she would be all right or I would never have left
her.''

Adam heard the guilt in her voice and saw her chin
tremble slightly. Was she a great actress or an innocent
bystander? He wanted to believe the latter. Again he reminded himself of Lisa. ''About what time did you last
see her?''

Susan noticed that the coaxing I-want-to-be-your-friend

tone he'd used yesterday was gone. Well, she had been behaving coolly, both last night and today, letting him know she didn't want his friendship. And she didn't. The thought of letting him get close to her, was definitely frightening. Even now, with him regarding her in that official, frosty manner she was wondering what his mouth would taste like. And such thoughts could lead to danger. "We parted company about nine-thirty or a few minutes after. She was exhausted. We both were. I thought she'd go directly to bed." Tears brimmed in her eyes. "I wish I could turn back the clock."

Adam again fought the urge to take her in his arms and comfort her. *If Mrs. Kinter's death was foul play, she's one of your prime suspects,* he reminded himself curtly.

Fitting the key into the lock, Susan's hand shook. Guilt over Linda and this unwanted attraction she was feeling for the detective were too much for her to handle. She wanted to escape into the cool, quiet solitariness of her home. "Is that all? It's been a long morning, I didn't sleep well last night and I've got a throbbing headache."

Adam ignored the dismissal in her voice. "There are a few more questions I need to ask." Hearing giggles, he glanced over his shoulder and saw Angel Carter walking up the street with a slightly chubby, brown-haired girl. Catching him looking her way, she grinned, gave her hair a playful, flirtatious toss, said something to her friend that caused the other girl to blush, then gave her friend's arm a tug so that they changed direction and headed back toward Angel's home. Promising himself he'd catch up with the teenager later, he returned his attention to Susan Hallston. "I think you'd prefer that we talk in private."

The warning in his voice surprised her. It suggested he thought she had something to hide. She didn't, but she did want a cold drink and a couple of aspirin. With a shrug that said she didn't understand his warning, she entered her house and headed to the kitchen. Behind her, she heard

Detective Riley's footfalls. "Would you like some iced tea?" she offered without looking back.

"No, thanks."

Hoping that was a sign he wasn't planning to stay long, she set her briefcase on the table, ran some water, got out two aspirin and took them.

Adam decided on the direct approach. He waited until she'd swallowed the pills and turned back to face him. Studying her for any signs of reaction, he asked, "Are you having an affair or have you ever had an affair with Ken Kinter?"

Startled, for a moment she stared at him in dumb silence. Then finding her voice, she said, "No. Never. I've never thought of Ken in romantic terms. He's a friend, that's all." Her voice firmed. "And Linda was a friend. And they were both devoted to each other."

She looked and sounded innocent. But looks could be deceiving. "Don't you think it's an intriguing coincidence that nine years ago Ken Kinter found your dead husband and yesterday you discovered the body of his wife?"

Susan's stomach began to churn and the pain in her head sharpened. First he'd asked her about a possible affair and now he was bringing up the discovery of Lyle's body.... She wasn't certain where he was heading but she was certain she wasn't going to like it. "Coincidences happen."

"Granted, they do." That she suddenly didn't look too well wasn't lost on Adam.

She heard the cynical edge in his voice. He didn't like the coincidence theory. Her shoulders straightened defiantly. "Just exactly what are you implying?" she demanded.

Adam studied her narrowly. "I have to consider all the possibilities. Maybe you and Kinter are a couple of terrific actors. Maybe he wanted his wife out of the way for some reason. And could be, he helped you do away with your husband so you helped him get rid of his wife. A favor for a favor." He didn't really buy this theory. Neither the doctor nor Judd had any suspicions that Kinter had been involved in Lyle's death. But it couldn't hurt to throw out a red herring before he hit her with what he considered the most likely possibility.

"That's absurd! Ken loved Linda. And neither of us did away with Lyle. He managed to kill himself!" She'd known some people thought she'd been instrumental in her husband's death but no one had ever said it aloud and given her the opportunity to deny the charge. It was almost a relief to get this declaration out in the open…almost.

"Or maybe you got rid of your husband on your own and got away with it? So you decided to try murder again to get someone you considered a nuisance out of your life. Could be you wanted Kinter for yourself so you decided to take the wife out of the picture."

Susan glared at him, anger hiding her fear that he might really believe what he was saying. "Where would you come up with such a ridiculous notion?"

"Rumors are that you and Kinter were sweet on each other once. Maybe you never stopped having feelings for him. Could be you two even had an affair going on behind the wife's back?"

"We did not! And, like I've already told you, we were never 'sweet' on each other. That was nothing more than idle gossip. We were and have always been just good friends." Her head was pounding. She wanted him gone. "If you're finished asking ridiculous questions and making absurd accusations, I've got work to do. We have to squeeze an entire semester into only a few weeks."

Normally Adam didn't mind rattling people he suspected might be involved in foul play. But in this case, he found himself reluctant to continue. He didn't have any real evidence that Linda Kinter's death hadn't been self-inflicted. Besides, if Susan Hallston was guilty in any way of contributing to her neighbor's demise, he'd made her nervous and nervous people made mistakes. It was time to back off, wait and watch. "Then I won't take up any more of your time for the moment."

Keeping a couple of paces behind, Susan followed him to the door. His accusation reeled in her mind. As he reached for the handle, she asked tersely, "Do you really think Linda was murdered?"

Adam turned back to face her. "It's my job to consider all possibilities."

For a long moment she regarded him mutely, then said, "I can't imagine anyone intentionally killing her." Challenge entered her voice. "Do you have any evidence that she didn't take her own life?"

She looked so stricken, he was beginning to hate himself for putting her through what he'd just put her through. Lisa had looked stricken, too, he reminded himself. "No. I'm simply making certain I don't miss anything."

The sudden thought of the gossip that would ensue if his suggestion that Linda had died at the hands of someone else ever became public knowledge brought an icy chill. She could still remember the behind-the-hands whispers she'd endured after Lyle's death. "What you're doing, Detective, is turning an already painful situation into one that could damage innocent people. Linda's death was tragic. But it was either a horrible accident or she did it to herself. Either way, I'll live with the guilt of having left her on her own until the day I die. But tossing around unsubstantiated innuendos isn't going to bring her back."

"I'll keep that in mind," he replied. Again he found himself disliking what he was doing, but it was his job and he still had a few problems with this case. One was that there had been no note. Admittedly, that could be explained if the woman hadn't intended to die. Secondly, he was fairly certain the husband had had an affair. Love triangles led to all sorts of problems. He also didn't like coincidences involving dead spouses.

Susan stood stiffly as he left. Her marriage had been a horrible mistake, one for which she'd paid dearly. Now this policeman was threatening to drag everything out into the open again. Her stomach churned and she was forced to make a dash for the bathroom. After she'd been sick, she rinsed her face with cold water and ordered herself to think calmly. Adam Riley was wrong about Linda's death but that didn't matter to him. He was probably bored in this little town and wanted to add some excitement to his case no matter who he hurt in the process. He went to the top of her hate list.

"Not a hate list," she muttered to herself. Her grandmother never approved of hating anyone, except of course for Lyle. But then, Lyle had been the personification of evil.

Adam Riley went to the top of her Persons I'd Least Like to See Cross My Path list, she corrected. Then, hoping work would help ease the dread spreading through her, she went down to the kitchen and opened her briefcase.

Leaving the Hallston house, Adam Riley spotted Angel and her friend sunbathing in the Carters' yard. They were stretched out on lounge chairs placed where they had a clear view of the traffic on Willow Street as well as Oak. The brown-haired girl's suit was modestly cut but Angel's bikini was one of the scantiest he'd seen. She filled it better than most twenty-year-olds and he wondered if she'd chosen the location so that she could keep an eye on the comings and goings of the neighbors or because she liked providing as many people as possible with an eyeful. Most likely a little of both, he decided.

Angel wasn't the only one watching the comings and goings today, he observed as he approached the girls, only to have Pauline Carter come off her back porch and head in their direction as well. Clearly she wasn't going to allow her daughter to say anything outside of her hearing. Silently, he cursed under his breath. He'd hoped for a more private interview.

"Afternoon, Detective Riley," Pauline Carter called out, reaching the girls a little ahead of him.

She reminded him of a mother hen protecting her brood. A natural reaction, he admitted. It was rare when he ran into a parent who didn't want to be present when their child was being questioned by the police.

"Afternoon, Mrs. Carter, Miss Carter." He left his notebook in his pocket. He'd noticed that most people tended to be more careful about what they said when he was jotting down their words and he wanted Angel off her guard.

"Afternoon, Detective." Angel remained prone, eased her sunglasses down the bridge of her nose until she could see the policeman over them, then eased them back in place.

This girl was never off her guard, Adam decided.

Angel waved a hand toward the brown-haired girl in the adjacent lounge chair. "This is my friend Melissa Colby." She turned to Melissa. "Now that you've seen him up close, you have to admit I was right. He's not what you'd call handsome, but he is a hunk."

Melissa flushed. "I suppose so."

Adam felt sorry for the friend. Angel was using her to try to embarrass him or at least shake him up some. But he'd dealt with a lot tougher and more brazen adolescents than Angel Carter.

"Really, Angel!" Pauline Carter admonished.

"You said yourself he was a hunk," Angel returned flippantly.

Pauline flushed. "That was a private observation."

Not a nice kid, Adam noted silently. She'd not only embarrassed her friend but her mother as well. And she'd enjoyed it. Subtlety, he decided, would get him nowhere with her. "You suggested earlier that Ken Kinter might be having an affair with one of the other women in this neighborhood. I want to know who."

Shock showed on Pauline's face. "That's preposterous. I've never known a more devoted husband than Ken. He'd never look at another woman." She scowled at Angel. "My daughter wants to be an actress. Sometimes she suggests things that aren't true simply to elicit emotions in others or see if she can convince them to believe her."

"I'm sure Angel didn't mean to cause any harm," Melissa spoke up quickly.

Adam caught the beginning of a catlike grin at one corner of Angel's mouth before she stopped it and schooled her expression into one of pure innocence.

"My mother's right," she said. "It's preposterous to think that Mr. Kinter would have an affair. He was crazy about his wife."

Adam saw the gleam of amusement in her eyes and knew she found her mother's naiveté laughable. He also caught the glitter of defiance and knew she wasn't going to give him a name. Asking all three if they'd seen anyone other than Susan Hallston or Linda Kinter enter or leave the Kinter house on Saturday, he got curious glances.

"You really are considering the possibility that she was murdered," Pauline said barely above a whisper.

"No. I'm merely trying to sort out all the facts," Adam replied, noncommittally.

Angel was now eyeing him with interest while Melissa's expression was one of horror. Suddenly Angel laughed. "He's just being a policeman, Mother. They ask a bunch of questions and get everyone stirred up over nothing. That's what policemen do. Isn't that right, Detective?"

"Yes, that's what we do," he replied, choosing to look the part of being overly zealous rather than start a flurry of rumors that, if Linda Kinter had taken her own life, could harm innocent people unnecessarily. What did surprise him was that it was Angel who had helped him. He would have thought she would have enjoyed seeing everyone suspecting each other of the foul deed. But then, a teenager's mind was incomprehensible. Maybe she'd done so just because she guessed he'd expect her to want turmoil.

Thanking them for their cooperation, he left.

"I need a break," he muttered.

A couple of hours later he was sitting at his desk finishing a pizza and going over his notes when the phone rang.

"I just got a call from my friend at the state lab," Dr. Miller said from the other end of the line. "There were traces of the drug in the wineglass. None in the bottle, which is reasonable if she wanted to make certain she got the full dose. Also, her prints were the only ones on the bottle and wineglass. They were also the only ones on the bottle of morphine."

With the evidence they did have strongly supporting suicide, Adam felt like a heel for the accusations he'd tossed at Susan Hallston. Mentally he kicked himself; he'd overreacted to learning about her husband's death because of Charlie and Lisa.

An uneasy edge crept into the doctor's voice. "However, there was something in the results that was peculiar."

Adam's self-recriminations came to an abrupt halt. "Spit it out, Doc."

"She'd eaten fudge all right, but it wasn't the fudge in the tin. The fudge in the tin was made with nearly fat-free ingredients. What she ate was the real stuff. Of course it could be that she kept the low-fat fudge around for Ken. He had a cholesterol problem. He didn't like watching his diet and she once told me she was secretly changing ingredients in the food she was feeding him and he'd never noticed. As for herself, she might have been a purist about her chocolates and kept a private stash."

Adam's jaw hardened into a grim line. "I didn't find any other fudge in the house. In fact, there were no other sweets. Looked to me like the lady followed a real healthy diet."

The doctor hesitated, then said, "Although I still find it hard to believe anyone would want to do her any harm, I suppose if someone had wanted to do her in, they could have hidden the drug in the chocolate and she'd never have noticed. After she'd eaten it, they could have added a drop to the bottom of the wineglass and taken the rest of the tainted candy away with them.'' His voice hardened. "However, my friend is a real stickler for detail, and he swears she definitely opened the morphine bottle herself. The prints and smears were all in the right places.''

"Keep this to yourself, Doc,'' Adam ordered.

"You bet I will. My vote is that she had a stash of fudge and what she ate was the end of it. That's why you didn't find any.''

"You could be right,'' Adam admitted.

The doctor gave a snort. "I wouldn't even consider the possibility of foul play if you hadn't brought up Lyle Bartram. I still think he deserved to meet his maker, but I'd like to know for certain I didn't let someone get away with murder.''

Susan Hallston was sitting on her front porch when Adam Riley returned and entered the house next door. The urge to go inside, lock the doors and curl up in a dark corner where she couldn't be found was strong. But nothing, she was being forced to realize, could stay hidden forever.

An hour later, when he exited the house, she was still sitting in her porch swing wishing she'd spent more time listening to her grandmother. Hattie had never liked Lyle. She'd warned Susan that she had a bad feeling about him. But Susan had been sure Hattie was simply afraid of being left on her own once Susan was married. Her grandmother had had a good head on her shoulders and a loving heart. Susan had ignored one and come close to breaking the other.

"Evening.''

Susan groaned silently. She'd been hoping the detective would climb back in his car and drive away. Instead, he was mounting the steps to her porch. "Go away,'' she said, her thoughts blurting out before she realized what she was saying.

Reaching the level of the porch, Adam leaned against one of the round pillars supporting the roof. He experienced a surge of sympathy for her. Immediately he steeled himself. "I have a couple more questions."

She glared at him. She'd been attracted to two men in her life. The first had nearly killed her and now this one wanted to hang her. "I've told you everything I know."

Adam ignored the dismissal in her voice. "When you and Mrs. Kinter went out to dinner, what did she eat?"

"She said she really wasn't hungry. She ordered a salad, no oil or onions, and coffee. But she didn't eat much of it."

"Any candy or popcorn at the movies?"

"No."

"I found a tin of fudge on the coffee table in the Kinters' house. It looked homemade."

Susan frowned in confusion. "What's fudge got to do with anything? You said she died of an overdose, not food poisoning. Besides, you can't get food poisoning from fudge, can you?"

Ignoring her question, Adam asked, "Do you know if Mrs. Kinter made the fudge?"

Angered that he'd refused to answer her question, Susan glared at him for a long moment, then said, "Yes, Linda made it. Ken loved homemade goodies. Fudge was his favorite. She always kept some on hand." A bud of hope bloomed. The thought that someone could die from bad fudge seemed almost sacrilegious but she was willing to accept anything that would put an end to this investigation. "Was something wrong with it?"

"No."

Frustration swept through her. "Then why ask about it?"

Again Adam ignored her query. "Did Mrs. Kinter ever share her recipe with you?"

Susan continued to frown at him, wondering what he really wanted to know and how he planned to get there with an idiotic conversation about fudge. "I never asked for it."

"You don't like fudge or you didn't like her fudge in particular?"

"I tried making fudge once and ended up with chocolate syrup. My grandmother, now there was a woman who could make homemade candies you would die for." Susan flushed. *Very bad choice of words.*

"Mrs. Kinter's wasn't as good as your grandmother's?" Adam persisted.

She felt guilty about sounding critical of her friend's cooking. "Linda's was very tasty but it wasn't the real thing. It was a low-fat recipe she'd worked up herself." Susan breathed a tired sigh as she recalled Linda watching her expectantly while she bit into a square of fudge. "It was a secret. Linda experimented until she developed a recipe we both thought would fool Ken. She was worried about his cholesterol. If she told him something was low in fat, he said it had no taste. So she swore me to secrecy and used me as her taste tester."

So, she knew about the fudge. And she hadn't claimed that Linda ate any candy at dinner or the movie. Adam experienced a surge of pleasure. Those were definite points in her favor. "Mrs. Kinter ate some regular fudge just before she died. Do you have any idea where she might have gotten it?"

Susan shrugged. "Maybe she kept a stash hidden away. Sometimes only the real stuff will do and Saturday could have been one of those times." Her gaze leveled on him as a reason for his questions suddenly occurred to her. "Are you suggesting that someone gave her fudge with the morphine in it?"

"All I know is that she ate the real stuff and I didn't find any in the house."

Susan continued to refuse to believe that anyone would

murder Linda. "Maybe she pigged out and ate all she had," she snapped. "You're making mountains out of molehills, Detective. You're looking for villains where there aren't any."

"I want to know what's going on!" a male voice demanded.

Susan looked past Detective Riley to see Ken approaching.

"I want to know when I can get back into my house." He had reached the policeman. Lowering his voice, he continued curtly. "My mother is hovering over me like a brooding hen. I know she means well, but she's driving me nuts. I need my own space. I need time to grieve on my own."

The desperation in the man's voice struck a sympathetic chord in Adam. "You can move back in tomorrow morning."

"Why not tonight?"

Adam watched Kinter for any reaction. "I'm going to make one more sweep of the place. I'm not satisfied that your wife's death was by her own hand."

For a moment Kinter studied him in mute silence, the color draining from his face. "You really are considering the possibility that Linda was murdered?"

"Everyone who knew her, when first questioned, swore she never used drugs," Adam said. "And there was no note."

Ken's expression was one of a man holding a mental debate with himself. Then he said grimly, "I haven't been entirely honest with you. About four years ago my wife confessed to me that she'd had a drug habit. She'd been in the accident that killed her parents. Her back was injured and she was in severe pain for a long period of time. It was then that she became addicted to painkillers. By the time we met, she'd gotten herself clean. The only reason she told me about her addiction was because she'd injured herself and I couldn't understand why she wouldn't take the painkiller Dr. Miller prescribed. She explained that she was afraid any backsliding could resurrect her habit full force.'' He sighed. ''But I guess even her best intentions couldn't keep her from doing a little backsliding after all.''

''Do have any proof of what you're saying?'' Adam asked.

''She told me the name of the clinic where she went. It's in her address book. She made me promise I'd take her there if she ever got hooked again.''

Hattie had been proved right again, Susan mused. Everyone had their secrets.

''Why in the hell didn't you tell me that right at the start?'' Adam growled. ''With a history like that, morphine would have been her drug of choice.''

''I wanted to spare her memory. It never occurred to me that you'd honestly try to make a murder case out of this.''

Adam wanted to take a punch at the grieving husband. Knowing that Linda Kinter had had a drug habit made a huge difference. The doctor's theory about her having purchased the drug but not used it so that she could cleanse her system to have a child was now very probable. And, she, most likely, hadn't intended to take enough to kill herself, thus there'd be no note. As for the fudge, she could easily have had a private stash and eaten all of it. She was, after all, distraught. As for the coincidence of Kinter finding Susan's dead husband and her finding his dead wife, even that didn't seem so far-fetched. Their lives had been closely entwined. ''Go back to your mother's place, Mr. Kinter. I should have this wrapped up soon.''

Ken turned to Susan. ''Would you offer me sanctuary for an hour or so?''

Susan tossed Adam a defiant glare. ''A *friend* would never turn down a *friend* in need,'' she replied.

Adam got the message. She and Kinter were only friends. As for himself, he guessed she considered him lower than the dirt under her feet.

As the policeman left, Ken looked down at Susan.

"What was that all about? I thought you were actually going to spell out the word *friend* there for a minute."

"It was nothing important," she replied. "You want some iced tea?"

"No, I just want to sit quietly." Sinking into the rocking chair, he closed his eyes and began to rock.

Respecting his need for silence, Susan propped the pillow on the arm of the porch swing and lay back. Seeing the first bright star of the night in the sky, she made a wish that Adam Riley would stop his wild-goose chases and let them grieve for Linda in peace.

Chapter 5

Adam stood a little away from the group of mourners gathered to say their last goodbyes at Linda Kinter's grave. Armed with the knowledge that Linda Kinter had turned to drugs as a crutch in the past, after a final examination of the evidence, he'd found no proof she hadn't died by her own hand. In the end, he, Dr. Miller and Chief Byrne had all concurred to label the death an accidental overdose. And now, studying the tearstained faces of her friends and loved ones, Adam was satisfied he'd done his job properly.

His gaze again came to rest on Susan Hallston. He'd read the file Judd had on Lyle Bartram and seen the photos taken of Susan after one of the beatings. He, like the doctor and Judd, concluded that if she had been instrumental in her husband's death, it had been self-defense.

He owed her an apology. But he wanted to do more than that. He wanted to ask her out on a date. He guessed she'd slam the door in his face. Still, he'd give it a try. She haunted his dreams. He couldn't forget how good she'd felt in his arms. No woman had had that kind of lasting effect on him.

The minister finished his final blessing and the group around the grave began to break up.

Now, however, was not the time to approach her, Adam decided, and headed to his car.

Out of the corner of her eye, Susan Hallston watched the detective departing. When she'd returned from school two days ago to find the barriers removed from Ken's house and been told by Carol that the body had been released for burial and the death declared an accident, she'd hoped she could relax and stop worrying about her past being resurrected. And she had until she'd seen Detective Riley at the service. She'd felt his eyes on her several times. Recalling the accusations he'd thrown at her, the nagging fear that he was going to reopen Lyle's case plagued her. She was innocent but that would make very little difference to the gossips. Her life would be a living hell, filled with askew glances and behind-the-hands gossiping.

She told herself to ignore him. Instead, she was suddenly striding through the graves on an intersecting course, catching up with him as he reached his vehicle.

"I thought the case was closed," she said curtly.

"It is."

"Then why are you here? Are you so disappointed this case wasn't a murder that you're considering trying to prove I had something to do with my husband's death? Well, you'll be disappointed again. The only thing resurrecting that case will do is to make my life miserable."

He couldn't blame her for thinking he was that crass. He had allowed memories of Charlie and Lisa to cause him to act overzealously. "I came today to pay my respects. I also want to apologize to you for any suggestions I made that you were involved in Mrs. Kinter's death and for bringing up your former marriage. As you pointed out, coincidences happen."

Relief spread through her. "Yes, they do."

He smiled, hoping to lessen her dislike of him. "I hope you'll forgive me."

He was flirting with her. For one brief moment the temptation to flirt back almost won. Then suddenly Lyle's image was in the forefront of her mind. Last night she'd woken in a cold sweat from a nightmare about him. Fear of making another mistake swept through her. "I suppose you were just doing your job," she said stiffly. Seeking safety, she added, "I really have to go," and hurried quickly toward the limousine provided by the funeral home for the family.

Adam had seen the fear in her eyes. Clearly, her former husband had left some very deep scars. If he chose to pursue a relationship with her, he'd have to overcome the taint left by her previous marriage as well as the anger she must still feel toward him because of the accusations he'd tossed her way during his investigation. "She's worth the effort," he murmured, watching the sway of her hips.

Susan was aware of the detective's gaze almost as if it were a physical touch. Suddenly she was recalling the feel of being in his arms, and deep within her, sensual stirrings began to awaken. Then again Lyle's sneering face filled her mind and cold fear spread through her.

"What was he doing here?" a woman's voice asked in hushed tones.

Susan glanced to her left to see that Carol had fallen into step beside her. "He came to pay his respects."

"I suppose that was the polite thing to do." The detective forgotten, Carol glanced back toward the casket and grimaced. "I really do wish I could turn back the clock. I still think Ken should have told Linda the truth from the very beginning, but I should never have opened my big mouth, either."

Tears threatened to again flood Susan's eyes. "We'd all like to turn back the clock. I wish I'd known about her previous drug use or realized how depressed she was. I would never have left her on her own.''

Carol placed an arm around Susan's shoulders and gave her a squeeze. "Let this be a lesson to all of us. No man is worth dying for.''

"No, they're not,'' Susan agreed, ordering herself to put Detective Riley completely out of her mind.

"Looks like Ken and his mother are coming,'' Carol said in hushed tones. "I'll just run along. He's still angry with me and Claire suggested I stay out of his path today.''

Lucky you, Susan thought. Immediately she felt guilty. Not surprisingly, none of Linda's relatives had come. As for Ken and Claire's family, there were a couple of distant cousins still living in town but they rarely saw them and the cousins had not called or shown any concern. Susan had been forced to realize that she and Carol were the closest to family Ken and Claire had. And, with Carol being persona non grata at the moment, Susan was left on her own to see them through this ordeal.

Trying to be supportive and provide both of them with a strong shoulder to lean on, she'd fought to hold her own grief under control but the strain of the day was wearing on her and she wanted it to be over.

"I'm so glad Ken had the foresight to hire Mable to brew the coffee and make certain the food was all laid out,'' Claire said as, with Ken's help, she worked herself into the back of the long gray car. "I feel so drained, I don't think I could do a thing.'' She flexed her fingers with painful slowness. "And on top of everything, my arthritis is worse.''

"It's the strain you've been under,'' Susan sympathized, climbing in and taking the seat opposite her. "It causes the arthritis to worsen. I know whenever my grandmother was upset, her ankles would swell unmercifully.''

"I suppose these after-the-funeral gatherings are necessary,'' Ken grumbled, sliding in beside his mother. "But I don't know how much more I can take.''

He looked like hell, Susan thought. "I'll try to see that no one stays too long."

"You are a dear," Claire declared. "I don't know what we would do without you."

As they passed through the stone pillars at the entrance of the cemetery, Susan wondered if she'd ever get rid of the guilt she felt for leaving Linda on her own.

It was three hours later when, finally alone and emotionally drained, Susan climbed her own porch steps. Too exhausted to even go inside and change, she collapsed into the rocking chair that had been her grandmother's favorite, kicked off her high heels and propped her feet up on the short milking stool Hattie had used as a footrest. A monumental headache throbbed at her temples. She closed her eyes and leaned back.

"Miss Hallston?"

Susan opened her eyes to see a subdued Angel Carter standing a couple of feet away. She'd expected Angel to talk her parents into allowing her to skip the funeral. But the teenager had not only accompanied them to the service, she'd gone to the Kinters' house afterward. Even more surprising, Angel had hung in the background remaining as unobtrusive as possible. Maybe seeing Linda lying dead in the coffin had had a sobering effect on the girl, Susan mused. If so, her friend's death had not been entirely in vain. "What is it, Angel?"

The teenager hesitated a moment, then said, "I was sort of wondering why Detective Riley was at the funeral. I saw you talking to him. Have the police changed their minds about how Mrs. Kinter died?"

"No." Susan was certain she saw the hint of a smile begin at the corner of the teenager's mouth, then it was gone and the girl's expression was once again solemn. The reaction made Susan uneasy. "Do you know of any reason why they should?"

Angel shrugged. "Not me." A glimmer entered her

eyes. "But I'll miss having the detective around. He had a manly face, filled with character, don't you think? And a nice physique. All in all I'd classify him a hunk. Wouldn't you?"

Susan was in no mood to discuss Detective Riley. "I hadn't noticed."

This time Angel did smile. "I figured as much." As if Susan had just confirmed a suspicion the teen had held for a long time, Angel's gaze flickered over her with cold contempt, then the girl descended the steps and headed down the block in the direction of her home.

Mentally, Susan kicked herself. Letting the teenager's question about Linda's death throw her off guard, she'd played right into Angel's hands. She should have been noncommittal about Detective Riley. Instead, her response had given the teenager what she'd obviously really come looking for...fuel for making incorrect assumptions about Susan's sexual preferences. Clearly, Linda's death had not had a subduing effect on Angel's malicious nature, after all.

"That child has a vicious mind." Carol's voice cut into Susan's thoughts.

Susan glanced to her right and saw the woman approaching from around the corner of the house.

Mounting the porch steps, Carol stood regarding her narrowly. "I do hope she's not right in her insinuation. I'll admit that men can be the scum of the earth but there's no substitute when it comes to bedroom games."

"She's not right," Susan assured her.

Carol continued to study her reprovingly. "Of course I can understand where she'd get that idea. You haven't dated much since your unfortunate marriage."

"My 'unfortunate marriage' made me cautious."

Carol seated herself in the swing. "Too cautious. The men you've dated belong on the Top Ten Most Boring Men in Town list. And lately you've stopped dating entirely as far as I can determine."

"In case you haven't noticed, this town isn't overrun with eligible males," Susan returned in her defense. "And I've been too busy to look elsewhere."

"How about as far as your nose? Angel is right. Detective Riley might not be the handsomest man in the world but by Bandits' Gorge standards, he's a real hunk and the first fresh meat to come along in a long time."

Susan's jaw firmed. "I'm not interested in Detective Riley."

Carol frowned. "Admit it...you're scared of him. You're afraid he might start your juices running again. You've got to get past what Lyle did to you and get on with your life."

Susan scowled back. "Detective Riley thought I was having an affair with Ken, and that I might have done away with Linda so that Ken and I could marry."

Carol's eyes rounded. "He thought that? He thought Mr. I Worship the Ground My Wife Walks On was having an affair? Where in the world would he get a notion like that?"

"I have no idea."

Carol abruptly smiled. "You should consider the upside."

Susan regarded her dryly. "Upside?"

"He obviously considers you a femme fatale. That's a heck of a lot better than a dowdy, spinsterish high school teacher. There could be hope for the two of you getting together yet."

"And you have a very twisted sense of humor."

"And you are in danger of turning into a dowdy spinster."

"My life suits me just fine."

Carol's hands flew up to cup her face in a mock exaggeration of shock. "Oh my god, you've already metamorphosed into Miss Hanson."

Susan's scowl darkened. Miss Hanson had been her second grade teacher. Miss Hanson had been her mother's second grade teacher. The woman's whole life had revolved around her teaching and her pupils. After she'd been forced to retire, she'd sat on her front porch rocking, looking like a lost soul cast out from the world she loved. She'd died in that rocker. Jack Connelly had found her. He'd been driving by on his patrol. It was nearly midnight and she was still out so he'd stopped to check on her only to discover she was dead. "I am not going to end up like Miss Hanson," Susan assured her. "I plan to travel when I retire, see the world."

Carol looked her up and down. "It seems to me you're already spending too much time alone sitting in that rocker or on this swing watching life pass you by. And, I'm not the only one who's noticed. I heard Harriet Beecher at the beauty parlor the other day making a crack about you being a second Miss Hanson."

Susan's headache had never gone away. Now it was throbbing worse than ever. "I'm going to take a nice long bath. This has been a very difficult day." As she rose to go inside, Carol was suddenly on her feet laying a restraining hand on her arm.

"Did Ken say anything about me?" she asked in lowered tones. "Am I still on his black list? Claire doesn't take death well. I remember when her husband died in that boating accident. She went to pieces. We've been friends for better than thirty years and I hate not being able to be with her right now."

Susan had to admit that as irritating as Carol could be at times, she had a good heart. "Ken said he blames himself for not having told Linda the truth but he'd still prefer not to see you for another couple of days."

Carol breathed a relieved sigh. "I can handle another couple of days of avoiding him." Smiling, she left.

"I am not a Miss Hanson clone," Susan muttered under her breath as she went inside.

Adam was normally a patient man, but he couldn't get Susan Hallston off his mind. He'd reasoned that he should give her a couple of days to get over Linda Kinter's death before he called on her. But he didn't want to wait.

Sitting slumped on his couch, he grimaced wryly. He hadn't experienced this strong an attraction to a female since junior high when his hormones kicked in full force. He thought he was well past that stage of life or at least had himself under more rational control. "Looks like I was wrong."

Already on his feet, he headed out the door.

It was dusk when he parked in front of her house. He'd thought about bringing her flowers but decided that would probably just remind her of the funeral. Candy was his next thought, then he'd recalled their conversations about Linda's fudge. He didn't want to do anything that would heighten her memories of his investigation.

In the end, he'd settled on something he hoped would make her smile and get him an invitation for a cup of coffee.

Following her bath, Susan had dressed in her favorite cotton nightgown and soft terry cloth robe and curled up on the living room sofa to watch television. The knock on the door brought a low groan and she considered not answering it. She'd had all she could take for one day. But her sense of duty was too strong. Worried that Claire or Ken might need her, she pushed herself to her feet. Opening the door, she stood mutely. Detective Adam Riley was the last person she'd expected to find on her threshold.

"I brought an apple pie as a peace offering," he said, extending the bakery box from the grocery toward her. "An apple for the teacher..." He let the phrase trail off as he mentally kicked himself. He should have waited a couple of days. The strain of the day was etched into her features and there were circles caused by exhaustion under her eyes.

"I'm not sure what to say," Susan said honestly. The contrite expression on his face made him look incredibly handsome. Again a very feminine response began to awaken within her. It was quickly squelched by fear. She had played this game once and lost badly.

Adam told himself to leave but she looked delectably cute dressed for bed, her hair mussed and her feet bare. He didn't want to go, not yet. "You could invite me in. I'll make us some coffee and we can share the pie."

Refusal was on her lips, then she thought of Miss Hanson and found herself stepping aside to allow him to enter. "All right, sure."

The protective urge she'd inspirited in him the first time he'd seen her grew stronger. "On second thought, I'll bet you haven't eaten. How about if I take you out to dinner? Or, if you're too tired to get dressed, I can go get us something."

The concern in his voice had the effect of making her feel as if she were being wrapped in a cozy blanket and she found herself wanting to be in his arms again, her head resting on his shoulder. Again fear curled through her. Thoughts like that could lead to danger. "It's been a long day. I appreciate the pie and the dinner invitation, but I'm really tired."

The dismissal in her voice held no compromise. Adam cursed himself for not being more patient. He'd probably gone to the top of her list of insensitive boors. "You're right, it has been a long day. I apologize for barging in on you. But I wanted to make certain you know how truly sorry I am for any pain I caused you. I'll see myself out."

As he turned to go, the image of Miss Hanson dying alone on her porch came vividly into Susan's mind. Torn between the fear of taking a chance and the fear of not taking a chance, she wanted to scream in frustration. Instead, she heard herself saying, "If you're free on Sunday around two you could drop over for that cup of coffee." Her insides felt like jelly as she waited for his response. A part of her wanted him to accept while another part hoped he wouldn't.

Adam grinned. Maybe he hadn't made such a bad impression on her after all. "Two on Sunday," he confirmed.

A cup of coffee was safe, she told herself, standing at the door watching him walk to his car. So, why were her hands shaking?

Adam could feel her eyes on him and grinned triumphantly as he climbed into his car.

Sunday morning Susan barely heard the sermon. Ever since Friday night, she hadn't been able to get Adam Riley out of her mind. In her dreams she'd become lost in the brown depths of his eyes but just as she was moving into his arms, he'd suddenly become Lyle and she'd woken in a cold sweat. Awake, when she thought of him, she experienced bouts of girlish giddiness only to have them quickly countered by memories of the abuse she'd suffered at Lyle's hands.

By the time the church service was over her stomach was churning. "You can't live out your life in fear," she growled at her image in the rearview mirror. But instead of going directly home to prepare for Adam's arrival, she drove to the edge of town and parked at the far end of a long dirt drive. It was practically overgrown with weeds now and the house at the end of the drive was in a bad state of disrepair. The property belonged to Jess Bartram, Lyle's uncle. He'd built himself a more modern, fancier house down the road. When Lyle and Susan had wed, he'd offered them this place, rent free, until they could get financially on their feet. Since Lyle's death it had remained abandoned.

Memories of the terror she'd suffered inside those walls assailed her. Suddenly flooring the car in reverse, she filled the air with a cloud of dust. On the main road she left rubber behind when she shifted from reverse to drive and again floored the gas pedal, running from a past she wanted to put behind her but couldn't. In the safety of her home, she dialed Adam's number with shaky hands.

"I'm sorry, but I'm going to have to break our date today," she said without any preamble when he answered. "I think I have a touch of the flu." Hanging up before he could respond, she ran to the bathroom and threw up.

Adam frowned at the receiver. She'd sounded really sick. Dropping the receiver in the cradle, he strode out of his apartment.

Susan was splashing cold water on her face when the knock sounded on her door. Ignoring it, she dried her face and stood staring at the ashen image in the mirror. Lyle had nearly destroyed her once and she was still letting him rule her. Tears of anger and rage flooded her eyes. She hated the fear he made her feel.

The knocking sounded again. Whoever was there hadn't gone away. Steeling herself, she went to the door.

"I thought you might need someone to look after you." Her paleness scared Adam. "I think I should take you over to Dr. Miller's place. You look like hell."

"I feel like hell," she admitted, too upset by her anger at allowing Lyle to continue to haunt her to be embarrassed. But when he opened the screen door, removing that barrier from between them, she discovered that her fear was still stronger than her ability to fight it. Again nausea bubbled up inside her. She held up a cautioning hand and took a step back. "But I'll be fine on my own. I just need to get some rest."

Adam wasn't convinced. "Maybe I should stick around for a while."

"Really, I prefer to suffer on my own when I'm sick," she insisted, furious with herself for being so weak.

Don't push so hard, Adam ordered himself. He didn't like people around when he was sick, either. "I'll call in a couple of days," he said, his voice holding a promise.

Susan nodded and managed to fight back a second bout of nausea until he was gone.

Chapter 6

Tuesday morning at 6:12, just a week and two days since he'd been summoned to the Kinter house...the day Adam had planned on calling Susan Hallston for a date...he stood frowning down at Angel Carter's lifeless body. The girl was lying on her back near a large lilac bush by the side of the house toward Willow Street. This time, there was no doubt he was dealing with a murder. Her face had a purple hue and her eyes were bulged. Around her neck was a dark circle of bruising. A scarf lay nearby on the grass.

She was fully clothed and there was no visible evidence that anyone had made any attempt to undress her. One of her sandals lay a few feet away. The other was still on her foot. She'd struggled a little but not much.

He cursed under his breath. If there had been any evidence, it had been destroyed or would be useless in a court of law. The damp, dew-coated grass surrounding the body looked as if it had been trampled by half a dozen pairs of feet. He turned to Jack Connelly, flanked by two paramedics. "Who found the body?"

"The mother, as far as I can determine," the patrolman replied. "By the time I got here Trevor and Deborah Oliver were getting everyone to move away from the body. Being lawyers, they realized the scene shouldn't be disturbed. But the damage had already been done." He indicated the culprits with a twist of his head toward a couple of clusters of people standing in the Carters' backyard.

Most were wearing pajamas and robes. From the center of the largest gathering came the sound of a woman crying hysterically and Adam caught a glimpse of Pauline Carter dressed in a jogging outfit.

"Looks like she was strangled," the heavier set of the two paramedics volunteered.

Adam swung his attention back to them. "Did you touch the body?"

"I felt for a pulse," the heavier one replied.

Adam scowled.

"I asked him to. She looked dead but I didn't want to take a chance on making a mistake," Jack spoke up.

"I've known Angel all her life. Never figured I'd see her like this. 'Course when I heard she was running around with Polaski, I knew she was asking for trouble." This time, it was the slimmer paramedic who had spoken.

On closer inspection, Adam realized he was much younger than his partner. Barely out of school, he guessed. "Polaski?"

"Wayne Polaski. He works at Casey's Garage. Lives there, too, with old man Casey. Used to carry a switchblade and cut locks of girls' hair off in school for kicks just to frighten them. One of the girls got so scared she told a teacher. The teacher tried to take the knife away and he threatened her with it. That got him expelled. Can't say anyone missed him."

Adam jotted down the name. "Any relation to Councilman Polaski?"

"His sister's kid. She never said who the father was," the older paramedic replied. He grinned as if recalling a pleasant sight. "She was a beauty. Liked to party." The grin vanished. "Wrapped her car around a tree when the kid was still real young. His grandpa raised him after that. Good God-fearing man but the boy's ma's wild blood was too strong in him. When the grandpa died, the councilman took him in. The kid caused nothing but trouble. When he got kicked out of school, I guess Lewis figured he'd had enough, too. He kicked him out of his house."

Sounded as if the man and his young partner had already found their suspect, Adam noted. "Thanks for the information. You can go now."

"If I were you I'd get a call out to pick up Polaski," the younger paramedic advised. "'Course he's probably over the state line by now."

The older man scowled at his young counterpart. "The police know what to do. It's not up to us to tell them their job." A voice came over the walkie-talkie strapped at his waist interrupting any further reprimand. "We've got another call. Hurry it up," he ordered, jogging toward their vehicle.

"I didn't mean to tell you your business," the boy apologized quickly, then followed his partner.

"Maybe we should put out an APB on the Polaski kid," Jack suggested as the ambulance pulled away.

"You do that. Be sure to tell whoever picks him up, not to tell him why he's being picked up. I want to see the look on his face when I tell him Angel's dead. And, don't let anyone else near the body until I take pictures." Adam started toward the people gathered a short distance away, then turned back. It was going to take time to get this crowd settled. He didn't want to give nature a chance to disturb the scene any further. "Jack," he called out.

The patrolman stopped halfway to his car and looked back.

"You know how to use a camera?" Adam asked.

"I'm the official family photographer at all of our reunions," Jack replied.

Adam tossed his car keys to the patrolman. "The camera's in my trunk. Cordon off the area around the body, then take photos of the body from all angles and get shots of the yard in general. Make sure you get some close-ups."

Jack nodded. "You got it."

Adam returned his attention to the people surrounding the sobbing mother. Susan was there looking so shaken, he wanted to order her home immediately but duty refused to allow that. Forcing his attention from her to the others, he recognized Claire Kinter, Carol Hawkins, and Barbara and Ted Reynolds. Ray Carter was standing next to his wife, his arm around her shoulders, his face ashen.

A little apart from this group, was a foursome. The only one Adam recognized among them was Kay McFay, but he felt safe in assuming the man with his arm around her waist was her husband. The other two were a young couple. He guessed they were the Olivers.

Color flowed into Ray Carter's cheeks when he saw Adam approaching and anger distorted his features. "It was that Polaski kid! I told her to stay away from him. You'd better find him before I do."

Susan experienced a rush of relief at the sight of Adam Riley. The shock of Angel's death had numbed her. His presence gave her strength and she began to think more rationally. "Maybe it would be better if we got Pauline inside," she suggested.

"I don't want to leave my baby!" The woman's sobs became even louder and more gasping.

"Susan's right. We should move inside. We don't want to trample any evidence the detective needs to collect," Carol coaxed.

Too late for that, Adam thought dryly. But he liked the idea of getting Pauline Carter where her daughter's body wasn't in her line of vision. He needed to ask some unpleasant questions and he didn't want her any more hysterical than she already was. "It would be better if you moved inside." His voice carried a command.

Pauline cast him a look of protest.

"You do want to help the police find whoever did this dreadful thing," Claire Kinter coaxed.

Fury replaced the protest on Pauline's face. "Yes. Yes, I do." Without further hesitation, she allowed her husband to guide her inside. The group that had been surrounding them followed.

The McFays and the younger couple hung back.

"We really can't be of any help. We hardly knew Angel," Kay McFay addressed Adam, a plea to be dismissed in her voice. "And I should be getting back to my children. I don't want them coming out here and seeing…" Her words catching in her throat, she was forced to nod toward the body in an unspoken finish to the sentence.

"We're the Olivers, Deborah and Trevor." The male of the younger couple extended his hand toward Adam. "We live next to the McFays. I'm afraid we don't know anything, either. We just heard the screams and came running." He frowned impatiently toward the Carter house. "By the time we got here, they'd all gathered around the body. I'm afraid they did a lot of damage to any evidence."

Adam accepted the handshake. "I appreciate your help. You can all go home. I know where to find you, if I need to question you."

Relief showed on their faces. Immediately they started across the lawns to their own residences.

Entering the Carter house, Adam found The Backyard Society as Susan Hallston had once referred to this small social clique, gathered in the living room. Pauline Carter was seated in an overstuffed, upholstered chair near the front window, her face buried in her hands. Her husband was in the companion chair. Claire Kinter had chosen a straight-back chair close enough to Pauline's to allow her to reach out and pat the grieving woman's arm. Like two sentries standing guard, Carol Hawkins and Susan Hallston stood behind and to the side of Pauline's chair. The Reynolds had also remained standing, taking a position on the other side of Ray Carter, Barbara clinging to her husband. All looked at Adam as he joined them as if expecting him to make some monumental pronouncement.

"Who found Angel?" he asked.

"I found my daughter." Pauline lifted her head. She'd stopped crying. Her complexion was a grayish white making her reddened eyes even more prominent. "I was going out for my morning run. I always go out for a morning run." Her chin trembled. "I saw her lying on the ground. I thought she'd fallen. I knew she sneaked out her bedroom window every once in a while but I never thought about her falling. I assumed she came out onto the porch roof and used the trellis to climb up and down. It was built real sturdy. She'd seen to that."

Ray Carter glared at his wife. "She was sneaking out at night and you didn't tell me?"

"You were too restrictive. She was sixteen. She wanted to go out and have fun. You wanted to keep her locked up in the house. I knew you'd ground her and that would only make her resent us. I didn't want her to feel trapped."

"Just because your parents were overly protective doesn't mean you should have allowed her do whatever she wanted!"

"You refused to allow her to go out more than two nights a week and even then you set an eleven o'clock curfew."

"Mr. Carter. Mrs. Carter." Adam interrupted.

Both flushed. "Sorry," Ray apologized. He shot an accusatory glance at his wife. "I just wish I'd known. I would have found a way to stop her."

"She would have run away!" Pauline retorted. "She had a will of her own."

"You found the body when you went out to jog. That

was at what time?'' Adam interceded, again trying to take control.

"Five-thirty. I like to get an early start." A fresh flood of tears streamed down Pauline's cheeks.

"Did you touch her?"

Pauline trembled and looked as if she were going to be sick. "Her face was so purple and her eyes…" She paused and swallowed.

"Did you touch her?" Adam asked again, keeping his tone gentle but firm. He hated putting the woman through this but he had to know.

She nodded. "I unfastened the scarf from around her neck. I thought maybe that would help. Then I saw the horrible bruising beneath. I knew she was dead. I couldn't move. I just started screaming."

"I was still in bed," Ray Carter spoke up. "I heard my wife, grabbed my robe and went running out."

Adam turned his attention to the husband. "Did you touch the body?"

"Maybe. I think so. I think I shook her hoping she'd wake up." Ray Carter began to cry. "It's like a nightmare."

Adam's gaze traveled over the rest of the assembly. They all looked uncomfortable. Catching Susan Hallston's eye, he cast her an encouraging look and was pleased when she smiled back weakly. So maybe she wasn't still holding his previous behavior against him.

Forcing his attention off her, he turned to Ted Reynolds. "The 911 operator listed you as the caller."

Ted nodded. "Barbara and I heard the screaming and came running over. When we saw what was going on, I came in here and called."

Barbara was crying now. "I stayed with Pauline. I didn't touch Angel."

"I heard the commotion and called Susan," Claire said when Adam looked in her direction. "She'd had a first-aid course and I thought she might be of some help. I know a little myself but these old hands aren't of much use any longer.''

Noting the woman's swollen wrists and finger joints, Adam agreed. He turned his attention to Carol Hawkins. She was the only one in the group besides Pauline Carter who was dressed in street clothes.

''I was just going out for my early morning walk,'' Carol said, when she realized his gaze was now resting on her. ''I heard the screaming and came to see if I could help.''

Adam groaned mentally. Like good neighbors hurrying to the rescue, they'd all come running and trampled any evidence that might have been anywhere near the scene. ''Did any of you see or hear anything last night that might shed some light on Angel's death?''

All shook their heads in the negative.

Deciding he'd learned everything he was going to learn from them for the moment, Adam said, ''I'll need to take a look at Angel's room.''

''Upstairs, the last door on your right,'' Ray said, absently.

''She doesn't like anyone going through her things,'' Pauline protested, starting to rise.

Susan placed a restraining hand on her shoulder. ''If you want Angel's killer brought to justice, you have to let Detective Riley do his job.''

Pauline didn't look happy, but she did sink back into her chair.

Adam cast Susan a grateful glance, then headed upstairs.

''I give that marriage about a week past the funeral,'' Carol said as she and Susan helped Claire home a few minutes later. As soon as Adam had started up the stairs, the elderly woman had complained of feeling faint. Barbara Reynolds had volunteered to remain and look after Pauline and Ray, thus freeing the others to return home. Susan felt a little guilty about leaving, but then Pauline was closer to Barbara than any of the others, so having Barbara stay was the reasonable choice.

To avoid the onlookers and the cordoned off area, they'd gone around the corner to Spruce Street and were now crossing the McFays' property on their way to Claire's backyard.

"You could be wrong. I've always thought they suited each other very well." Susan tightened her grip on Claire's arm as the woman stepped on uneven ground and her arthritic ankles threatened to twist.

Carol gave Susan a wry look. "I can't believe it. You still want to believe in fairy-tale marriages."

"I want to believe a couple can grow old together, stay in love and be comfortable companions to each other like my grandparents. I know it wasn't a smooth path but they made it," Susan replied. "And my parents have a solid marriage, too."

"I suppose some people take the bumps better than others," Carol conceded. She glanced sideways at the Carter house. "But this is one hell of a bump. And for Ray to find out Pauline had been letting Angel sneak out isn't going to smooth the road any."

Claire sighed. "My Ward and I would have survived." They had reached her porch and her manner became apologetic. "I'd ask you in for coffee but I'm feeling too tired. This has been such a shock. And on top of Linda's death."

"I couldn't come in anyway," Susan said. "I have to be getting home and dressed. I've got a class to teach." She grimaced self-consciously. "I know that sounds callous but the truth is I've got to do something to get the image of Angel out of my mind." In spite of the heat, she shivered. "She looked so grotesque."

"We understand, dear," Claire said soothingly. "I think we would all like to have been spared that sight."

Carol nodded her agreement, then turned to Claire. "You rest awhile. I'll stop by later." As if a light had suddenly clicked on, she frowned and glanced toward

Ken's house. "Ken must be sleeping soundly. Of course, it's probably for the best that he missed this."

The tiredness on Claire's face lessened. "He's at Ruth's estate in Maine visiting with his son. He was so depressed by Linda's death, Ruth and I thought that being with the boy might help."

Susan recalled that Claire had been in the pictures with Ken and his son. And from Claire's tone, it sounded as if she were quite friendly with Ruth. Experiencing a sense of betrayal on Linda's behalf, Susan reminded herself that it was only natural for a grandmother to want to see her grandchild and if that meant befriending the mother, then she shouldn't really blame Claire. Still, it bothered her. "What about Ruth's father? Aren't you afraid he'll find out?"

"He died several months ago. Ken didn't tell me until after Linda's funeral. He was afraid that if I knew, I'd pressure him to tell Linda about the boy so my grandson could come visit me." Claire's gaze shifted to her son's home. "Linda was so set on having a child of her own, he was afraid of how she would take the news. Obviously, he had reason to be." A tear trickled down Claire's cheek. "I need to go lie down now."

Carol shook her head as she and Susan left Claire's porch and started across Ken's backyard. "Now there's a marriage that would have lasted if both Linda and Ken hadn't behaved so stupidly. He should have been honest with her and she should never have let herself get so depressed she turned to drugs. As cynical as I've become, I honestly believe they loved each other and would have worked things out."

Susan nodded her agreement.

Carol lowered her voice. "However, I wouldn't have placed any bets on Claire and Ward."

Surprised by that statement, Susan frowned. "That's ridiculous. They got along just fine."

Carol lowered her voice even more. "On the surface

Ward Kinter acted as if he loved his wife and I know Claire was crazy about him. It was always 'Ward this' and 'Ward that.' There were times when I got so sick of hearing about how wonderful he was, I wanted to puke. But it's my opinion that it was pure luck she was the one who survived that boating accident.''

Through the years Carol had said a lot of things that had shocked Susan but this was the most startling. ''I can't believe what you're suggesting.''

Carol's manner became even more confidential. ''Claire was too shaken to be of any use and Ken wasn't much better. They asked me to help go through Ward's papers. And guess what I found?''

Susan's scowl deepened with impatience. ''I'm really not in the mood for guessing games.''

''There was an insurance policy. A very large one on Claire's life.''

''Claire and Ward believed in insurance. There was a very large policy on Ward's life as well,'' Susan reminded her.

''Yes, but that one they'd had since Ken was born. Claire had never tried to hide it. In fact, she used to love to tell the story about how, right after Ken was born, she'd held him in her arms and suddenly had a panic attack worrying about how she would take care of him on her own if anything happened to Ward.''

''I know the story,'' Susan interrupted impatiently. ''She made Ward go out that day and take out a policy.''

''Right. But the policy I found on Claire was a shock to both her and Ken. She'd known Ward had a small policy on her to cover a proper burial and a few medical expenses she might have incurred. But the policy I found was a new one and for a great deal of money. And, it had been taken out only a few months before the accident. Both of them refused to believe Ward had any ulterior motives. Like you, they insisted on pointing out that he was a firm believer in insurance.''

"And he was," Susan insisted, refusing to buy into Carol's paranoia.

"You can't possibly be that naive. Claire hates being in a boat. She has a terrible fear of the water. She only went fishing with Ward that day to please him. Then he goes and hooks a fish so big trying to get it in causes them to capsize?" Carol raised a cynical eyebrow. "If he hadn't hit his head on the edge of the boat when he came back up, I'd take odds on him being the one alive today and Claire being in her grave."

"Claire was wearing a life jacket."

"When I was trying to comfort her after the funeral, she got to blubbering about how Ken could have been orphaned. She told me that Ward had talked her into keeping her life jacket unfastened so she could cast more easily and that she almost lost it in her panic when she fell in."

Susan's jaw tensed. "I refuse to believe Ward Kinter tried to kill his wife."

"You believe what you will." Carol glanced over her shoulder toward the Carter house. "But I'm going to start locking my doors. I don't feel safe around here anymore."

Susan breathed a tired sigh. "I've always thought of our little neighborhood as being a sanctuary. The whole town, actually. Compared to the rest of the world it seemed to be a haven of peace and goodwill." Her chin trembled. "Now it seems to reek with death."

Carol gave Susan's shoulders a squeeze then shoved her gently but firmly in the direction of her house. "Go get dressed and teach your class."

Entering her screened back porch, Susan pictured Ward Kinter. Carol was wrong about him. He'd been a nice man. She could still remember him crying while burying the puppy he'd bought for Ken's fourteenth birthday. The short stocky brown ball of fur had been a handful. He'd chewed on everything...shoelaces; socks left lying on the floor; the leg of the dining room table; Ken's baseball bat. But no one had minded too much. He was so cute. Then he chewed on the beans from the castor bean plant in the corner of the yard. Their poison caused a painful death. Ward had cut the plant down right after he'd buried the puppy and forbid Claire to ever plant another. It had been quite a scene with Claire bawling and vowing to always check on the toxicity of any plant she put in her garden after that.

Susan gave her shoulders a shake and shoved the old memories out of her mind. Entering her kitchen, she glanced at the clock on the wall. She was due at the school soon. Even a room full of students who didn't want to be there would be a welcome diversion today.

Halfway to the stairs, she stopped, returned to her back door and threw the dead bolt into place.

After a quick cursory survey so that he would know if any evidence had been tampered with during his absence, Adam issued strict orders to the parents to stay out of Angel's room, then he sealed the door. He'd go through her things more thoroughly later. Right now, he wanted to see what the body could tell him.

The Carters had been cooperative when they weren't bickering, but they hadn't given him much to go on. The mother had no idea when the girl had sneaked out. She assumed Angel had met with Wayne Polaski, but she didn't know for sure.

Outside, Adam found Dr. Miller waiting with Jack. "I don't like it when my patients die young," the doctor said. "I expect you to find whoever did this."

"I intend to," Adam assured him. He jerked his attention to Jack. "Did you get the photos?"

"Three rolls. I didn't want to take a chance on missing anything." The policeman handed the camera to Adam. "I put in a fresh roll in case you wanted to take a few yourself."

Adam nodded. He trusted the patrolman but liked to be thorough. He snapped the full roll, put the camera away and got out his evidence-collecting kit. After slipping on a pair of latex gloves, he began searching the body hoping for a clue as to who she had been going to meet.

Angel was wearing a pair of hip-hugging denim cutoffs, a halter top and an oversize shirt. From the pocket of the shirt he extracted a small pouch of greenish plant matter. A quick sniff told him it was marijuana. He also found cigarette papers and matches. "Maybe she tried to stiff her dealer and ended up being the stiff," he muttered as he bagged the evidence.

"He'd strangle her over that little bit?" the doctor asked incredulously.

"Maybe she owed him from before," Adam replied.

He searched the front pockets of her shorts and came up empty. Turning her on her side, he saw a bulge in the pocket over her right buttock. Slipping his hand inside he pulled out a wad of bills. They were all hundreds. Holding them between his finger and thumb and using his pencil to separate them, he made a quick count. "Looks like a thousand dollars here."

"I doubt she'd stiff her dealer with that amount of cash in her pocket," Jack offered.

"Where would she get that kind of money?" a man's voice demanded gruffly.

Adam looked over his shoulder to discover the father approaching. "Don't come any closer," he barked.

Ray Carter froze in his tracks. "I wanted to make sure you were treating her body with respect," he growled.

"The utmost," Dr. Miller assured him. "I brought this girl into the world. I'll take care of her now."

Ray's attention had returned to the money. "None of this makes any sense." Tears began to spill from his eyes. "I trust you, Doc," he said, and stumbled back inside.

Adam turned to the doctor. "Thanks."

The doctor nodded his acceptance of Adam's gratitude, then frowned. "But where did she get that money?"

"When we know that, it's my bet, we'll have our

killer,'' Adam replied. Noticing other people from the neighborhood beginning to gather along the sidewalk and across the street, he finished his inspection, then said, ''You do what you need to do, then let's get her moved as quickly as possible.''

A few minutes later the doctor drove away with Angel in a body bag in the back of his station wagon. Returning to where the girl had been lying, Adam made a close inspection of the lawn hoping to spot something he'd missed. He was cursing under his breath at the fact that anything near the body had most likely been trampled, when his beeper sounded.

He called in to find out that they had the Polaski boy at the station. Leaving Jack to make certain the cordoned off area remained as it was until he could made a second thorough sweep, Adam headed back to the station.

Pausing in the doorway of his office, Adam studied the nineteen-year-old male seated in front of his desk. His frame was lean with strong shoulders and well-defined arm muscles. This was someone who could hold his own in a street fight or strangle Angel Carter with very little effort. From the length of the legs stretched out in front of the chair, Adam guessed the boy's height to be around five feet, eleven inches. His thick black hair was cut in a fifties style with sideburns and a ducktail. In keeping with that era's ''bad boy'' look, he wore a black leather vest over a white T-shirt, worn blue jeans, and black biker boots. The face was handsome in a gaunt, sullen way…the kind that appealed to girls looking for excitement or danger or both.

''I'm Detective Adam Riley.'' Approaching the boy, Adam extended his hand.

Wayne rose, accepted the handshake then shoved his hands into the pockets of his jeans and squared his shoulders defiantly. ''I want to know why I'm here. All they'd tell me is that you wanted to talk to me. I've gotten my act together. I work for a living. Casey expects me to be there to help him open up. We've got a tune-up and three oil changes lined up for this morning.''

Adam was determined to cover all the bases. He didn't want a judge throwing out evidence because he wasn't careful enough. "You're not under arrest. You can leave if you want to."

Wayne eyed him suspiciously. "You planning to charge me with something? Because if you are, you've got the wrong guy."

Adam kept his voice noncommittal. "I just want to ask you a few questions."

Wayne shifted uneasily, then his jaw firmed. "I haven't got anything to hide. Go ahead, ask your questions."

Adam noted that he looked nervous, but even innocent people got nervous when brought in for questioning. "You've been dating Angel Carter."

The boy's manner became more defiant. "Yeah, so what? It's a free country." Enlightenment showed on his face. "What's happened? Her father drum up some charge to cause me trouble? Well, whatever he's saying, it's a lie. He's just trying to split me and Angel up."

"Angel was found murdered this morning. Strangled." Adam had broken the news bluntly because he wanted to observe the boy's reaction. Now he felt guilty. Wayne looked as if he'd taken a hard punch to the stomach.

"Dead? Angel's dead?" Wayne's posture slackened and he sank into the chair.

"Are you all right? You want some water?" Adam asked. His gut instinct was to believe the boy hadn't known. Wayne's shock appeared genuine. But then, Adam reminded himself, appearances could be deceiving.

Wayne shook his head.

"Do you know of anyone who was angry enough at her to kill her?"

"She was always saying something to tick someone off just to get a rise out of them. She wanted to be an actress.

She'd study their response then mimic it later. It was all a game to her."

"Maybe someone didn't like her games."

"I can't believe she would've ticked anyone off so bad they'd kill her. She wasn't stupid. She knew how far she could push people."

"A real manipulator?"

Wayne scowled at him. "She was her own person. She knew what she wanted and she went for it. She was exciting. She never clung. She always kept me guessing." A wistful smile played at a corner of Wayne's mouth. "She was a challenge. We kept each other hot."

"Did she ever tick you off? Make you jealous just so she could study your reaction?"

The hint of smile vanished. "I knew her game. She wanted me to be the James Dean type so I played along. When Angel was happy, she made me real happy."

"Did you see her last night?"

"I was supposed to meet her in the parking lot of the Lutheran church around eleven but she called around seven, said she had a headache and canceled our date."

"That's the church on the corner of Oak and Elm?" Adam asked, making a quick note.

Wayne nodded. "Yeah, that's the one."

"And you weren't angry or suspicious when she canceled your date?"

Wayne studied the squared toes of his boots. "Okay, so I thought maybe she was seeing someone on the side. Lately, she's been a little cool. I decided to check on her. I called her around ten-thirty. She has a private line so I wasn't worried about getting her father. She answered. But I got the impression she was anxious to get me off the line so after I hung up, I went over to her place. I left my bike a couple of blocks away in the parking lot of the Presbyterian church, walked to her place and stood by the bushes between her house and the old lady next door's place. I saw her up in her window real soon after I got there, but she didn't come out. Then I got to wondering what I'd do if she did. I knew we'd only get into another fight if she found out I'd been spying on her. Besides, Angel was going to do whatever she wanted. There was nothing I could do to stop her. So I left.''

''Are you sure you didn't stick around, see her leave with someone else, wait until she got back, get in an argument and strangle her?''

''Yes,'' Wayne growled.

Again Adam found himself believing the boy. Normally, he would have remained staunchly skeptical. The scenario he'd just described had been played out a million times throughout history. But there was the money in Angel's pocket. Why was she carrying around such a large amount? *Drugs* was the answer that kept coming to mind. Of course, that didn't rule Wayne out. It just changed the motive. ''Angel had marijuana on her. Do you know where she got it?''

''No.''

''Are you sure she didn't get it from you?''

Wayne straightened in the chair. ''I don't do drugs.''

Glancing through the young man's rap sheet, Adam rounded his desk and seated himself. Closing the file, he returned his gaze to Wayne, his expression dry.

''All right. All right.'' Wayne shifted uncomfortably. ''So maybe I smoked a little pot once. But after I crashed my bike, they made me go to rehab. I saw what could happen to a person who got really hooked on drugs, decided I didn't want to go that route and swore off the stuff. That was over a year ago. I tried to get Angel to stay away from it, too. But, like I said, she had a mind of her own.''

Adam changed direction. ''Angel had a large sum of money on her when we found her. Would you have any idea where that came from?''

Wayne looked genuinely surprised. ''No.''

''Casey called to tell me that my nephew had been brought in,'' a new voice interrupted briskly. The owner...tall, distinguished, in his early fifties, his features not unlike those of the boy...strode across the room. His authoritative manner coupled with the gray, pinstriped three-piece suit, a watch fob dangling from the pocket of the vest, would have caused Adam to guess the new arrival was a lawyer. But he didn't have to guess. He knew this for a fact.

"Good morning, Councilman," he said, rising and extending his hand.

Lewis Polaski ignored the greeting. Coming to a halt in front of Wayne, he frowned down at him. "I heard about the murder. I told you that girl was trouble but you're just like your mother. You never listen to good advice."

"Angel liked to be dramatic. That's all. She wasn't bad," Wayne retorted.

Interested in what the two would say, Adam seated himself so as to remain as unobtrusive as possible.

"She was selfish and self-centered," the councilman growled.

Wayne's complexion reddened with rage. "She's dead. Show some respect."

"Whatever happened, I've no doubt she brought it on herself." Councilman Polaski's gaze narrowed on his nephew. "Did she finally make you so angry you killed her?"

Tears welled in Wayne's eyes. "I could never have harmed her. I understood her and I accepted the way she was. I loved her."

Adam suddenly found himself the target of the lawyer's gaze. "My nephew has the same flaws as my sister. He's too headstrong and wild for his own good. But I believe him. If you have any evidence against him, I want to know what it is."

Adam wasn't ready to admit he didn't have any evidence against anyone yet. "I've just begun my investigation. Your nephew was merely brought in for questioning because he knew the victim. He's free to leave." Adam turned to Wayne. "Just in case I need to talk to you again, don't leave town."

Wayne levered himself out of the chair. "I've got a job and no vacation time coming anytime soon. I'll be here."

"Wait in my car. I'll give you a lift back to Casey's," the councilman offered.

Wayne continued toward the door. "Thanks, but I'll walk. I need the fresh air."

"Then I'll stop by Casey's later. We need to talk," the councilman insisted.

Wayne shrugged as he exited. "Yeah, sure. I'll be there."

The hostility Adam had expected between the two of them wasn't there. It was obvious they weren't the best of friends, but there wasn't any animosity, either.

Closing the door behind his nephew, the councilman then approached Adam's desk. Placing his hands flat on it, he leaned forward until his face was only inches from Adam's. "I'm going to tell you a story," he said, his voice hushed and harsh. "If you repeat it, I'll swear you're lying and sue for defamation of character."

Adam didn't like being threatened, but he wanted to hear what the councilman had to say. "I'll consider this privileged information."

"Angel Carter had a vicious core. When she was only fourteen, she came on to me at the Fourth of July Picnic. I was drunk and didn't notice what was going on until she'd gotten me alone in a clump of trees by the lake. Then she started unbuttoning her blouse...slowly, in a teasing way. Even then she was built better than most women." A lecherous gleam sparked in the lawyer's eyes, then they turned icy. "I knew it was wrong but she got me hot and bothered real fast. She'd just gotten to her bra when out of the blue she says she wonders how my wife would feel if I got taken to court for raping a minor. I'll tell you, I sobered in a split second. I could hear her laughing as I took off back to the picnic. She had a nasty sense of humor. It's my guess that's what got her killed.''

The councilman straightened and his voice returned to its normal authoritative mode. "The next time you want to talk to my nephew, you call me in. People around here think I threw the boy out. He and I let that stand. The truth is, he left because of my wife. They didn't get along. She's very conscious of her social standing. Wayne didn't fit into her vision of her world. It just made life easier for all of us if he left. But he's family. And I don't turn my back on family.''

Adam watched the man leave. He'd heard that it was the wife who had all the money. Could be the councilman wasn't being totally honest. Could be he'd been willing to give in to her wishes to maintain a life-style he liked. Or maybe he honestly loved his wife and was merely trying to maintain harmony in his married life. Adam chose to give him the benefit of the doubt. It wouldn't be the first time a man was caught between a rock and a hard place when it came to his family versus his wife.

Besides, the councilman's marriage wasn't his concern. It was the story Lewis Polaski had had to tell that was important. Adam wondered how many others Angel had played games with. A headache began to build at his temples. He'd come to this small town nestled in the mountains of western North Carolina looking for a peaceful slice of old-fashioned America...a place where neighbor helped neighbor and goodwill reigned. Mentally he shook his head at his naiveté. Human nature in all its forms, both good and evil, existed everywhere. He'd known that. He'd just hoped he was wrong.

He pulled out his notebook. He'd asked Angel's parents for a list of names of her close friends, anyone she normally hung around with. They'd given him two...Polaski's and Melissa Colby. He dialed the girl's home number.

Chapter 7

Susan sat at her desk grading papers. At the end of each daily session, she gave a short quiz covering the material they'd discussed in class. She'd hoped this ploy would encourage her students to remain awake. It was only partially successful. Raking a hand through lightly sweat-dampened hair, she admitted that she, herself, had trouble concentrating on these hot summer days. Fans kept the air stirring but, a heaviness remained, lolling the mind into a haze.

Summers were for lying in the sun in a meadow full of daisies or sitting by a stream with your feet dangling in the cool waters, she mused wistfully. Normally she would have taken the tests home, changed into shorts and stretched out on a lounge chair on her screened back porch or sat in the front porch swing and graded them. But today she wasn't in any hurry to return home...to pass where Angel's body had been found and have that image again fill her mind.

"What happened? Do you know?" a young voice, shaky with emotion demanded.

Susan looked up to see Melissa Colby standing in the doorway. The girl's face was distorted in grief.

"I went by Angel's. Her mother told me she was dead and to go away. She wouldn't tell me anything else. I saw where the police had put that yellow tape around in the yard. Is it really true? Is Angel really dead?"

"I'm afraid so." Worried the girl was going to faint, Susan rose and approached her. "Maybe you should sit down."

Melissa allowed herself to be led to one of the desks. Tears began to stream down her cheeks as she slipped into the seat. "How did she die? Did she fall off her roof? She used to sneak out that way at night."

"No. She didn't fall."

"How, then?" Melissa demanded.

Susan hesitated. She didn't like being the one to break the news to Melissa but the girl was going to find out sooner or later. In a voice soft with sympathy, she said, "Angel was strangled."

Melissa moaned, wrapped her arms around herself and rested her forehead on the desk.

"I'm really sorry." Susan placed a hand on the girl's shoulder.

Melissa straightened abruptly. "When she started seeing Wayne, my mom told me about your bad marriage. She said Angel was headed down the same road only in her case it was more obvious. She said that everyone thought your husband was an okay kind of person, even a good catch. But you just had to look at Wayne to know he was bad news."

Susan's stomach knotted. She'd hoped her marriage had been forgotten. Finding out mothers were using her as an example of how horrible a mistake a person could make in choosing a mate came as a blow. Nothing in this town is ever fully forgotten, she reminded herself.

"I tried to get Angel to talk to you but she just laughed at me," Melissa continued. "She said she knew how to handle Wayne and that your advice wouldn't be any good, anyway. She said you were sour on men."

Susan heard the implication behind Melissa's words. "I'm not sour on men. I'm simply a great deal more cautious about those I date," she said, taking the opportunity to set the record straight. If people were going to gossip about her, she wanted it to, at least, resemble the truth.

A knowing expression spread over Melissa's face. "I figured that. I saw you out with Mr. Fausas, the math teacher. Angel said that proved her point. She said Mr. Fausas was so boring that only a woman who wasn't interested in men would go out with him. But I think he's nice."

"He is nice," Susan affirmed. But Alan Fausas was also boring, she confessed silently. But safe, she added. She'd known from the beginning, she could never be sexually attracted to him.

Melissa drew a shaky breath. Suddenly she paled even further. "Wayne must have found out..." Abruptly she clamped her mouth shut.

"Found out what?" Susan coaxed.

Melissa's chin trembled and a fresh flow of tears ran down her cheeks. "I promised Angel I wouldn't tell."

"Under the circumstances, I don't think Angel would mind you telling me," Susan prodded gently. If Wayne Polaski had killed the girl, and Susan didn't doubt that he was capable of it, she wanted him caught. He was much too dangerous to be allowed to roam freely.

"She was going to Los Angeles. She was going to be a star," Melissa sobbed.

"I knew her plans. I'd promised to take her there," a male voice growled.

Susan had been vaguely aware of heavy-booted footsteps in the hall but she'd been too intent on Melissa to notice when they stopped in her doorway. Now she looked up to discover the Polaski boy standing there. Terror swept through her. She took a step back knocking into the desk behind her.

"She wasn't going with you. She was leaving this weekend. It was a secret. She didn't want you to know. She was afraid of you. She was afraid you might do something violent to stop her. And you did. You found out and you killed her. I know you did," Melissa yelled between sobs.

"That's crazy." Wayne took a step into the room, his features distorted in anger. "I would never have hurt her. She knew that."

Susan's heart was pounding in panic. Wayne Polaski was one person she avoided at all costs. When he'd started working at Casey's she'd started having her car serviced elsewhere. If she saw his motorcycle parked at the grocery, she waited an hour before shopping. She moved farther back causing the desk behind her to scrape the floor loudly. "I think it would be best if you left, Mr. Polaski." She tried to speak with the authority she used to keep her class under control but the words came out shaky.

He turned his gaze on her. "I didn't come here to cause any trouble. I came here to set the record straight."

His hands had been in the pockets of his jeans. As he took another step toward her, he pulled them out. Both Susan and Melissa screamed in unison.

Wayne cursed and came to an abrupt halt, holding up his palms to show that they were empty.

Running footsteps sounded in the hall. Susan was swallowing a second scream when Hal Logan, the principal, and Adam Riley came into view behind Wayne.

"What's going on here?" Hal demanded. He was an ex-football player and coach. Besting Wayne by better than four inches and fifty pounds, he was a formidable match. "Polaski, you know you're not allowed on school grounds."

Wayne's jaw firmed with resolve. He took another step forward then pivoted and took a step backward in the direction of the blackboard so that he could see both Susan and Melissa and the newcomers. "This time I'm not running. I figured the police would get around to talking to Miss Hallston and I wanted to set the record straight." His gaze leveled on Susan. "I never meant to snap the blade out at you. I was going to hand you the knife but I got nervous. I knew my uncle would go ballistic and his wife was just looking for an excuse to toss me out. I'd just been fooling around with that girl. She and her friends all thought they were better than me. I usually ignore people like that, but she was giggling at me and it got on my nerves. I just wanted to frighten her a little. Teach her that she wasn't any better than anyone else. But I never meant to scare you. I pressed the button by accident. When you got hysterical and started screaming, I figured no one would believe me so I ran."

Susan could still picture him holding the knife in front of her, the blade pointed at her. Her stomach twisted in fear. "Stay away from me," she ordered.

He scowled. "What I told you is the truth. I would never have harmed you." His gaze jerked to Melissa. "And I didn't kill Angel!" He stomped toward the door.

Hal Logan looked to Adam to see what the policeman would do. When Adam stepped aside to let the boy pass, Hal frowned disapprovingly but did the same.

Before Wayne was even out the door, Adam had breached the distance between himself and Susan. "Are you all right?" he asked, still shaken by the sound of her scream.

She nodded, taking deep breaths to calm her nerves. The incident, three years ago, that had caused Wayne to be expelled from school played through her mind. "I suppose it could have happened the way he said," her fair side forced her to admit. "I thought I had the situation under control, but when I saw that knife blade suddenly pop out at me, I lost it."

Hal had joined them. "Switchblades are not allowed in

school. He would have been expelled simply for having it here. And, I'd had other complaints about him. I was gathering information on him and just about ready to go to the school board when the incident happened."

Adam gave Susan an encouraging smile. "We've got to stop meeting this way."

His attempt to lighten the mood of the moment was surprisingly soothing. Even more, his presence made her feel safe. A crooked smile played at one corner of her mouth. "Most definitely."

"I don't care what he said, I know he killed Angel!" Melissa snapped.

Realizing he'd been momentarily oblivious to everyone else in the room except for Susan, Adam was stunned that she could make him so completely forget why he was there. He forced his gaze away from her and to the teenager. "I've been looking for you. Your mother said you might be here at the school."

"Why didn't you arrest Wayne?" Melissa demanded, beginning to sob once again. "I know he did it."

Adam took out his notebook, letting her know he considered what she said important enough to jot down. "How can you be so certain?"

Melissa looked to Susan, the guilt of betraying her friend's confidence clearly visible on her face.

"I think, for Angel's sake, you should tell Detective Riley everything you know," Susan encouraged.

Melissa turned back to the policeman. "Angel was going to leave town. She was going to L.A. to be a big star. She didn't tell her parents because she knew they'd try to stop her and she didn't want Wayne to find out, either, because she knew he'd insist on going along and she said she'd outgrown him. But he must have found out she was dumping him for good and he killed her."

Adam recalled the bundle of money in Angel's pocket. Hopefully, Melissa would prove the solution to where it came from. "How was she going to pay for this trip if her parents weren't helping her?"

"She said she had a couple of angels." Tears again began to trickle down Melissa's cheeks. "'Angels for Angel,' she said."

"Angels?"

Melissa gave him an impatient look. "Patrons. All great artists have patrons."

Susan recognized that look as one of Angel's and guessed Melissa was parroting what her friend had said.

Recalling what the councilman had told him, Adam wondered if Angel's "patrons" were willing contributors or had been coerced. "Who were these 'angels'?"

Melissa brushed at her tears. "I don't know. Angel said they'd sworn her to secrecy."

"I found a thousand dollars in Angel's pocket. Do you think it could have come from one of her 'angels'?" Adam persisted.

Melissa's eyes rounded in surprise. "A thousand dollars?" Admiration for her deceased friend showed on her face. "It must have. I don't know where else she would have gotten that kind of money."

"Someone gave Angel a thousand dollars? In cash?" Susan looked from Melissa to Adam and then back to Melissa with disbelief.

Melissa gave her a rueful look. "Angel was a great actress. She would have paid them back and more. She would have been a star."

Wanting to make certain the child didn't become sullen and uncooperative, Susan said, "I'm sure she would have."

Melissa's eyes gleamed with admiration. "She was wonderful. She should have had the lead in the school play but Mrs. Graywell hates her. She's jealous that Angel had more talent in her little finger than Mrs. Graywell has in her entire body."

Susan decided that now was not the time to point out

that Angel had skipped classes so often she had been in danger of being suspended and Mrs. Graywell needed someone she could depend on to play the lead.

"I also found marijuana on her," Adam said, again taking charge of the conversation. "Was she a heavy user?"

"She never used any hard drugs," Melissa replied quickly in her friend's defense, then added reluctantly, "but she did have a joint every now and then. She liked to sit in her window late at night with a smoke and watch what went on in her neighborhood. She said she saw some real interesting things, stuff that would really shock some people." Suddenly she flushed and turned to Susan. "She never said she saw you doing anything weird, though."

Adam's policeman's instinct tweaked. "Who did she mention?"

Melissa shrugged. "She was vague when it came to details. I think maybe most of what she saw was just made up...fantasy stuff, you know, caused by the drug. Spirits and demons. The kind of things that go bump in the night sort of stuff. She liked adventure. Sometimes it was a little hard to separate fact from fiction where Angel was concerned. She had a great imagination. That was what was going to make her a great actress." Tears again began to roll freely down Melissa's cheeks.

Spirits and demons? Definitely a dead end, Adam decided. "Do you know who her dealer was?"

Melissa wiped at the flow with the palm of her hand, glanced out of the corner of her eye toward the principal, then shook her head violently. "No, and I never asked. I didn't want to know."

"If you're finished with your questions, I think I should take Melissa home," Hal interjected, his concern for the child evident on his face.

Deciding he'd learned all he could for the moment, Adam nodded. "I'm finished for now."

"I've got my bike here," Melissa blubbered, looking uncertain about what to do.

"We can't have you crying and steering out in front of traffic," Hal replied. "I promised your mother that if we found you, we'd see you got home safely. I'll throw the bike in my trunk."

She nodded and rose shakily. Once on her feet, she stiffened and faced the principal. "I took a couple of puffs once from one of Angel's joints but I didn't like the way it made me feel. I never used it again and I honestly don't know where she got her stuff."

"I believe you," he soothed. "Come along. You've had a shock. You need to go home." He glanced toward Susan. "I can give you a lift, as well."

"Thanks, but I'll walk. I need the fresh air," she replied, refusing the offer.

Adam stepped back allowing the principal and Melissa to leave. Lingering just inside the door, he watched Susan as she went to her desk and began gathering papers together and putting them into a briefcase. She still looked shaken. "Do you think Wayne Polaski did it?"

"I don't know," she said honestly. "I'm obviously not very good at predicting what people will or will not do."

She looked on the verge of tears. Unable to resist, Adam approached and captured her face in his hands, tilting it upward to meet his gaze. "I won't let him harm you."

Susan's breath locked in her lungs. She'd never looked into eyes that held so intense a promise of protection. "You do look like the kind of man who could protect a woman."

Adam smiled. "To protect and serve, that's what I've been trained to do," he drawled. Her lips looked as if they needed to be kissed.

Susan saw his mouth coming closer. The heat of his hands was sending a warmth through her and the stirrings he'd woken before were growing stronger. Twinges of desire prickled within her. Suddenly she was thinking of Lyle. He'd woken those same urges. And he'd also vowed to protect and care for her. Terror surged through her and she jerked away, moving backward until the blackboard stopped her.

Adam read the fear on her face. "I wasn't going to hurt you. I was only going to kiss you," he said soothingly.

She swallowed down the bile in her throat. "I know. It's not you. It's me. I don't trust myself. They say people continue to make the same mistakes. I don't trust myself to pick a man who won't turn out like my ex-husband."

Adam's jaw tensed with anger at the implication in her words. "I would never strike a woman."

His anger fed her fear. "I'd like to believe that."

Realizing he'd frightened her even more, Adam drew a calming breath and relaxed his jaw. "Look, I'm sorry. I seem to be saying and doing all the wrong things. But I would like to be your friend." He smiled beseechingly. "Actually, I'd like to be more, but I'll settle for being a friend right now. You look like you could use one."

"I could," she admitted, then added shakily, "I'm just not sure if I can."

"You don't have to be afraid of me. I swear," Adam coaxed.

Susan again thought of Miss Hanson and it gave her courage. "All right. We'll work on the friendship part."

Adam grinned and extended his hand. "Shake on it."

As she accepted, the heat that traveled up her arm awoke sensations that were well beyond friendship...sensations she wasn't ready to face just yet. "I'd better be getting home," she said, working her hand free.

"I'm going that way myself." Adam picked up her briefcase. "I'll give you a lift."

The urge to refuse was strong. He'd already cracked her barriers and they were in danger of crumbling at her feet.

Adam read the hesitation in her eyes. If he was going to win her trust, he had to convince her to spend time with him. "I'm offering as a friend," he said, his voice reminding her of the pact they'd just made.

She fought down the desire to flee. It was time to stop

letting fear rule her life. "How can a friend refuse a friend?" she said. "Lead me to your chariot."

In spite of her attempt at jesting, Adam noted that she remained tense as they walked to his car. Hoping to take her mind off of her fear of learning to like him, he asked, "What did the Polaski kid do that caused you and Melissa to scream?"

Susan's cheeks turned scarlet. "He pulled his hands out of his pockets. I thought he had a knife. I suppose Melissa thought so, too. He didn't." Again guilt that she might have misjudged the boy three years ago nagged at her. She figured she owed it to Wayne to be completely honest. "By the time I finished college and came back here to teach, I thought I had put the night my husband died behind me. The nightmares had stopped being so frequent. I was sure I was in control of my life. But when Wayne flashed that knife in front of me three years ago, I was back in that house again with Lyle threatening to slit my throat. That memory caused me to overreact toward Wayne then and today."

Adam couldn't rid himself of the thought that she hadn't been entirely honest with Judd or the doctor; that there were circumstances surrounding her husband's death that weren't letting her conscience rest. "It might do you good to talk about your husband," he suggested. "Exorcise the demons."

Susan made no response as she climbed into his car. She didn't like talking about Lyle. But then, maybe Adam was right. Maybe she needed to. "Lyle Bartram was evil," she said as they pulled out of the parking lot. "I wanted to leave him after the first time he hit me, but he threatened to kill me if I did. After the next beating I was willing to take my chances. But he said he'd kill anyone who helped me. I knew he meant my grandmother. I couldn't risk her life. That last night when he tried to kill me, I vowed that I'd never go back to him. And, I promised myself that if he got within ten feet of my grandmother, I'd kill him."

She breathed a grateful sigh. "But I guess someone up there..." She paused to look heavenward, then continued. "I guess someone up there must have been looking after me. Lyle died and I was free."

"But the nightmares didn't end," Adam prompted.

Her chin trembled. "No, they didn't."

Adam knew he was in danger of alienating her once again, but he had to get at the truth for both their sakes...hers because it would finally free her and his because he wanted to trust her and he couldn't until everything was out in the open. "Maybe there's something about that night that you've suppressed. Something that won't let you put it behind you."

Susan turned to look at him and saw the same suspicion she'd seen in the doctor's eyes, in those of Detective Claymont and others as well. "I didn't kill Lyle, if that's what you're suggesting." Her jaw hardened. "And a friend wouldn't think such a thing." She reached for the door handle. "Stop this car and let me out."

Afraid she'd open the door while the car was still in motion, Adam pulled over, but before she could climb out, he laid a restraining hand on her arm. Seeing the panic spread across her face, he immediately released her. "Look, give me a second to explain," he pleaded.

Her stomach was churning. She'd come very close to trusting him. Now she didn't know what to think. "All right, explain," she said stiffly.

"I'm trying to do us both a favor. Sometimes good people with strong consciences block out events they can't face. It could be that if you were involved in your husband's death, you've blocked it out and that's why you can't put the past behind you. Somewhere deep in your subconscious, it continues to haunt you because you feel guilty."

Susan felt betrayed. "Is that why you've befriended me, Detective? You think I killed my husband and that I'll snap and confess and you'll have another notch in your policeman's belt? Well, I haven't blocked out anything. I didn't kill Lyle.''

Adam frowned at her accusation. ''I'm not after a notch in my belt. I'm trying to ease some of the pain I see in your eyes.''

''Well, you've got a real funny way of showing it.'' Opening the door, Susan got out and slammed it closed. Not only were mothers using her marriage as an example of how badly things could go wrong, but even the new cop in town thought she'd killed Lyle.

Adam climbed out of the car and caught up with her before she'd gone two paces. ''If you were instrumental in Bartram's death, I'm convinced it was self-defense. All I want is for you to face the demons that are haunting you so I'll have a chance to get to know you better.''

''The only demon that is haunting me is my fear of making another mistake,'' she growled back. ''And right now, you seem like a big one. Friendship is based on trust. You obviously don't trust me and I certainly don't trust you. Looks like we don't have any foundation to build on. So just stay out of my life.''

Adam watched her stride away. He'd done what he felt he'd had to do. He could only hope that after she'd thought about it, she'd forgive him. Some flowers and candy wouldn't hurt his case, he decided. Returning to his car, he made a detour to the local florist and ordered a bouquet sent to her. On the card, he wrote, ''Friends are honest with each other. I apologize if I upset you. I was only trying to help.''

Once that was done, he headed to the Carter house.

Adam stood at Angel's bedroom window. She'd had a bird's-eye view of the backyards of the Reynolds' house as well as that of Claire Kinter's, Ken Kinter's, Susan Hallston's, the Olivers', the McFays' and Carol Hawkins'. Admittedly trees barred some of the view but not all of it. He could see the door of Susan Hallston's back porch as well as the doors leading onto the porches of both the Kinter houses. In the other direction, the Reynolds' back-yard was fairly open as well as that of the Olivers'.

A couple of shade trees in the McFays' yard were positioned so that they would block the view of their comings and goings out their back door but he could see the major portion of their back property. Carol Hawkins' yard was open with the trees being at the corners of her property. Adam lifted the pair of binoculars he'd found on the girl's desk to his eyes. If anything went on in those backyards, or even on portions of the street in front of the houses, Angel could have seen it. And, judging from the entries in her diary, she had.

The problem was knowing what she'd seen and what the marijuana had caused her to imagine. Adding to his difficulty, the entries, in many cases, were cryptic. Many were poems or rhymes and the pages were populated by creatures from fairy tales or characters from books. The reason for this was made obvious on the flyleaf. There, there was a message to her mother and father warning them that trying to snoop on her by reading her diary would be futile.

She'd had nothing kind to say about her neighbors. She'd picked out their flaws and concentrated on them in a bitchy, self-flattering way. But she wasn't as clever as she'd thought. Adam had easily been able to figure out who represented Wayne. At first he was her knight on a black steed, then he became her knave. And Adam was fairly certain Carol Hawkins was the flower woman.

But the couple that had caught and held his attention was Romeo and Juliet. According to Angel, they met regularly "in wooded lanes like children hiding from the peeping eyes of adults or in secluded country inns" and she hypothesized these lovers' trysts had been going on for some time before she'd discovered them. From the hints Angel had cast during his investigation of Linda Kinter's death, Adam was fairly certain Romeo was Ken Kinter and Juliet was one of the neighbor women. But there was no clue on those pages as to which one she was.

Adam again read Sunday's entry. "Chose not to confront Romeo. Juliet has more to lose. I made the right choice. Juliet is willing to pay for her secret to be kept!" had been scribbled with an excited hand. "But a thousand dollars will not go far in California. Will contact 'The Dancer' tomorrow."

Monday's entry stated that The Dancer would pay even more handsomely. "Five thousand! And I'm sure I can get more if necessary," Angel had written. Paging back through the diary, Adam had not been able to find any earlier mention of The Dancer.

On the night of her death, Angel had written, "Tonight's the night. First I meet with Juliet and then Dancer."

Closing the diary, Adam tagged it and added it to the items he was taking away with him.

For a long moment he stood indecisively, mulling over what he'd learned. Juliet had agreed to pay and the thousand dollars in Angel's pocket had most likely come from her. That was the sum agreed upon and Angel had said that The Dancer would pay more.

So if Juliet had paid, why kill Angel and leave the money behind? Lack of time? Fear of being seen? Or maybe the killer had been the Polaski boy. He could have returned, seen Angel meeting with Juliet, waited until she left, confronted Angel, found out the girl intended to dump him and killed her in a jealous rage.

Or maybe Juliet had told Romeo about the blackmail and after Juliet had paid, Romeo decided to end the extortion once and for all. Adam recalled that Ken had not been among those who had rushed to the scene this morning.

Or maybe The Dancer had decided not to pay.

"One step at a time," Adam told himself. He looked toward Susan Hallston's house and the frown on his face deepened. Had he let himself be played for a fool again?

The gossip he'd uncovered during his investigation of Linda Kinter's suicide made Susan his prime candidate for Juliet.

But why pay? Linda was dead. What harm could the truth do now other than cause a lot of unpleasant gossip? But then that could be deterrent enough for some and it was his guess that Susan Hallston fell into that category. His jaw tightened further. Or maybe Juliet had a more pressing motive? And, as she handed the money over, she'd begun to worry about the blackmail continuing and decided to get rid of the threat.

He didn't like the scenarios playing through his head. He wanted to discount Juliet and concentrate on Romeo and The Dancer. He cursed under his breath. Why couldn't Angel have left some clue as to who The Dancer was?

Resealing the room, he went in search of the Carters.

He found them in the living room. Claire Kinter and Carol Hawkins were also there. Carol was refilling everyone's iced tea glasses as he entered. Earlier she'd come knocking on Angel's door and offered him some refreshment. He'd refused.

"Would you like that tea now?" she offered.

He needed information and he figured the Carters might not speak freely in front of their neighbors. Besides, he wanted to question the others individually and he didn't want them knowing the questions beforehand. "I'd like to speak to the Carters alone."

Pauline forced a weak smile, her gaze encompassing Carol and Claire. "You've both been very helpful. But really, my sister should be here soon. She's driving up from Atlanta. We'll be fine on our own."

Claire hesitated, her manner that of a mother hen overseeing her brood. "Are you sure?"

"Yes, really."

"Mrs. Kinter, I didn't see your son this morning," Adam said, keeping his tone casual.

"He's out of town," Claire replied. "He left Sunday morning."

Adam hid his disappointment. If Kinter had left before Angel confronted Juliet, he might not even know about the blackmail. On the other hand, Juliet could have phoned him and he could have returned. "A business trip?"

"No. He's visiting with his son." Claire smiled weakly. "Ruth and I are hoping that being with Jason will help ease the pain of losing Linda." A fresh tear trickled down her cheek. "To be honest, I'm glad he wasn't here."

Clearly worried that Claire was going to break down and begin sobbing, Carol took her arm and began guiding her toward the door. "You call us if you need anything," she instructed the Carters, over her shoulder.

Adam saw the curiosity in her eyes when she glanced his way and knew she was wondering why he'd asked about Ken. Claire Kinter merely looked tired and relieved to be released. He made a note to check on Ken Kinter's alibi, then turned his attention to the Carters. "I need to trace your daughter's movements for the past few days. Who did she visit or talk to? Did she do anything unusual?"

"I was so proud of her this past week." Pauline spoke slowly as if getting the words out were an effort. "It was as if she'd matured overnight. I know it was Linda's death. That was a shock to all of us." Her voice became stronger and the pride more evident. "I couldn't believe it when I saw Angel helping Carol weed. She used to hate gardening. And she tried to cheer up Jane Reynolds. The child had been badly shaken by Linda's death. She's at a very impressionable age, you know. Angel obviously recognized Jane's pain and tried to take her mind off the death by playing Monopoly with her. She even let Jane win."

Tears brimmed in Pauline's eyes. "And just yesterday she took Claire grocery shopping and helped her put the groceries away when they got back. Linda used to take care of that chore. Claire can't drive herself and her arthritis makes lifting and carrying difficult. And Ken's been worthless. He can't seem to get over Linda's death.''

The tears overflowed and Pauline grabbed a fresh tissue to wipe at them. "Our Angel had finally grown up and was behaving like a caring adult. I even saw her speaking to Susan. After Susan gave her a C in history, she'd been unhappy with her. I told her that holding a grudge was not healthy but until this past week, she'd persisted in remaining cool to Susan.'' Abruptly, as if the strain of talking were too great, Pauline stopped.

Adam turned to the husband. "Can you add anything?''

"I sure can,'' he growled. "A couple of days ago I told her I wanted to talk to her about that Polaski kid. She knew I didn't approve of her seeing him. Usually when I brought up his name, she'd start accusing me of not trusting her and storm out of the house. This time she didn't. She simply told me not to worry and that she respected my judgment. She didn't actually say so, but I had the impression she was considering breaking up with him. Now, I'm certain I was right.'' His scowl turned to a glower. "She broke up with him and he killed her in a jealous rage. He'll skip town if you don't do something.''

"We can't arrest anyone without evidence,'' Adam said. "And he doesn't show any sign of skipping town.''

"He's not going to announce his intended departure,'' Ray retorted.

"We're keeping an eye on him.''

"You'd better!'' Ray slumped back in his chair as if he, like his wife, had expended his energy.

Adam rose. "I want to thank you for your cooperation. I apologize, but I have to keep your daughter's room sealed for a little longer. And if you think of anything else, please give me a call.''

Both simply nodded.

Leaving the Carter house, he decided to begin with Carol Hawkins and work his way around the horseshoe of neighboring houses, ending at Susan Hallston's place. He didn't lie to himself. He was looking for evidence that would point to anyone but the brown-eyed teacher as a candidate for Juliet.

Carol Hawkins was weeding her front garden when he arrived at her house. As they settled into a couple of rocking chairs on the woman's front porch, she glanced around to assure they would not be overheard, then said, "I don't like to speak ill of the dead, but if ever a girl spent her time looking for trouble, it was Angel."

"I understand she'd changed her ways these past few days."

Carol grinned. "No more than a leopard can change its spots. Oh sure, she suckered me in for a few minutes…came over here and began helping me weed. I figured Linda's death must have been a real shock for her to consider getting her hands dirty doing some physical labor. At first we talked about the flowers, then suddenly I found myself telling her—" Carol abruptly clamped her mouth shut.

"Telling her what?" Adam prodded.

"Just talking about things that happened in the past." Carol shrugged. "Nothing important."

The woman was not a good liar. "This is a murder investigation, Mrs. Hawkins. I need to know what was on Angel's mind these past few days."

"I'm sure that what we talked about had nothing to do with the murder."

Adam's tone became more demanding. "What did you talk about?"

Carol eyed him nervously. "I'm already in trouble for gossiping. If anyone finds out about this, no one may speak to me again."

"Unless it becomes relevant to the case, whatever you tell me will be in the strictest confidence."

Carol glanced around uneasily, then said in hushed tones, "She maneuvered me into talking about Susan's marriage. She was particularly interested in how Susan's husband died. She wanted to know what had gone on that night.''

Adam experienced a surge of self-directed anger. It was looking more and more like he'd let himself be suckered in by a pair of soft brown eyes. ''And what did you tell her?''

''I told her that Lyle had gotten into a rage, gone after Susan with a knife, tripped and killed himself.''

''And how did Angel react to this information?''

Carol again shifted uneasily. ''She asked me if I didn't think it was peculiar how tragic deaths seemed to happen around Susan.''

''And how did you respond to that?''

''I told her that some people were just unfortunate enough to have more grief in their lives than others.''

Adam detected a growing hint of uncertainty in her voice. Carol Hawkins might have believed that when she told Angel, but she wasn't so positive about it now.

Chapter 8

Susan Hallston sat on her front porch swing. Closing her eyes, she laid her head on the nest of pillows on one end and propped her ankles on the arm at the other. She couldn't count the number of lazy summer days she'd lain like this as an adolescent and then as a teenager, listening to the birds, surrounded by the perfume of the lilacs. She'd been so innocent then. What she'd considered problems, she realized now had merely been slight nuisances.

"Miss Hallston?"

Susan recognized the young female voice. Opening her eyes, she saw Melissa standing at the foot of the porch steps, her expression that of a lost child. Shifting into a sitting position, she smiled encouragingly. "What can I do for you?"

"Could I sit here with you for a while?"

Susan would have preferred to remain alone, but the plea in the girl's voice tore at her. "Yes, of course."

Melissa mounted the steps and sat down in a nearby rocking chair. "You didn't like Angel either, did you?"

Susan wasn't in the mood to lie but being totally frank didn't seem like a good idea at the moment. "She knew how to hold a grudge," she replied noncommittally.

Melissa nodded. "My parents and the other kids, they all say how sad and terrible it is that she was murdered, then they start in on how she brought it on herself. I think some of the kids are actually glad it happened."

"I doubt that *glad* is the right word to use," Susan soothed. "But she did have a way of treating other people as if they were inferior to her. That's not an endearing quality."

Melissa's chin trembled. "You think she deserved to die, too! I knew the two of you didn't get along but I thought you had a softer heart." She rose, intending to leave.

Susan reached out and touched the girl's arm. "You're right, we didn't get along. But I don't think she deserved to die."

Looking relieved, Melissa sank back into the chair. "All the other kids do is tell stories about things Angel did to prove she was always looking for trouble." A tear trickled down Melissa's cheek. "But they're wrong. They just didn't understand her. She wasn't like them. She was smarter and more clever and didn't sit around mooning over boys or complaining about her life. She set goals and worked toward them. I tried to explain to them that she only did the things she did so she could study their reactions but they said she just had a mean streak. They even blamed her for Sarah Ann getting pregnant."

"Angel did go after Sarah Ann's boyfriend," Susan said, recalling the incident. The results of Angel's actions had proved to be particularly tragic and had caused a lot of anger toward her among some segments of the school population.

"Well, Sarah Ann practically dared her. And it wasn't Angel's fault that when Tom did ask her out, Sarah Ann decided the only way to keep him was to get herself pregnant. Angel said the girl was stupid. She said, Sarah Ann should have known that trying to force a boy into marriage wasn't a way to keep him.''

''And she was right,'' Susan conceded. ''But that doesn't change the fact that, when Tom refused to marry her, Sarah Ann got scared about how her parents would react and, instead of seeking good medical help, ended up dying from a botched abortion.''

Melissa frowned down at her hands. ''I'm not saying Angel was perfect. And I did feel real bad about Sarah Ann. But Angel did, too. She told me so. She said that was the kind of thing she would recall when she needed to cry in front of the camera.'' Melissa's gaze shifted to Susan. ''All Angel ever wanted to be was a great actress. And she would have been.''

Susan didn't like to think badly of the dead, but if she was Melissa's mother, she'd be breathing a sigh of relief that Angel was out of her daughter's life.

''And she was always doing something that would help her.'' Melissa continued, her gaze traveling to the tree-lined street. ''Right after she got her driver's license, she started practicing tailing cars in case she ever got to play a policewoman or a private eye.''

Susan stared at the girl in shocked surprise. ''She tailed cars?''

''It was more than just tailing. She did a surveillance. She was real scientific. She picked out a woman she code-named Juliet and observed her activities whenever she could. She even kept a notebook. At first, it was kind of dull. She was even considering following someone else. Then one morning she came to school all excited. She told me she'd followed Juliet to a place by one of the lakes in South Carolina and that Juliet had met a man there. Angel code named him Romeo. I don't think she was really surprised. I got the feeling she'd suspected Juliet was having an affair. Then she made me promise not to mention what she'd told me to anyone. I don't think she'd really wanted to tell even me but she'd been so excited she had to share it with someone." Melissa suddenly flushed. "You said it wouldn't count as a betrayal if I told our secrets now."

"No. It won't matter to her now." But the thought that what the girl knew might matter to someone else made Susan uneasy. "Do you know who this Juliet was?"

Melissa shook her head. "No. Angel was real secretive about that and she could get real angry if I tried to pry information out of her. So I didn't ask. Besides, I'm pretty sure Juliet was someone around here in the neighborhood and Angel was afraid I'd look at her funny or something and tip her off that we knew." Melissa grimaced self-consciously. "And she was probably right."

Recalling the thousand dollars in Angel's pocket, Susan wondered if it could have been extortion money. She wouldn't put it past Angel to try something like that if it suited Angel's interests. And if that was the case and Angel had been killed to keep a secret and the killer found out Melissa had been Angel's confidante, the girl could be in danger. "I think it might be best if you don't go mentioning this to anyone else."

Melissa's eyes suddenly rounded as if a new thought had occurred to her. "Do you think Juliet might have found out that Angel knew her secret and murdered her to keep her quiet?"

"It could have happened that way," Susan replied.

Melissa paled. "That thousand dollars. Do you think Juliet was trying to buy Angel's silence and then got worried and murdered her?"

"What do you think?" Susan asked.

Melissa chewed on her lower lip. "Angel did want to get to Los Angeles real bad. They were casting a part in her favorite soap and she was sure she would be right for it. I suppose she might have asked Juliet for some money." She frowned. "But if Juliet murdered Angel then why would she leave the money?" Her frown darkened and she gave her head a firm shake. "No. I'm sure Wayne killed Angel."

"I want you to promise me you won't tell anyone else what you've told me," Susan said sternly.

"Cross my heart." Melissa made a crossing sign with her fingers on her chest. Suddenly her attention was averted by a florist's delivery truck parking in front of Susan's house. When the driver retrieved a large bouquet of flowers arranged in a basket from the back and headed their way, she looked toward Susan.

"He probably has the wrong address," Susan replied to the unspoken question on the teenager's face.

"Susan Hallston?" the man asked, reaching the steps.

"That's me." Stunned, Susan rose to accept the bouquet.

"Enjoy them," the man said, handing it to her, then quickly returned to his truck.

"Who are they from?" Melissa demanded excitedly.

Carrying them inside with Melissa following, Susan set them on the hall table, then read the card. "They're from Detective Riley." Recalling their last conversation, she wasn't certain if she wanted to keep them or throw them on the floor and stomp on them.

"You don't look very happy about getting them," Melissa noted.

"I'm surprised," Susan replied.

"He must like you." Melissa's eyes were gleaming with interest.

"Maybe." Susan wasn't ready to trust him. Men, she knew from experience, could be devious when it suited their goals.

Melissa sighed wistfully. "They're really pretty. I can't wait to get my first bouquet from a suitor."

"I wouldn't go so far as to classify Detective Riley a suitor." A wolf in sheep's clothing might be more accurate, she added to herself.

Melissa didn't look convinced. Then glancing at the

clock, she said, "I have to go home." A plea spread over her face. "Could I come back and talk another time?"

Better me than another Angel, Susan thought. "Sure."

Accompanying the teenager out onto the porch, in the distance, Susan heard Claire Kinter's and Adam Riley's voices. She'd seen the detective come up the street earlier and go up the walk to the elder Kinter's house. Now she realized he was bidding Claire goodbye and heading her way.

Melissa saw him, too, and grinned knowingly up at Susan. "I'll see you soon."

Susan laid a restraining hand on her arm. "There is one person you need to tell about Juliet," she said and nodded toward the detective.

Melissa looked as if she were going to balk.

"You want the person responsible for Angel's death to be caught, don't you?" Susan coaxed.

Melissa nodded.

"Afternoon, ladies," Adam said, reaching the level of the porch. He was having a hard time keeping his manner civil toward Susan. Nothing he'd discovered had pointed to anyone but her as Juliet. Not only that, he now knew that Angel had been asking questions about her.

She read the coldness in his eyes. Obviously, after he'd sent the flowers, he'd had second thoughts about taking the friendly approach. Mentally, she congratulated herself for not falling for his line. "Melissa has something she needs to tell you."

The teenager didn't appear happy about parting with any information, Adam thought. He noticed her glance toward Susan as if uncertain this was the right thing to do.

"He should know everything about Angel," Susan coaxed firmly.

Melissa's expression became solemn as she turned back to the detective. "I'm not a snitch, but Miss Hallston's right."

Adam listened while she told him all she knew about

Juliet. It wasn't much but it confirmed his suspicions about Romeo and Juliet being residents in the neighborhood. As the girl left he studied Susan Hallston. He didn't doubt that she could have sworn Melissa to secrecy and trusted the girl never to say anything. Either Miss Hallston was as innocent as she claimed or exceptionally clever. And he didn't trust his instincts to choose. "Looks like you've found a new friend," he said.

"One," she confirmed, her tone letting him know he didn't fall into that category.

And he'd be smart to leave it that way, Adam told himself. "Do you have any idea who Juliet might be?"

"None."

His gaze leveled on her. "If I was a betting man, my money would have to be on you."

Recalling earlier accusations he'd flung at her, Susan had a suspicion as to where this was leading and she didn't like it. "Then you'd lose." Challenge flickered in her eyes. "If I was, would I have had Melissa tell you about her?"

"You might have realized that I'd probably find out about Juliet on my own. Having Melissa tell me was simply a way of throwing me off guard."

"If I was seeing someone, I'd have no reason to go sneaking around."

"Unless your Romeo is a married man or was a married man. Ken Kinter, for instance."

She'd been right about where he'd been heading. "I have no Romeo in my life," she said firmly. "And like I told you before, Ken and I are friends, *just* friends. We have never been more than that."

Adam wanted to believe her. Curtly, he reminded himself of Lisa. "I'm trying to track Angel's movements during the past few days."

"Angel and I weren't on the best of terms. I didn't pay much attention to her."

Adam studied her narrowly. "The question is, did she pay much attention to you?"

The defiance in her eyes increased. "If she did, I'm sure she got quickly bored."

Adam told himself to leave. He was going to learn nothing useful here. But it was as if he were one pole of a magnet and she was the other. "Have dinner with me."

Susan didn't try to hide her surprise. "You're joking, right? You think I killed my husband and had an affair with my best friend's husband. Next you'll probably be accusing me of killing Angel." Seeing the slight twitch in his jaw, her tirade came to an abrupt halt. For a long moment, she regarded him in silence, then barely above a whisper managed to ask, "You think I killed Angel?"

"She could have threatened to expose your affair with Kinter if you didn't give her a little something to help her on her way to L.A. And maybe you paid because you didn't want to be the object of some ugly gossip. Then you got worried she wouldn't keep quiet after all."

Susan paled. "I did no such thing."

"Then have dinner with me. We can talk. Your neighbors have had their say. Now it's your turn to tell me about them."

Panic threatened to take control. "There's nothing to tell."

"Or maybe you're afraid that if you spend time with me, I'll see through your lies," he challenged.

"I haven't told you any lies." A counter to his accusations occurred to her. "Even if I was Juliet and Ken was my Romeo, neither of which is the case, I'd have no reason to keep it a secret now that Linda is dead."

"Unless you had something to do with Mrs. Kinter's death," Adam returned, voicing the suspicion that had been eating away at him. "It could be that after killing your husband and getting away with it, you settled on murder as a way of getting rid of all your problems. You wanted Ken Kinter but Linda Kinter stood in your way."

Susan turned ashen. "You actually think I'm capable of three murders?"

Adam hated himself. If she was innocent she woul never forgive him. Curtly he reminded himself that he ha a job to do. He also reminded himself of Lisa and ho she'd played Charlie for a fool and nearly blindsided hin as well. "A detective has to be able to come up with variety of scenarios. Then we rule them out, one by one So, how about dinner?"

Her mind reeling, she wanted to demand that he leave But her more rational side reasoned that if she spent som time with him, she might be able to convince him she wa innocent. "I have a chicken baking in the oven. I wa going to have an early supper. You can join me if yo want." Without waiting for a response, she went inside.

Adam followed.

Pausing in the hall, Susan nodded toward the bouque "Since you've obviously stopped playing the I-want-to be-your-friend game, you can take that with you on you way out."

Adam's control snapped. "I wasn't playing a game." His gaze bore into her. "I want to believe you're innocen but I've been fooled before. I won't be fooled again. I'n just following where the evidence leads me."

"And it led you to my front door?" Numbed by panic she continued to the kitchen.

She looked bewildered, Adam thought, as if she'd sud denly found herself surrounded by danger and didn' understand how she'd gotten there. *Some of the most in nocent-looking of nature's creations are the most deadly* he reminded himself sternly, still his desire to trust he remained.

Susan told herself to say nothing more, but the admis sion that she was his prime suspect along with his sug gestion that she might have had a motive to kill Linda ha her badly rattled. "I thought you ruled Linda's death a an accident."

"That's the official line."

His tone made it obvious that he was reconsidering th

official line. Too shaken to make a response, she concentrated on putting dinner on the table.

Watching her take the chicken out of the oven, Adam found himself wishing they were together under much different circumstances. Curtly, he ordered himself to keep his mind on business. Suddenly the fact that she'd baked a whole chicken took on a suspicious nature. "Looks like you were expecting company. Ken forget to tell you he was going out of town?"

Anger replaced her panic. He was looking for reasons to find her guilty. Indignation etched into her face, she turned to him. "What Ken does with his time is of no interest to me. Cooking for one is boring. I usually cook enough for several days."

Adam mentally kicked himself. He was trying too hard not to let his hope that she was innocent take control. "Sorry," he apologized. "That was unfair."

That he'd admitted he'd gone too far surprised her. But her guard remained up. He could merely be playing mind games with her. She raised the carving knife to cut the chicken. "Do you prefer white meat or dark meat?" This was the polite behavior her grandmother and mother had taught her. Suddenly she didn't feel so polite. "Never mind." She placed the platter along with the fork and carving knife on the table. "You can cut your own piece."

The thought that she could have turned on him with that knife played through Adam's mind. He tried picturing her with murderous intent on her face. He couldn't. Or, maybe he just didn't want to.

He watched as she took two plates out of the cupboard, cut the baked potato in half and placed a half on each. Next came a bowl of salad. She set that beside the chicken along with three containers of different blends of salad dressing. "Looks good," he said, seating himself in the chair she indicated with a wave of her hand.

"It is good. My grandmother taught me to cook."

"But she never taught you the art of making fudge,"

he mused dryly, determined not to let the cozy atmosphere of the kitchen influence him.

"So we're back to the fudge, are we?" Susan's stomach knotted and she wished she'd refused his company. If he was determined to convict her, he might be able to twist her words around and make her look guilty. She faced him squarely. "No. I decided that bit of expertise wasn't important. Both Claire and Carol make terrific fudge. If I want some, I just hint around and one of them suddenly gets the urge to make some."

Suddenly, very tired of his job, Adam picked up the carving knife. "What kind of meat would you like?"

"White." She regarded him dryly. "You know what's ironic about this whole situation? I actually wanted to trust you."

His gaze again leveled on her. "And I want to trust you. But like you, I learned the hard way that people aren't always what they seem at first glance." His jaw tensed. "My partner fell in love with the sweetest, cutest, most domesticated-appearing female I've ever met. He doted on her. They got married and less than a year later, he was found dead in an alley. At first, I figured his death was related to one of the cases we were investigating. But I couldn't pin it on any of our suspects. Then I found out Lisa—that was his wife's name—had taken out a huge insurance policy on him. I investigated her and found out she'd been using an alias and that she'd been married four times before and left four dead husbands in her wake...and each had had huge insurance policies. I caught up with her just before she could skip town with Charlie's insurance money."

Enlightenment flashed in Susan's eyes. "She's the one who shot and nearly killed you."

"The one and only. Dear, sweet Lisa."

"So, now all innocent-appearing women are your prime suspects?" she accused.

"No." His gaze burned into her. "Only the ones I suspect of lying to me."

"I have never lied to you," she replied in clipped tones.

"Several of your neighbors mentioned you and Ken as a couple. They said you were close during your youth and your teenage years and they were surprised when the two of you didn't marry."

"A lot of men and women are friends but would never consider marrying each other." Tired of denying a romantic relationship with Ken, she decided that ignoring Adam was the best ploy and turned her attention to her food. She forked a bite of chicken into her mouth, chewed and swallowed. It tasted like cardboard and threatened to stick in her throat.

Adam followed her example. Swallowing down his bite, he watched her putting sour cream on her baked potato. She looked green around the gills and he wished he didn't have to continue, but he did. "Just for discussion's sake, let's say Linda Kinter was murdered."

Susan gave up any pretext of eating, set her utensils aside and faced him. "I really find that hard to believe, impossible actually."

Adam, too, set aside his utensils. "I have two deaths within three houses of each other in less than two weeks. I have to ask myself if they're connected. If they are, then maybe it was something Angel knew about Mrs. Kinter's death that caused her own."

Susan's stomach knotted more tightly and she wished she hadn't swallowed down that bite. "You're grabbing at straws. Angel made enemies easily."

Adam operated on the theory that if he gave a murderer enough rope, they'd hang themselves. But the thought of a noose around Susan's neck was not a sight he wanted to see. Still, he forced himself to continue. "I'll tell you what. I'll outline a scenario and you can punch holes in it."

"Fair enough." She wasn't certain what his game was,

but was afraid not to play along for fear of making herself look more guilty in his eyes.

"Assume Mrs. Kinter was murdered. There were no traces of the drug in the wine bottle. However, there were traces of it in the wineglass. The drug in the glass could have been added after she was dead or the drug could have been administered in her wine. It could also have been in the fudge. In either case, the murderer would have to have been there with her while she ate and drank to be certain she consumed enough. So, what does that tell you about the killer?"

"Considering her mental condition that night, it would have to have been someone she knew, someone she trusted."

"And who would that have been?"

Susan swallowed down a sudden rush of bile. "It would have to have been one of our small social group...one of the women. Linda's life centered around Ken. She had no one she ran around with on any kind of regular basis outside of our small social circle." The color drained from her face. What he was suggesting was too horrible to comprehend. Her jaw tensed. "I refuse to believe one of us murdered Linda. Her death was a tragic accident. And, most likely, the Polaski boy murdered Angel."

Adam found himself wanting to console her, wanting to accept her theory of what had happened. A twinge caused by the scar on his chest reminded him of Lisa. "That's one possibility," he conceded.

"But you're not buying it."

"If Polaski did it, my guess is that he'd have used his hands not a scarf."

"If Angel was wearing the scarf, he might have used it simply because it was there," Susan argued.

"Maybe," Adam admitted.

He didn't sound convinced and Susan admitted that she wasn't either. "You have a point about Wayne," she conceded. "But that still doesn't mean it was one of us who did Angel in. She was good at making enemies."

Adam decided it was time to really rattle her cage. "Suppose I told you that I have evidence that Angel was going to meet with Juliet last night and that it was, most likely, Juliet who gave her the thousand dollars."

"Why pay and then murder the blackmailer? That doesn't make sense," Susan argued.

"Unless, after handing over the money, Juliet suddenly had second thoughts and became worried Angel might continue the blackmailing and killed her. In which case, Juliet could have been so shocked by her actions she forgot to retrieve the money or too scared to take the time to retrieve it."

Susan scowled. "Just because you had one bad experience doesn't mean every time you go looking for a suspect it has to be a woman. One bad apple doesn't mean all the others are rotten."

"It would seem you don't entirely believe that where men are concerned." Adam leaned closer. "Or maybe your standoffishness is merely a facade. Maybe you've been biding your time until a certain married man would be free once again."

Mentally she wailed in frustration. He'd run her around in a circle and brought her back to Ken. "I haven't been biding my time. I just don't want to make another mistake."

"And neither do I."

She glared at him. "Why not suspect Romeo? Why couldn't it be the man who committed the crime?"

"She had no plans to meet with him. However, I haven't ruled anyone out." Adam made a decision. "She did have a second appointment though, with someone she referred to as The Dancer. She expected to collect money from that person, as well. Any ideas?"

"Everyone I know has two left feet." A sudden thought struck her. "Maybe Angel was playing the part of Lolita on the side. Maybe she had an older boyfriend, maybe even a married man. If she was asking for money from him, he could have been afraid his wife would find out. Or maybe Wayne found out and murdered her after Juliet showed up and before Dancer came.''

Considering the promiscuity of some of today's youth, and Angel's behavior in particular, Adam had to admit that scenario could work. ''That's a possibility.''

Susan toyed with the food on her plate. ''If you'd asked me two weeks ago where I thought the safest place in the whole universe was, I'd have said right here. Now I'm beginning to wonder if there is a safe place.''

''Human nature being what it is, probably not.''

''You are a cynic.''

''I'm a cop. I've seen too much not to face reality. Most people are good, decent, mostly law-abiding citizens. But there's always a percentage who will stop at nothing to get what they want.''

The stress of the day caught up with Susan all at once. Tiredness swept through her. ''Eat your dinner, then take your flowers and go away, Detective. Go find your murderer and leave me alone. I need to rest.''

The strain on her face caused a rush of guilt. ''You do look beat.'' He didn't feel much like eating, either. ''I'll take a rain check on the meal.''

She cast him a look that said, it'd be a hurricane before she'd ask him back. Letting him show himself out, she sat at the table. Her chin trembled and tears welled in her eyes. It was as if an evil had invaded her world and was threatening to engulf her.

Chapter 9

The persistent ringing of her doorbell woke Susan. After clearing away the dinner dishes, she'd noticed that the bouquet was still in her hall. She'd thrown it away with the rest of the trash. Then seeking a diversion from the thoughts that plagued her, she'd plopped on the couch and turned on the television. Almost immediately, exhaustion born of stress had overwhelmed her and she'd escaped into sleep.

A glance at the clock told her it was a little before nine. Through the window, she could see the last faint rays of dusk. The doorbell rang again. Levering herself to her feet, she went to answer it.

"I've got to talk to you." Susan had to step back to keep from being trampled as Barbara Reynolds entered, closing the door behind her. Brushing past Susan, she strode into the living room where she paced nervously.

Knowing that Barbara and Pauline were close, Susan became concerned that Pauline was having a dire reaction to her daughter's death. "Is Pauline coming unhinged?"

Barbara stopped pacing. "I'm counting on our friendship and your discretion to keep this conversation just between us." Without pausing to give Susan a chance to respond, she continued curtly, "I need to know if the police can take fingerprints off of money."

"Why...?" The question died on Susan's lips as the answer popped into her mind. "You?"

Barbara drew a terse breath and nodded. "Yes, I was the one who gave Angel that thousand dollars." Starting to tremble, she collapsed into a nearby chair. "But I didn't kill her. She was alive and happy when I left her. Gleeful, even."

"I think they can get fingerprints off the money." Susan's mind was reeling. Barbara was the last person she would have suspected of being Juliet.

Tears began to roll down Barbara's cheeks. Rising, she began to pace again. "That little demon found out I was having an affair and blackmailed me."

Susan was still having trouble believing this turn of events. "You're in half a dozen car pools just so you can get your kids to all of their activities. You're active in the PTA and the Girl Scouts. You make gourmet meals for Ted. You even iron his underwear. Your house is immaculate. When in the world did you have time for an affair?"

Barbara sat down again. She'd stopped crying and was brushing at her tears with the palms of her hands. "A person has to have some time to herself."

Susan handed her a box of tissues. "I would have thought you would have collapsed in front of the television. Or you could have read a good book."

"Thanks." Barbara accepted the tissues, then frowned up at her. "A person sometimes needs a little excitement in her life. Ted's a wonderful husband, but he's very pedestrian in bed. I can't entirely blame him. It's not easy being inventive with kids around. Even when you lock your door, you never know when one of them is going to get sick and come knocking. Or sometimes they get into

squabbles. They never seem to realize that parents need
time to themselves.''

''Your children are ten and twelve. Surely they give you
and Ted some privacy now.''

Barbara flushed, then shrugged. ''The affair started
when they were much younger.''

''And Ted has never suspected?''

''I'd tell him I had a school meeting or that I needed a
break from the kids and was going to a movie. He liked
staying at home with them. He's always been a terrific
father. Besides, he hated school meetings. Could I have a
drink of water?''

Manners! Where were her manners? Susan admonished
herself dryly feeling as if she were in a surrealistic play.
''How about some iced tea?''

Barbara smiled. ''That'd be great.'' Following Susan
into the kitchen, she stood leaning against the counter. ''It
wasn't as if I was really betraying Ted. Emotionally, there
was never any involvement on either side. The man I've
been seeing loved his wife and I love Ted. It was just fun
and games. Even now that the kids leave us alone, Ted is
very missionary in his approach to sex. Sometimes I crave
something a little more exciting.''

Susan was not interested in discovering what Barbara
meant by exciting. She already knew more about her
neighbor's sex life than she'd ever wanted to. ''Who are
you having the affair with?'' she asked bluntly, handing
the woman the drink.

Barbara suddenly became guarded. ''I really don't think
I should say.''

''It could be important,'' Susan insisted. ''If Angel was
blackmailing you, she could have tried blackmailing him
as well and he might not have been so willing to pay.''

''She hadn't contacted him. She figured he didn't have
anything to lose now. Besides, he couldn't be the murderer. He's out of town.''

Susan wasn't certain what it was...the downward flicker

of Barbara's eyes or the flash of guilt on her face or the realization that Barbara had used the past tense in reference to the love her paramour felt for his wife and that Angel had discounted him as a possible source because he had nothing to lose...but a suspicion as to who Barbara had been seeing flashed into her mind. "Ken. You and Ken?" Even as she said it, she was finding this even more incredible to believe than Barbara having an affair. She expected the woman to burst into laughter.

Barbara didn't. Instead, panic spread over her features. "Please, you promised to keep this secret. I know you've been sweet on him ever since you were a kid, but he's always thought of you as a sister." Tears again began to stream down her cheeks. "You're not going to tell Ted, are you?"

"I'm not going to tell anyone. And I am not, nor have I ever been, sweet on Ken."

Barbara didn't look convinced. "Claire is certain you've always been in love with him."

"Well, she's wrong." Susan fought down the urge to stand on her front porch and scream that she had never and would never be romantically involved with Ken.

For a moment Barbara appeared relieved, then her panic returned. "Ted can't find out. Please, you've got to help me."

Susan was only half paying attention. She was remembering the animosity she'd sensed between Linda and Barbara. "Do you think Linda suspected you and Ken were having an affair?"

Barbara shook her head. "Even if she had thought Ken was running around on her, which she didn't, she'd never have suspected me. She was always looking down her nose at me. I know she thought I was dumpy and frumpy."

Recalling remarks Linda had made about Barbara, Susan had to admit that Barbara was correct in her assessment. Linda had certainly behaved as if she considered herself superior to the other woman. Still, Susan couldn't help wondering if some primitive instinct deep within Linda hadn't sensed a competition between herself and Barbara, something she couldn't define but a feeling that the other woman was treading on her territory. That would explain the nearly instant animosity that had developed between them.

"And I know she thought she would make a better mother than me," Barbara added. "She was always hinting around that I was ruining my children's health by feeding them too much sugar and butter." Her shoulders squared with pride. "My kids are happy and healthy." Tears again welled in Barbara's eyes. "My kids! What will they think of me if they find out about the affair? And the congregation at my church? My minister! Ted will never forgive me." She looked pleadingly at Susan. "What am I going to do?"

"You're going to talk to Detective Riley." Susan didn't leave any room for compromise in her voice. "Maybe if you come forward on your own, he might be willing to try to help protect your secret provided you can convince him Angel was still alive when you left her."

"I swear she was." Barbara's expression suddenly brightened. "And I can prove it. Will you call Detective Riley for me?"

Adam Riley sat across from the red-eyed woman on Susan Hallston's sofa. The doctor had not been able to pinpoint the time of Angel's death precisely. Somewhere between midnight and three in the morning, had been his best guess. If Barbara Reynolds was telling the truth, she'd narrowed that down to between 1:15 and three.

"You claim Angel was alive when you left her," he said.

"Alive and giggling. My husband saw her. He woke up, saw I was missing and came down to the kitchen to find me. He saw me out on the lawn with her and started out to investigate. I didn't want him getting near her. She had her money and, being the vindictive little brat she was, I was afraid she might decide to tell him just for fun. I hurried home before he could get halfway across our lawn. I made up something about seeing her out there and going out to find out if anything was wrong. I assured him there wasn't and we went back inside.''

''How did you plan to cover up the missing money?'' Adam asked.

''I handle the finances in our house. Ted would never know it was missing.''

''You didn't get worried that Angel might continue to blackmail you and go back a few minutes later to make certain she'd never have the chance?''

Barbara's shoulders stiffened with righteous indignation. ''No, of course not. I'll admit I was worried she'd want more money. Los Angeles is expensive. But Ted was wide awake and so was I, and the kids were asleep, so he and I fooled around a bit, then watched an old movie on television. He didn't go back to sleep until nearly three. I figured Angel was inside by then.'' Bright red spots of fear showed on her cheeks. ''But I never thought about killing her. I just thought about getting her word that she'd leave me alone but then I realized that trusting her word would be lunacy. I settled for hoping she got on the first plane for California and that would be the end of her.''

''I'll need to check out your alibi with your husband,'' Adam said, reaching for the phone. If she'd just come up with this story, he didn't want to give her time to clue Ted Reynolds in on it. ''What's your number?''

''What are you going to tell him?'' Barbara demanded, panicked.

''I'll be the soul of discretion,'' he promised.

She gave him the number and he punched it in. When Ted Reynolds answered Adam identified himself, then said, ''I'm at Susan Hallston's house. Your wife is here and has mentioned that the two of you saw Angel alive a little after one last night.''

"Yes, we did," Ted answered. "Is that important?"

"It's helpful. I'm trying to pinpoint the time of death," Adam replied. "You didn't see or hear anything after that?"

"No. Our kids were asleep so I took the opportunity to have some intimate time with my wife. If you had children you'd know what I mean. What went on outside of our bedroom was of no concern to me."

Adam thanked him and rang off.

Barbara's chin had tightened defiantly. "May I go home now? I've got an awful headache."

"Just one more question," Adam said. "Did Ken Kinter know about the blackmail?"

"No. He'd left town by the time Angel confronted me and I didn't see any sense in contacting him. He has enough on his mind. You will try to keep our affair confidential?" she asked in a pleading tone.

Adam nodded. "For now, I'll keep your affair in confidence. But don't leave town."

She scowled at him. "I would never desert my husband and children."

Adam remained in Susan Hallston's living room while she saw Barbara Reynolds to the door. He had his Juliet and he knew who her Romeo was. But this was one scenario he'd never figured on.

"Apparently I'm the only one you aren't willing to give the benefit of the doubt to."

He looked up to see Susan glaring at him.

"Maybe she and Ted cooked up her alibi before she came here."

"I am considering that possibility," he admitted. "But as long as the husband sticks to his story, it's going to be hard to prove."

Susan continued to glare at him. "I'd like an apology."

She looked so damn cute...furious but cute...Adam couldn't stop himself from grinning. "I apologize." His expression abruptly turned serious. "Do you think she killed Angel and the husband is willing to cover for her?"

Her eyes widened into an exaggerated expression of incredulousness. "You're asking *my* opinion? First, you practically accuse me of three murders and now you want my opinion regarding the guilt or innocence of my neighbors?"

He shrugged. "This case is full of surprises. I don't see any reason why my behavior should be any more predictable than anyone else's."

Susan breathed a tired sigh and sat down. "She might have, if she was panicked about being exposed and losing her kids." An unnerving thought struck her. "What about Linda? Do you think Barbara could have decided she wanted to be with Ken on a daily basis and hoped that if Linda was out of the way, she could divorce Ted and marry him?"

Adam shook his head. "She has an alibi for the night of Linda Kinter's death. One of her kids was sick. She was up all night with him." The frown on his face deepened. "And if Barbara's husband is telling the truth, she couldn't have murdered Angel."

Susan straightened and glowered at him. "I should have known you'd do that. You've dismissed Barbara as a suspect with barely a second thought. While, on the other hand, you were able to come up with a multitude of theories involving me."

"I never said I wasn't going to give Mrs. Reynolds a second thought." Adam had been fighting not to allow his euphoria at learning Susan was not Juliet to cloud his judgment. It was taking a great deal of willpower to keep reminding himself that this new information didn't mean she wasn't guilty. "You forgot about The Dancer. I have reason to believe Angel was expecting a great deal more money from that meeting and it was supposed to occur before three. I only found a thousand, which means that either she was killed before The Dancer showed up or The Dancer chose not to pay and killed her.''

"So now you've decided that I'm The Dancer.'' Susan's voice turned sarcastic. "Well, I hate to break the news to you, but you've just lost your motive. I wasn't the one having the affair with Ken.''

"Just because you weren't having an affair with him doesn't mean you aren't in love with him. And since you didn't know about the affair, you might have figured you could land him if he was free. If you did his wife in to get him, Angel could have seen you coming and going from the house. She had a bird's-eye view of the neighborhood.''

Unnerved by his persistence in keeping her a suspect, Susan pointed to the door. "Get out of my house.''

Adam toyed with the key in his pocket. Reaching a decision, he rose. "Come on. You're coming with me.''

The panic Susan had been suppressing bubbled to the surface. "You're going to arrest me? You can't possibly have any evidence against me. All you've got is a misguided, absurd theory.''

"I'm not arresting you. We're going to take a walk down memory lane.''

He was back to Lyle's death again. She was certain of it. "We've already been there. I'm not interested in going again.''

"You want me to believe you, don't you?'' he challenged. "As long as you've been telling the truth, you've got nothing to worry about.''

"I have been telling you the truth.''

He held his hand out to her, to aid her in rising. "Prove it.''

Her jaw hardened with righteousness. "Fine, I will!'' Refusing his help, she rose on her own.

A few minutes later Adam parked in front of the old two-story frame house on the outskirts of town where her nightmares had begun.

A shiver ran along her spine. Darkness had fallen, leaving only the light from the half-moon to cast its eerie glow over the landscape. That night, nine years ago, when she'd fled for her life had been a lot like this one. The moon had been only a little more than a crescent then but, like tonight, the sky had been clear and filled with stars. They had lit her way.

"I thought you were taking me to have a polygraph test done." She worked herself deeper into the upholstery of her seat. "I don't want to be here."

"Polygraphs can lie." Adam left the car, came around and opened her door. "I want you to walk me through the night Lyle Bartram died."

She flattened her feet against the floor and shoved herself harder into the seat. "I will not. I lived it once for real and in nightmares for years afterward. I still have them."

"You'll never get rid of the demons that are haunting you if you don't face them head-on."

She continued to remain tightly wedged in the seat. "That's only a theory."

"The only way I'm going to believe you didn't kill your husband is for you to come inside and show me what did happen."

She was tempted to tell him she didn't care what he thought. But she did. She had to. He was trying to pin a murder on her...three murders on her, she corrected.

Easing out of the car, she stood and looked at the house. Even at this distance, her heart began to pound violently. After Lyle's death, she'd refused to come back even to pack her things. Her grandmother and mother had done that. On her instructions, they'd left Lyle's things for his family to pick up, and she'd had Ken arrange to sell the furniture.

Adam studied her drawn countenance. Whatever had happened here had left a mark of terror deep within her. He considered stopping, but forced himself to go on.

"How did the confrontation between you and your husband start?"

Susan continued to stare at the house. The sound of Lyle's ugly, angry voice echoed in her ears. "The same way they all did...over something ridiculous, something he'd made up to get himself worked up." There were things Susan had never told anyone, not even her grandmother. But Adam Riley had backed her into a corner. Besides, maybe he was right. Maybe if she spoke the words aloud she would be freed from the horrors that lurked in the dark recesses of her mind. "I was a virgin when I married. During our courtship, Lyle never pressured me. He said he wanted our wedding night to be special. He was so sweet while we were courting. If we had the slightest disagreement, he'd be on my doorstep the next day with a bouquet of flowers and a box of candy."

Susan drew a shaky breath. "My grandmother didn't like him. She said he was too good to be true. But I thought she was just afraid of being left alone once I'd married. I should have known better. But Lyle was handsome, from a good family and considered one of the best catches around. That he'd even paid attention to me was flattering. He could have had his choice."

"Don't try to play Miss Naiveté with me," Adam warned. "You've got enough qualities to attract any man's eye."

She jerked her gaze to him. "I suppose I should be flattered by your assessment. But I'm not and I'm not trying to appear naive. There was no line of suitors standing at my door. I knew I wasn't ugly, but I wasn't the kind who had boys fighting over who was going to carry my books, either. I was quiet, studious. I blended in with the crowd."

Adam found it difficult to imagine her blending in with any crowd. But then, he reminded himself, others didn't see her the way he did. This attraction he was feeling was like nothing he'd ever experienced before. "Apparently, Lyle Bartram thought you stood out."

"Actually, I discovered after we were married, it was the fact that I didn't stand out, that I hadn't had a string of boyfriends, that attracted him to me. He wanted a virgin wife. That meant a lot to him." Her gaze returned to the house. "I learned how much on our wedding night." She turned back to Adam, her voice bitter. "You see, he couldn't perform until it was a rape of someone he considered pure. He had a very twisted psyche. Once he told me that good women didn't enjoy sex but it was their duty to satisfy the males of the species so they had to be taken by force. It was all a power thing with him. At first I was too humiliated, too degraded to tell anyone. By the time I realized I had to get out, I was too scared of what he might do."

Adam recalled her telling him about the threats to her life and her grandmother's. Lyle Bartram deserved death for what he'd done to her! The urge to stop now was close to overwhelming. But the haunted look in her eyes told him that she needed to face that night. And, he couldn't turn back, either. He had to know the truth. If she'd murdered once and gotten away with it, she might have murdered again. This thought caused his stomach to knot. He wanted her to be as innocent as she claimed. "You are going to walk me through the night Lyle died," he said, firmly.

Susan started to balk, then her jaw stiffened with purpose. She'd relived this night hundreds of times in her nightmares. Retracing her steps for real couldn't be any worse. She headed to the house.

At the base of the porch steps, Adam laid a restraining hand on her arm. "You'll need this," he said, handing her a flashlight.

In spite of the fact that it was a warm summer night, she'd been feeling chilled. His touch sent an unexpected warmth coursing through her and she mentally glowered at herself. The man wanted to pin three murders on her. How could his touch bring comfort? "Thanks," she muttered, then added sarcastically, "Guess you wouldn't want your chief suspect falling and breaking her neck. You'd have no one to arrest."

"What I don't want is for you to be my chief suspect," he replied, curtly.

She looked at him and knew he meant it. "Then believe me when I tell you I'm being truthful with you," she pleaded.

"I want to." He unlocked the padlock on the door and pushed it open, then stepped aside to allow her to enter ahead of him.

Susan's knees threatened to buckle as she crossed the threshold. Inside, it smelled musty and rank. There was mildew on the walls and the paper was peeling off. It was a house of death, decay and evil, she thought. Entering what had been the living room, she saw a large hairy form scurry into the shadows and flashed her light in that direction. A mother raccoon with a new brood had claimed a corner of the room. She turned her light away from them, returning them to the dark.

Adam noted that she looked as if she were going to retch. He reminded himself of what good actresses some women could be. It didn't help. He felt like a heel. "Where did the confrontation begin?"

"We were in here," she answered vacantly, a part of her fighting recalling that night. "He was complaining about his dinner not being on the table when he walked through the door." She gave up the struggle and the memories came back clear and precise. "Then came the line about him needing to teach me a lesson. I could see him already getting excited. Suddenly I couldn't take any more. I told him that he was the one who needed to be taught a lesson. He laughed. He liked it when I fought back."

Susan moved back into the hall. "I started to the front door. He tried to block my way. I did something I'd never had the courage to do before, I kneed him." The hint of a smile played at a corner of her mouth. "It felt good." The smile vanished as abruptly as it had appeared. "He let out a yell. It reminded me of an animal in rage. I jerked free and ran for the back door. He'd bolted it. That slowed me down. Suddenly he was there, grabbing my arm, telling me I was going to pay dearly. I fought him. He ripped my shirt." She reached up and touched her upper arm. "I remember there were scratches here the next day. One left a small scar."

She had made her way to the back door as she spoke. Continuing to retrace her steps, she began backing toward the hall. "I managed to free myself again. That's when he grabbed the knife. 'You're going to die for this, bitch, and so is that grandmother of yours. She's probably the one who taught you that move.'"

Susan visualized Lyle in front of her, his eyes bulging, spittle foaming at the sides of his mouth. He'd reminded her of a rabid dog. "I knew he meant it. I figured he'd bolted the front door as well. I ran up the stairs and into the spare room at the back of the house. All I could think about was getting outside. It was as if this house was helping him hold me hostage. I heard him at the door taunting me and I knew that with one kick he'd have it open. I opened the window and climbed out. I hung from the frame hoping that would decrease the length of my fall. He came through the door at the same moment I released my hold. I hit the ground hard. There was a sharp pain in my ankle. Then I saw him at the window looking down and I didn't care about the pain. I knew that if I didn't get away from there, I'd die."

"And that was the last time you saw him alive?"

"That was the last time I saw him, period. I refused to even attend his funeral." Susan was standing at the window through which she'd made her escape. The need to again flee this place was too strong to be ignored. Leaving the room, she strode down the hall. "I figure he started to run after me and tripped on these steps,'' she said stiffly as she descended to the lower level. ''It was mere luck he drove that knife into his heart. Maybe the fates had decided I'd suffered enough for my mistake.'' She'd reached the front porch but she didn't stop until she was at Adam's car. Her shoulders squared with defiance, she turned to face him. ''And now I'm going home!'' Wanting nothing from him, she tossed the flashlight into his back seat, then started walking down the drive using only the light from the moon to guide her way.

Adam wasn't convinced she was totally innocent in the death of her husband. But the desire to catch up with her, pull her into his arms and tell her that if she had killed Lyle, he wouldn't blame her was strong. The policeman in him held him back. Still, he couldn't let her go off on her own. Sliding into the driver's seat, he turned the car around and pulled up alongside her, slowing to keep pace. ''Get in. I brought you here and I'm taking you home.''

''I don't need or want your help,'' she snapped back and kept walking. What she did want was a shower to bathe away the vile stench of filth that lingered from being in that house.

Adam's sense of being a heel quadrupled. She looked honestly ill. He reminded himself that he'd had no choice, he was looking for a murderer. That didn't ease his conscience any. ''I don't care how safe small-town America is supposed to be. It sure isn't as free of violence or abuse as I'd hoped. Now get in,'' he ordered.

Suddenly her legs were like lead weights and she realized the strain of reliving that night had sapped her. Besides, the sooner she was home, the sooner she could be scrubbing herself clean. Too angry to admit she wanted a ride, she simply stopped. When he stopped too, she opened the door and climbed in.

''I'm sorry I had to put you through that,'' he apologized.

She tossed him a cold glare. ''I doubt that very much.''

"I'm just doing my job." That sounded anemic, he chided himself.

"I'd say that investigating a death that occurred nine years ago is going pretty far above and beyond the call of duty, especially when that death was an accident," she snarled back.

"Officially an accident," he corrected.

Susan had no energy left to fight him. She centered her attention on the road ahead and fell silent. To her relief, he respected her desire not to talk. When he pulled into her drive, she opened the door and stepped out, but before closing it, she looked back inside. "You're searching in the wrong place for your murderer, Detective. Why don't you go stir up someone else's mud for a while." Slamming the door, she walked away.

Back in his room at Mallery's Boarding House, Adam stood, pretending to hold a knife in his right hand. If he fell forward, his reaction was to drive the knife forward or turn it to the side away from his body and try to catch himself on the palms of his hands. Maybe Bartram had knocked into the wall. He tried that. Going down the stairs, the wall was on the left side. He'd pulled the file. Bartram had been found facedown with his right hand wrapped around the knife. A hit against the wall would have knocked his left hand in front of him, but not his right. And even if he had fallen on the blade, it had to have been a million to one shot it would have been driven directly into his heart.

Sinking into his chair Adam frowned at the blank television screen. But then, like Susan Hallston had suggested, maybe the fates had decided to smile on her. Million to one shots did happen.

Or, maybe Kinter had lied. The doctor had said there wasn't any evidence against him, but both he and Judd had admitted they hadn't looked too hard into the case. Maybe when Kinter had gone to the Bartram house, he'd found

Lyle alive. They'd fought and Kinter had killed Bartram. If that was the case, then it would have to stay between Kinter and his conscience. There was no evidence to convict anyone in Lyle Bartram's death.

The scowl on Adam's face deepened. Was he letting the struggle not to allow the strength of his attraction for Susan Hallston to influence him, sidetrack him down a path that had nothing to do with Angel's murder or Linda Kinter's death?

Leaning back, he closed his eyes. Immediately Susan's drained countenance came sharply into his mind. He wanted to comfort her. Grimly he forced himself to remember the look of grief on Lisa's face at Charlie's funeral. It had fooled everyone. He'd stay away from Miss Hallston for a while. That was the only way to keep his mind clear.

Chapter 10

"My office, now."

Adam looked up from his notes to see Chief of Police, Philip Byrne, hovering over him. It was Thursday morning, a little more than forty-eight hours since the discovery of Angel Carter's body and he knew his boss wanted answers.

Following the chief into the inner sanctum, Adam paused to close the door. When he turned back Byrne had seated himself and was frowning up at him. "What have you got on the Carter murder?"

Adam never hedged. He knew the chief was not going to be happy, but he refused to promise anything he couldn't deliver. "Not much. If there was any footprint evidence it was trampled. The scarf could have been hers or not been hers. The mother wasn't certain. If it wasn't hers, it's going to be impossible to trace. It was inexpensive and could have been purchased in any number of stores in the area. Since people here go to Ashville, Hendersonville, even Charlotte and Greenville to shop, not to mention the small communities in between, there's no way we have the manpower to trace its origin. For all we know, it could have been mail ordered. And there were no makeup smears, hairs or any other evidence not belonging to the victim on it.''

"What about the Reynolds woman? You said she admitted to being blackmailed and worried that the Carter girl would tell even though she paid.''

"As long as her husband backs up her alibi, we can't make a case against her. I haven't confronted him. She swears he doesn't know about the affair and I want to wait until I'm certain she's a viable suspect before I face him with it and try to break his story.''

The chief nodded his approval. "We don't want any more trouble in that neighborhood, if we can prevent it.''

"I canvased the entire area. No one saw anything or heard anything. Of course we're talking about the middle of the night. But there are a lot of dogs in the three blocks surrounding the house and none of them woke their masters with excessive barking so I figure whoever met with Angel was either someone the dogs had grown accustomed to hearing or seeing at that time of night or the person didn't pass any of the houses. In other words, it was one of her immediate neighbors.''

"What about the Polaski kid? According to him, he and the Carter girl have walked that route from the church to her house on a regular basis.''

"His alibi holds, too. As Casey put it, 'I'm an old man. Nature calls frequently.' He claims that every time he was up, the boy was asleep on his couch.''

"Have you got any suspects?'' the chief demanded impatiently.

"Right now I'm concentrating on the immediate neighbors. The girl kept a close eye on them. Three don't have alibis. They were home alone. Claire Kinter, I've pretty much ruled out. Her arthritis makes it difficult for her to walk across a room and her hands don't look strong enough to open a jar. Carol Hawkins and Susan Hallston are the other two. But I can't pinpoint a motive.''

"I heard you took Susan Hallston out to the old Bartram place the other night. Do you think the Carter girl's death ties back to her husband's? Maybe there's a motive there?"

Adam shrugged, unwilling to implicate Susan without proof. "I'm just trying to cover all the bases." He frowned. "I thought I'd kept that trip discreet."

"You threatened Jess Bartram with obstruction of justice if he didn't give you the key to the place. That made him curious enough to keep an eye open. When he saw you heading out that way with Susan Hallston he couldn't dial my number fast enough to find out what was going on."

"What did you tell him?"

"I told him to keep his mouth shut unless he wanted his family's dirty laundry out airing again."

Adam kicked himself. He hadn't meant to feed the gossips. "And will he?"

"He will." Byrne's gaze hardened. "Now go find something solid on the Carter girl's murder. She wasn't particularly liked but people around here get real nervous when teenagers are murdered in their own backyard. And, if you're not going to arrest the Polaski kid, you'd better go explain your reasons to the father, in person. He's been calling here every half hour wanting to know if the kid is in custody and, if not, why. He's certain Polaski did it and he thinks we're playing politics because of the uncle. I don't need those kind of rumors getting started."

"I'll take care of it." Adam sounded more confident than he felt. Trying to convince Ray Carter to be reasonable wasn't going to be easy. The thought that the choice of his remaining in Bandits' Gorge or leaving might not be his, crossed his mind. If he didn't find the killer, the chief was going to need a scapegoat.

* * *

A short while later Adam sat in the living room of the Carters' house with the two parents. "There's no evidence that Wayne Polaski killed your daughter," he informed them. "In fact, he has a firm alibi for the time of death."

"Our daughter didn't have any enemies. There's no one else who would have killed her," Pauline insisted.

Being diplomatic hadn't gotten Adam anywhere. He decided that it was time to be bluntly honest. "You're wrong, Mrs. Carter. According to everyone I've interviewed, your daughter had a way of making enemies."

"That's a lie!" Ray started to rise, rage on his face, clearly intending to level a punch at Adam.

Pauline grabbed him by the arm, gave him a warning glance and pulled him back down beside her. Then with an expression of motherly pride, she turned to Adam. "Angel marched to the beat of her own drummer. People who do that sometimes tread on the toes of the slower, more mundane of the population."

"Well, it could be that one of those slower, more mundane of the population held a grudge that went deep enough to cause them to murder her," Adam said. "If you know of anyone who would fit in that category, I'd like the name or names."

Pauline glared at him. "She never did anything really mean enough to cause anyone to hold that strong a grudge."

Adam saw the flash of defensiveness in her eyes and knew she'd known that her daughter had a vicious streak. But alienating the mother wasn't going to gain him her cooperation. "Some people are easily hurt and hold strong grudges for even the smallest of offenses," he said.

Pauline's jaw firmed. "I refuse to believe Angel would do anything that would cause anyone to feel so...so hateful toward her."

Time to take off the kid gloves again, Adam decided. "I have evidence that suggests your daughter was blackmailing a couple of people to get the money she needed to go to Los Angeles.''

Pauline and Ray both turned red with indignation.

"Blackmail? Never!" Pauline snapped.

Ray's jaw hardened. "You think that's where she got the thousand dollars? Well, you're wrong. If anyone gave it to her, it was a loan."

Adam read the determination on their faces not to believe their daughter was an extortionist.

"You can't find her killer so you're trying to make our daughter out to be a bad person," Pauline accused. "I won't stand for you tarnishing her reputation."

"I'm merely telling you what I've discovered so far. I have no intention of tarnishing your daughter's reputation." Adam kept himself from adding that Angel had done a good enough job of that herself. Instead, he said, "And I assure you that I intend to find out who killed her."

"You'd better," Ray seethed. "And you'd better stop spreading vicious rumors or I'll have your badge."

Adam groaned inwardly. This was getting him nowhere. "Try to think of anyone who might have held a grudge against your daughter," he directed. "In the meantime, I'm going to take another look at her room."

Upstairs he hunted through Angel's wall calendar and the doodlings on her desk blotter for any clue that would lead him to The Dancer. He found nothing.

When he went back downstairs, Pauline Carter handed him a sheet of paper with a short list.

"Sarah Ann Johnson's family blamed Angel for their daughter's death. The girl got herself pregnant and died from a botched abortion." Pride mingled with anger on her face. "They were looking for someone other than themselves to blame." She nodded toward the paper. "The rest are old boyfriends Angel dumped and a couple of girls Angel didn't get along with."

Adam had a feeling that the list could have been a lot

onger, but he said nothing other than to thank the parents, then he left. The list had been more of a diversion, a way of taking their entire concentration off Wayne. The Dancer, he was certain, was the one he needed to find and he doubted he or she was on this list. Someone looking to seek revenge wouldn't be paying blackmail. And, even if she had something on someone on the list, teenagers didn't usually have access to five thousand dollars.

"I double-checked," Dr. Miller informed Adam. "What told you yesterday stands. The girl was strangled and hat's all. There was no sexual assault and she hadn't used any drugs."

"She must have wanted a clear head," Adam mused, recalling the makings of a joint in Angel's pocket.

The doctor studied him coldly. "I heard you took Susan Hallston out to the old Bartram house."

"I thought Jess Bartram was going to keep quiet about hat," Adam grumbled.

The doctor's gaze turned colder. "He called me after he talked to the chief. He was worried the case was going to be reopened. I gave him my word we'd let him know ahead of time if it was, so he could warn the family. For now, it won't go any further than him, me, the chief and whoever you tell."

"Good." Adam hoped, for Susan's sake, the doctor was right. If she was innocent, he didn't want to be the cause of revived gossip about her ill-fated marriage.

Doc Miller continued to regard him frostily. "Did it ever occur to you to wonder why the Bartrams didn't demand a more thorough investigation into Lyle's death? People around here are real strong on family ties."

"I assumed you and the chief told them there wasn't any evidence of foul play and they believed you. I'd also guess they didn't want their son's brutality to become front-page headlines," Adam replied.

"There was a lot more to it than that."

Adam raised a questioning eyebrow.

"This is strictly off the record, between you and me," the doctor stipulated.

"Off the record, strictly between you and me," Adam agreed.

"The father and the brothers were all set to demand that someone be punished even if the death had been self defense, but I made his sister and mother tell them the truth. Lyle had molested his sister when she was barely ten. The mother had brought her in to me. I'd wanted then to press charges, get help for him, but the mother refused. Neither wanted to face the public humiliation. The mother said she'd warned Lyle that she'd tell his father if he ever got near his sister again. Lyle was terrified of his dad. As far as she was concerned, he was cured. The truth was he just got slyer. When I got the mother to tell the other about the first incident, the sister broke down and confessed that he hadn't stopped. But he'd threatened to kill her, her mother and the rest of the family if she told. She said she was sure he meant it and I think he did. Some people are born with no conscience. Outwardly, they put on a facade of being friendly, charming, the kind of people you want to invite home to dinner. Inwardly, they have no soul. Lyle was one of them."

Adam recalled Susan's face when they'd walked through the Bartram house. If he'd been around nine years ago, he might have killed Lyle Bartram himself. "Thank for the information, Doc," he said and left.

Heading to his car he couldn't get Susan off his mind. She'd lived through hell and he'd forced her to revisit it. He felt lower than the dirt under his feet.

Chapter 11

Seeking solitude, Susan had remained in her classroom after the students had gone home. But she couldn't keep her mind on the papers in front of her. Ever since Detective Riley had taken her back to the old Bartram house, the old nightmares had returned full force. The past two mornings, she'd woken in a cold sweat, her body trembling with fear. Even awake, images of the past continued to haunt her.

Making her nerves even more tense, she was certain Adam Riley was building a circumstantial case against her and would arrive at any moment to arrest her for Angel's murder...and Linda's, if he could figure some way of proving that was a murder as well.

Deciding it was doing no good to linger in her classroom, she headed home. A summer rain had started. As the raindrops pelted her umbrella, she wished the torrent would wash away the ominous foreboding that was growing within her.

"Susan. Susan," Claire called out to her, as she started past the elder Kinter's house.

She didn't want to talk to anyone. She wanted to go
home, lock the door and hide in her private, snug litt
corner of the world. Anger flared. But there was nowhe
that was truly private and snug for her with Detective Ril
on her trail. That she was innocent didn't matter. He w
bullheaded and determined. He'd centered on her becau
of Lyle's death. It didn't seem fair that even from t
grave, her ex-husband could put her in danger. Stoppin
she forced a smile, looked toward Claire's porch a
waved.

"Come up here. I've got someone I want you to meet.
In spite of her arthritis, Claire gestured animatedly.

Susan breathed a resigned sigh. Approaching the wid
roofed porch, she saw a boy who looked to be around te
or eleven. Even if she hadn't seen the photos Linda ha
found, the boy's blond hair, blue eyes and facial featur
would have left no doubt in her mind that he was Ken
son. Seated in the chair next to him was a small, dar
haired woman Susan recognized as Ken's first wife.

"This is my grandson, Jason." Claire began the intr
ductions before Susan even reached the level of the porc
The elderly woman was beaming with pride. "Jason, th
is Miss Hallston."

The boy rose and extended his hand. "It's a pleasure
meet you."

His mannerisms were the same as his father's, Susa
realized in amazement. Talk about a strong gene poo
"It's a pleasure to meet you," she replied, accepting t
handshake.

As he reseated himself, Claire motioned toward th
woman. "And this is Ruth Valence, Ken's first wife.
believe you met her once many years ago." Susan saw th
uneasy glance that passed between Ruth and Claire.

Immediately Ruth was on her feet. "I realize you wer
a close friend of Linda's. I hope my being here is n
offensive to you. It's just that Ken was so terribly shake
by his wife's death and being with Jason seemed to eas

his sorrow. When he heard about the death next door, he became worried about his mother's safety and felt he had to come back. I was worried about him and followed.''

"Ken doesn't even know she's here," Claire said. "He came in late last night. This morning he rose early and went into the office." Tears of motherly concern brimmed in her eyes. "The day after Linda's funeral, even though it was the weekend, he began to throw himself into his work. He went into the office before dawn and didn't come home until well after midnight."

"I'm sure with all the memories it holds, he finds it difficult to be in his house right now," Susan said.

"Precisely." Claire nodded vigorously. "But I worry that he's going to make himself sick."

"That was why Claire called me and asked me to invite Ken up to visit with Jason," Ruth spoke up. "I'd been worried about him since I'd heard about his wife's death, but hadn't wanted to intrude on his grief. When Claire asked, I was happy to help."

Susan was relieved that Claire and Ken had found someone other than her to lean on at the moment. She was having enough trouble dealing with her own problems. "I'm glad you're here. Ken needs all of his family right now."

Relief showed on the women's faces.

"Ken has spoken of you often," Ruth said. "He thinks of you as a sister."

"I suppose he is as close to a brother as I've ever had," Susan conceded, glad that at least one person understood there had never been any romantic involvement between her and Ken.

"Would you like some iced tea?" Claire offered, clearly seeing this as a family gathering.

Perhaps some company was what she needed, Susan thought. "That would be nice."

"I'll get it," Ruth offered before Claire could rise. Her

gaze flickered to the elderly woman's swollen ankles. "You relax."

"I can get it for myself," Susan said, heading to the door.

"No, please, let me," Ruth insisted. "I like feeling useful."

"You're such a dear." Claire beamed at her former daughter-in-law.

"May I go watch some television?" Jason asked, reminding them of his presence.

"Yes, of course. My home is your home," Claire replied.

Bowing to Ruth's determination to act as hostess, Susan moved to a chair and sat down.

As Ruth and her son entered the house, Claire leaned toward Susan and lowered her voice. "You'd never know she has servants to wait on her hand and foot. She's just as sweet and unpretentious as she can be."

Susan's impression was that Ruth was trying overly hard to make a good impression but then she couldn't fault her for that. "She does seem very nice."

A twinkle showed in Claire's eyes. Still keeping her voice low, she continued to lean toward Susan. "I've noticed that Detective Riley is spending quite a bit of time with you. Have the two of you discovered you have a lot in common?"

"We have nothing in common." Seeing the confusion on Claire's face, Susan wished she hadn't responded so sharply.

Suddenly the confusion changed to consternation. "I realize that you and Angel have never been on the best of terms, but surely he doesn't suspect you of killing her."

Great work, Susan admonished herself. She didn't have to worry about others starting rumors that she might be the guilty party. She was doing a terrific job on her own. "He thinks I might be able to help him solve the case."

This wasn't a total lie. She was certain he was hoping she would do something to convict herself.

Claire nodded as if Susan's aiding the detective made perfect sense. "Of course. You know the high school kids and I noticed Melissa coming by to visit with you. Did she know anything that could be helpful?"

"No. Angel was very good at keeping her secrets."

Claire frowned. "I was hoping the murderer could be found quickly." Anger spread over her face. "I don't like feeling unsafe in my own home." As she spoke, she balled her hand into a fist and hit the arm of her chair. A cry of agony escaped.

"You really should be more careful," Ruth admonished gently, returning with Susan's iced tea just in time to witness her mother-in-law's pain.

A tear escaped from the corner of Claire's eye. "This darned arthritis. I can't even get around anymore. Everything I do hurts. If the murderer was to come after me, I might even welcome him or her."

"Now, now. You're just stressed." Ruth began to gently massage the older woman's hand. "Everything will work out just fine. You'll see."

"Yes, of course it will." Watching Ruth tend Claire, Susan experienced a surge of guilt. She should have been coming by and checking on the elderly woman more often. After all, Claire had been very good to her through the years. And Susan did like her. But the like was tempered with impatience. She'd always found Claire to be a bit too smothering and overly motherly. But Ruth appeared to truly enjoy being with the elderly woman.

"Maybe you would feel more comfortable if you came and stayed with me for a while," Ruth encouraged Claire, giving proof to Susan's assumption.

"That is a cheerful thought. But I couldn't leave just now. My friends need me." Claire looked toward the Carters' house. "But once this ugly business is cleaned up, I'd love to come."

Ruth smiled warmly. "The invitation is always open You know Jason and I enjoy your company."

Susan suddenly found herself recalling the photograph of Ken, Ruth and Jason that had also included Claire. Officially Ruth might not have been a member of Ken's family, but, Susan now realized, unofficially, Ruth had always been an integral part. Again she felt a sense of betrayal for Linda and the urge to leave was strong. She was considering various excuses, when a familiar car pulled up in front of her house.

Not wanting to be arrested in front of Claire, she rose "It looks as if I have company." She forced a smile for Ruth. "It's been a pleasure meeting you and your son."

"I'm sure we'll be seeing more of each other," Ruth replied.

"Looks like the detective brought along something," Claire said, her attention following the policeman, who had paused at the end of Susan's driveway and was looking their way.

Susan frowned at the white paper bag he was carrying. "Looks like," she replied, wondering what new torment he had in store for her. Halfway across Ken's yard, she began to catch the scent of Chinese food.

Adam met her at the foot of her porch steps. "I figured I owed you a meal," he said.

She couldn't believe her ears. "Fattening the lamb before the slaughter, Detective?"

"It's more of a peace offering. I'm sorry about what I put you through the other night," he replied.

He looked honestly repentant but she wasn't ready to trust him. "I'm not playing any more of your cat-and-mouse games. The only peace offering I want from you is for you to find Angel's murderer and leave me alone."

Ignoring her get-lost manner, Adam accompanied her up the steps. "You've obviously had a rough day."

"I have, thanks to you. Go away." She opened the door and stepped inside.

Inviting himself in, he closed the door to ensure their privacy. "I recognized the woman on Claire Kinter's porch from the photographs. She's Kinter's first wife."

"Yes."

Adam heard the ice in her voice. The apology he'd come here to make was forgotten as a curl of jealousy wove through him. "You don't like her. Is that because you're afraid she might foil your plans to net Kinter for yourself?"

Susan glared at him. "I realized that she's always been a part of his life and I feel betrayal for Linda."

"Are you sure it isn't for yourself?" he challenged.

"Linda was my friend and for the first time, I realize how hurt she must have been. I should never have left her on her own." Tears welled in her eyes. "For the zillionth time, Detective, I am not romantically interested in Ken Kinter. You know where the door is. You can show yourself out."

Adam frowned at her departing back as she went up the stairs. Her explanation was plausible. Carrying the food into the kitchen, he began putting it out on the table. He had gotten out plates and utensils and set them out as well by the time he heard her coming back downstairs.

Entering the kitchen, Susan glowered at him. "I can't believe you actually think I'm going to eat with you."

Adam leaned against the counter, his gaze traveling over her. Her feet were bare and she'd changed into shorts and a T-shirt. He didn't think he'd ever seen a woman look more sexy. Tired of fighting the thoughts running through his head, he said gruffly, "I'm attracted to you. Damn attracted. It's made me afraid I'd let that attraction cloud my judgment. So maybe I've overcompensated in the opposite direction."

For a moment she regarded him in a stunned silence, then said dryly, "That has to be the worst pick-up line in history. You're so attracted to me, you're trying to pin three murders on me. That's got to be one for the books!"

"I don't believe your husband's death was a murder. If you were instrumental in it, it was self-defense."

"And Linda?" she asked sarcastically, refusing to trust him.

"When I saw you on the stairs the morning I was called in on the case, you looked totally stricken. My instincts tell me that was an honest reaction. I want to believe them."

She regarded him ruefully. "But you want me to believe you can't, because you're so 'damn attracted' to me?"

"Yes." Approaching her, he cupped her face in his hands. "You have no idea how hard it's been for me not to kiss you."

Startled by the fire his touch was sending through her, she backed away. "This is some trick, some game you're playing," she accused.

"It's not a game." Scowling, he shoved his hands into his pockets. "I wish it was."

Susan continued to distrust him, but she wasn't going to throw away an opportunity to clear herself. "Surely you have other suspects."

"If I don't link Angel's death to Linda Kinter's...if I accept my previous conclusion that Mrs. Kinter's death was self-induced...that makes it a whole new ball game. The problem is discovering who Angel had information on other than the Reynolds woman."

Again the thought that he could so easily discount others while continuing to focus on her brought an acid edge to her voice. "So, you do think Barbara is innocent?"

"I don't know. I need to find out who The Dancer is."

"I can't help you, Detective. I wish I could," she replied.

Approaching her, Adam tilted her face upward with the tips of his fingers. "My gut instinct tells me that Linda Kinter was murdered and that Angel's death is somehow tied in to that murder. It also tells me that you're innocent.

The problem is knowing if the last part is true or just wishful thinking.''

Susan's jaw firmed. "I think you should stick to the evidence, Detective. Linda's death was a terrible, tragic accident and I'll never fully forgive myself for leaving her on her own. As for Angel's and Lyle's deaths, I had nothing to do with either."

Looking into her eyes, Adam was certain he saw honesty there. Unable to resist, he kissed her lightly on the lips. "Eat your dinner. I've got work to do."

He could feel her eyes on him as he strode down the hall and out of the house. Until the business with Lisa, he'd always trusted his instincts. And they hadn't been entirely off base in that case. He'd always thought she was a little too perfect to be real. And when he found out about the insurance policy, even though she'd sworn that it was Charlie's idea and her explanation had sounded plausible, he hadn't hesitated to investigate her.

The heat of Susan's lips lingered on his. But was it really instinct that was telling him she was innocent or was it lust? He looked back at the house before driving away and a wave of protectiveness washed over him, the same protectiveness he'd experienced the first time he'd seen her. What he was feeling was a great deal more than lust. And he refused to believe he could feel that way about a murderess.

Susan stood where he'd left her, the taste of his lips still on hers. Deep inside, the fires of desire smoldered. How could she be attracted to him, she raged at herself. Only a fool would believe he was really on her side. Tears welled in her eyes. Men! She would be smart to enter a cloistered convent and never have to deal with one of them again.

The smell of the food caused her stomach to grumble. As long as it was there, she might as well eat it, she decided. She carried a plateful out onto her screened back porch and eased herself onto the lounge. Forking a bite of sweet-and-sour pork into her mouth, she heard males laughing and looked toward Ken's house. He was coming out the back door with his son. She was in a shadowy corner and hoped they wouldn't notice her. They didn't. Ken was too intent on his son and Jason was only interested in the game of catch he and his father began to play.

Beyond them, she saw Ted Reynolds lighting his barbecue. The thought of Barbara and Ken together caused her appetite to disappear. She considered going inside, hoping that 'out of sight, out of mind' would allow her to forget about the affair. Instead, she sat watching the ball fly between father and son and wondered how she could have been so blind to all that was happening around her. But then, she was sure, other than Angel, no one else had guessed the truth, either.

Carol Hawkins calling out a greeting to Ken jerked Susan's attention to the house behind hers. Carol was heading her way. Susan noticed that Ken did not acknowledge the woman's greeting.

"I guess Ken's still angry with me," Carol said, entering the porch and seating herself across from Susan.

"It'll take time. Losing Linda was a shock," she replied.

"You were looking awfully grim yourself when I entered."

Susan sighed and pushed Barbara from her mind. Immediately Ruth entered and she heard herself saying, "I met Ken's ex this afternoon. It's obvious she, Claire and Ken have kept in touch and thought of themselves as a family. I suddenly found myself realizing just how betrayed Linda must have felt."

"Maybe you're the one who's feeling betrayed."

Susan fought to control the anger caused by hearing this sentiment echoed again.

"Maybe you thought you'd be the one to help Ken through his sorrow," Carol finished, her voice laced with motherly sympathy.

"I have never thought of Ken in romantic terms." Susan pronounced each word distinctly to give them emphasis.

Carol's expression brightened. "I'm so glad to hear you say that. Claire has always thought you never remarried because you were pining over Ken but I've never really believed that. If the two of you were going to get together you would have done it right after Lyle died. Both of you were in need of consoling and companionship at the time. Ken was getting over his divorce and you were getting over a bad marriage."

"Claire's definitely wrong," Susan affirmed. "I've told you before that there had never been any romantic involvement between Ken and me," she added impatiently. "I hope this time it sinks in."

Carol smiled her best motherly smile as if to say she forgave Susan for her sharpness, then returned her attention to the man and boy next door. "I got the impression Hattie was relieved the two of you never married each other. I don't think she relished the idea of Claire being an in-law. I think she thought the woman would be in your pocket and she was right. As dear a friend as Claire is, if she'd been my mother-in-law, I'd never have put up with living next door to her like Linda did."

Susan had to agree but then she wasn't Linda. "Claire and Ken took the place of the family Linda had lost. She enjoyed Claire's mothering. And she liked taking care of Claire. It made her feel needed and wanted."

Carol nodded in agreement. "Just a week before Linda died, Claire was telling me that no one could ask for a better daughter-in-law."

The thought that Ken's first wife was quickly filling Linda's shoes occurred to Susan, but she kept this to herself. If Carol's belief in her was the least bit tenuous, she didn't want to make any crack that might encourage the other woman to change her mind and think she was jealous.

"Actually, I didn't come over here to discuss Ken."

Anxiousness showed on Carol's face. "When Detective Riley came by to see me the other day, I told him about a conversation I had with Angel."

Susan guessed she was not going to like what was coming next.

"It regarded you." Carol grimaced self-consciously. "Angel had asked me about your marriage...about Lyle's death."

"And what had you told her?" Susan demanded coolly.

"I told her his death was an accident." Carol lowered her voice and leaned closer. "I'll admit, I've never thought it happened exactly the way the police said it did. But I know it was self-defense. Besides, he deserved to die."

Susan swallowed hard. So, Carol thought she'd killed Lyle. She'd known there were those who had held this suspicion...Doctor Miller, for one, and Detective Claymont for another. But she'd thought that most people had believed the official report.

"Anyway, even after I assured Angel the death was an accident, she asked me if I didn't think it was peculiar that tragic deaths seemed to occur when you were around. I told her that some people had more grief in their lives than others. And, I told the detective the same thing." A tint of embarrassment reddened Carol's cheeks. "I've always had the impression that he didn't entirely believe Linda committed suicide and I'll confess that after he left, I got to thinking that if you had been sweet on Ken like Claire claimed, you might have considered getting rid of her." Carol screwed her face up into a self-mocking grimace. "Then I realized how ridiculous that was."

That Carol had even considered the possibility that she'd killed Linda, shook Susan.

"Anyway, I thought I should warn you about what was said." Carol rose. "I don't want to be accused of telling tales out of school again."

"Thanks." Susan marveled that the word had come out so calmly. Inwardly, she was on the verge of panic. For the past two days, she'd been relieved that Carol had not been by. She'd wanted to be left alone. Now she realized that the reason for the woman's absence had been because Carol was working her way through her suspicions that Susan was a murderess.

Carol paused with her hand on the door. "I was surprised when Angel asked about Lyle. I wonder what got her to thinking about that?" She shrugged. "But then who knows how that girl's mind worked. I heard she had a thousand dollars on her and was planning to fly away to California to become an actress."

"I heard the same thing," Susan replied noncommittally. She was beginning to understand very well how Angel's mind worked. The girl had been asking about Lyle, hoping to find something she could use for blackmail. Angel had thought she'd found her pot of gold in the form of other people's secrets.

"If you ask me, it's the boyfriend. He found out she was leaving without him and strangled her. I know Pauline and Ray are convinced of that." Carol frowned. "I don't understand why he hasn't been arrested."

"I'm sure Detective Riley is gathering evidence for a conviction even as we speak," Susan said, feeling the noose tightening around her neck. She'd been right to distrust him. He knew Angel had been asking about her. No doubt he was convinced the girl had found out something that would be a motive for Susan to have murdered her. He was merely pretending to be on her side to give her enough rope to hang herself. The bite of food she'd swallowed felt like a rock in her stomach.

Carol nodded, then her gaze shifted back to the man and boy playing catch. "Looks like Ken's going to be needing some of Claire's special ointment tonight. That stuff is great. I used it last winter when I slipped on the ice and sprained my ankle. Too bad Claire's allergic to it. Talk about irony. The one person who needs it the most and she can't use it."

Susan felt the urge to laugh. She was terrified of being arrested for murder and Carol was making small talk about ointments. Realizing she was near hysteria and, knowing Carol could come up with enough inane subjects to stand for another half an hour with her hand on the doorknob before leaving, she rose. "I'm really tired. I need to go inside and lie down."

"This whole business has been a strain," Carol said sympathetically. Again she started to open the screen door, and again she paused to look back. "I wonder where Angel got that much money? You don't think she was selling her body, do you?"

"No." Susan didn't elaborate. The fewer who knew what Angel had been up to, the better.

"Maybe she was dealing in drugs."

"Maybe," Susan replied noncommittally.

"Most likely," Carol said and left.

The moment the woman was gone, Susan made a dash for her bathroom. There she splashed cold water on her face. She was innocent. She had nothing to fear, she told herself. But she didn't believe it.

A loud knocking sounded from her back door and she heard Ken calling her name. She didn't want to talk to him, but there was no polite way to avoid it. Forcing a smile, she answered the summons. Considering the rumors people were spreading about her and him, she felt uncomfortable inviting him inside. Instead she stepped outside, joining him on the porch.

"What do you think of my kid?" he asked, beaming with fatherly pride.

"He looks like you." She tried to keep the coolness out of her voice, but couldn't.

Ken's smile disappeared. "You're angry with me. Mom said you seemed a little uneasy when she introduced you to Ruth. I suppose you think I shouldn't have allowed her to come visit so quickly after Linda's death. It wasn't my idea, she came on her own. But I have to admit that I like having my son around.''

''I am feeling a little bit as if you're betraying Linda to have them here,'' she conceded. ''On the other hand, the boy is your son and a father and his child should spend time together.'' Again she'd tried to school the chill out of her voice, but the image of him and Barbara together had come back to taunt her and her effort had proven unsuccessful.

''Why don't I believe you mean that?'' he asked.

She scowled up at him. ''I do. It's Barbara Reynolds. How could you have an affair with her right under Linda's nose? Linda loved you and trusted you.''

Shock showed on his face. ''You know about my affair with Barbara?'' He glanced worriedly over his shoulder toward the Reynolds' house. ''Who else knows?''

''As far as I know, only Detective Riley. Barbara came to me because she was scared. Angel had tailed her and found out about the affair. Barbara was the one who gave the thousand dollars to Angel to keep her from telling Ted about your liaison. She was worried the police would get her fingerprints off the money.''

''Damn,'' Ken cursed under his breath. ''Barbara's a good friend, I hate seeing her get into trouble over a few fun and games.''

''Fun and games?'' Susan seethed. ''Linda adored you. How could you do that to her?''

''There was no emotional attachment on either side.''

Susan marveled at the lack of guilt in his voice. ''I don't understand how you can claim to love someone and then be unfaithful to them.''

''You're beginning to sound as if you're jealous.'' Ken studied her as if seeing her for the first time. ''My mother's always claiming you have feelings for me. I never believed it before.''

Susan flushed scarlet. ''I don't and I'm not jealous.''

"I'm sorry, I didn't mean to intrude." A woman's voice sounded from behind her.

Startled, Susan glanced over her shoulder and saw Ruth at the door of the porch. The uneasiness on the newcomer's face told her that Ruth had overheard Ken's accusation.

"You aren't intruding." Stepping around Susan, Ken moved to the door. "Susan was just throwing a little tantrum. I'm used to her kid-sister fits of anger."

Susan frowned. He'd made it sound as if it were normal for her to fly into rages. "I was not throwing a tantrum." She read the disbelief in Ruth's eyes and knew her protest had fallen on deaf ears.

Ruth turned to Ken. "I came to tell you that we're ready to go to dinner."

Ken smiled. "Then let's get going." He glanced back at Susan. "We'll talk again when you're in a better humor."

"You run along," Ruth said, stepping aside to allow him to pass, then entering the porch. "I want a word with Susan."

"She's really not in a very good mood," he warned.

Again Susan was rankled by his unfair implication that she had a foul temper. She took a couple of calming breaths.

"You run along. I'll join you shortly," Ruth insisted.

Ken glanced toward Susan, clearly worried about what she might tell Ruth, then with a shrug of resignation, he left.

"Claire has told me that you've always had a crush on Ken and I realize that my being here must be difficult for you," Ruth said as soon as Ken rounded the corner of the house. "Well, you're right to be jealous. I plan to win him back and this time I'll keep him. My son needs his father and Ken has been the only man I've ever loved. I know how much he cared for Linda. And I know his feelings for me are currently merely that of a friend, but he might be willing to marry me for our son's sake. I'll take him on any terms."

"You're welcome to him," Susan assured her. Ruth didn't look convinced and Susan realized that the woman thought it was pride that was talking. She was tempted to reveal his affair, but that would only make her sound like a jealous shrew. Even more, Ruth probably wouldn't care. She'd made it clear she was willing to accept him on any terms. That would leave Barbara being the only one harmed and Susan refused to follow in Carol's footsteps, blithely revealing secrets that ripped families and lives apart. "I just hope you're not disappointed."

"I won't be," Ruth replied, and left.

"And I should go lock myself in a closet and throw away the key," Susan muttered under her breath. If Detective Riley ever learned about this altercation, he'd be convinced she killed Lyle in a rage, did in Linda to get Ken, and strangled Angel to prevent being blackmailed.

Chapter 12

Susan stood at Angel's grave site listening to the minister's final words being spoken over the coffin. It was now four days since the murder. The casket had been closed. Only family and close friends had come to the cemetery. There had been a contingency of high school students at the church but Susan guessed they were there more out of curiosity than to mourn. Only Melissa, of all the teenagers present, seemed to honestly care. During the service, the girl's shoulders had been trembling as she fought to hold back the sound of her sobs. Now by the grave, she was crying openly, her tears dripping on the ground.

Susan saw Pauline looking around the assembly, her red, swollen eyes searching the faces of those present. She knew who the woman was looking for. Wayne Polaski. But he wasn't at the grave site. He hadn't been at the church, either. Susan hoped this was because he'd confessed to the murder and was now under lock and key. She'd heard that he was supposed to have an alibi. But maybe Casey had lied for the boy. The old man treated

Wayne like family, more so than any of his blood kin. Aware that Adam Riley was standing a few feet behind her, on the outer fringe of the graveside gathering of mourners, she was tempted to ask him. But this didn't seem like the right place or the right time.

"I hope you have that juvenile delinquent who killed my daughter under lock and key!" Ray was on his feet, glaring across the coffin at the policeman.

The minister, who had been cut off in the middle of the Lord's Prayer, stood mutely as all eyes turned to Riley.

Apparently she was the only one who thought this was not an appropriate time, Susan thought dryly.

"I haven't made an arrest yet," Riley replied calmly.

Melissa started sobbing louder. The minister took control, reminding Ray they were there to bid a gentle farewell to his daughter. Pauline jerked on her husband's arm.

Ray ignored them. "I want justice done," he demanded, continuing to glare at Adam.

"It will be," Adam assured him.

Pauline jerked harder on her husband's arm. This time he obeyed the unspoken command and returned to his seat. As the minister began the Lord's Prayer once again, Susan caught a glimpse of Detective Riley out of the corner of her eye. He was watching her, his expression unreadable.

Adam noticed her covert glance and wanted to give her a wink of encouragement, but decided that wouldn't be prudent with the rest of his suspects assembled around her. He didn't want anyone getting the notion he was playing favorites. That could damage his investigation and bring his credibility into account. Besides, she didn't believe he was on her side anyway. He'd have to prove her innocent to win her trust. And that's exactly what he planned to do.

By a process of elimination, he'd determined that either Carol Hawkins was The Dancer or one of the Olivers was, and they were covering for each other. His problem was coming up with a motive. Of course there was always Barbara Reynolds. But his money was on The Dancer.

* * *

Walking up Willow Street three hours later, Susan breathed a sigh of relief. After the service she'd gone with the others to the Carters' home, helped serve the food prepared by family and friends and listened to platitudes about Angel. Most people had talked about what a pretty girl she was. Almost no one had used the words *kind* or *sweet*.

Ruth had not been at the funeral nor come to the house Susan learned from Carol who'd gotten her information from Claire, that Ruth had stayed at home to look after her son. Besides, as Carol had pointed out, Ruth didn't know Angel so there was no reason for her to attend.

Barbara and her family had been at both the church and graveside ceremonies. And, they'd come to the Carter house afterward. Ken was also present at all functions but Susan noticed that he and Barbara kept their distance from each other. She'd chosen not to speak to either. Lately, it seemed that every time she opened her mouth, she put her foot into it. And both seemed agreeable to allowing her to avoid them.

Carol was back in Ken's good graces, at least enough for him to exchange a few polite words with her. As for Claire, she'd come to the service at the church but her arthritis had been aching so badly, she'd been afraid of being a burden on everyone if she tried to walk on the uneven ground at the cemetery. Instead, she'd gone directly from the church to the Carters' house, laid out the food, then gone home to rest and spend some quiet time with her grandson.

To Susan's relief, Detective Riley had not come by the Carter house following the graveside service.

Now the afternoon was fading into evening and Susan was on her way home, leaving Pauline and Ray in the capable hands of family. She found herself glancing over her shoulder and to either side as she walked. "You're being ridiculous," she chided herself, hoping to shake off the feeling that evil was lurking in the shadows. It didn't work. She wanted to go back to the fairy-tale time, before she'd learned her neighbors' secrets, when she thought of the couples as being faithful to each other and the children as simply going through difficult phases they would outgrow. She didn't want to know about their infidelities or that there could be such meanness in a child Angel's age. She wasn't naive. She'd been aware that those faults existed in the world. But she'd pictured their little enclave as being the epitome of old-fashioned, God-fearing, even puritanical America.

"Miss Hallston," a young voice broke into her thoughts as she mounted the steps of her porch.

Susan let out a small shriek.

"I'm sorry. I didn't mean to scare you."

Susan looked toward the porch swing to see Melissa sitting Indian fashion, clutching a pillow in her arms, looking pale with a tear slowly trailing down her cheek.

"I couldn't stand being in that house any longer and I didn't want to go home," the teenager said, brushing at the trickle of water with the palm of her hand.

"Won't your parents worry about where you are?" Susan had noticed the Colbys earlier at the Carter house quietly trying to get Melissa to leave with them, but the girl had insisted on staying.

"No. I told them to go on home and that I'd call them when I was ready to leave." Another tear trickled down her cheek.

Susan was tired. All she wanted was to take a long hot bath and watch some television, but it was obvious Melissa needed a friend just now. She sat down in Hattie's rocking chair.

Melissa lowered her voice conspiratorially. "Wayne was there at the cemetery. I saw him up on the hill watching from behind a tree."

So, the boy had come to pay his last respects, Susan mused.

Melissa scowled angrily. "I don't understand why Detective Riley hasn't arrested him."

"He has an alibi," Susan replied.

"Well, I don't believe it. Who else would have done it?" Melissa demanded.

Susan drew a tired breath. "I wish I knew."

Melissa's gaze traveled past her to the end of the block. "Do you believe we have souls, Miss Hallston?"

"Some people, not everyone," Susan replied honestly. "I think some people get born without them."

Again Melissa nodded. For a long moment she was silent, then said, "Angel told me she saw a soul once."

That sounded like a story Angel would make up, Susan thought dryly.

"It was the night Mrs. Kinter died. Angel saw it from her bedroom window. Angel said it was her soul...Mrs. Kinter's. She figured that because it was nearly two in the morning and the doctor said Mrs. Kinter died sometime around then. Of course, Angel had been smoking a joint when she saw it." Melissa stopped abruptly as if she felt guilty of gossiping.

Susan visualized Angel sitting in her window looking down at the backyards of their houses, her mind fogged by drugs. An uneasiness stirred within her. What exactly had the girl seen? "Tell me what Angel said about Mrs. Kinter's soul."

Melissa shrugged. "Not much. Just that it was all dark and shadowy. I remember she said it came out the back door and did sort of a twirling dance as if it were happy to be free, then it hurried on its way." Melissa grimaced crookedly. "She said it headed toward one of the neighbors' houses probably to do a little voyeuristic peeking before heading into the netherlands. Angel always liked to add a bit of risqué spice to everything she saw."

Susan's heart was beginning to pound frantically. "Did she mention which house?"

Melissa shook her head. "No. I told her I thought she'd been smoking too much pot and she got mad at me. She said that when people die under tragic circumstances, especially when they're real unhappy, it's not unusual for their spirits to roam around. She said she'd been too tired to enter the experience in her diary when it had happened. But she was going to devote a whole page to her feelings about souls when she wrote in it that night.''

Melissa shivered. "I told her she was scaring me. Suddenly her expression got real serious and she said she was sorry. She said she hadn't meant to upset me." Melissa smiled weakly. "Angel could be real nice when she wanted to. Anyway, she made me swear not to tell anyone what she'd said. She said that if anyone else heard about this they'd probably think she was nuts and try to put her in some drug rehab place. She said she wasn't even going to enter it into her diary, that it was much too ethereal an experience to be recorded and that we should never talk about it again…that it was too holy." Melissa sighed wistfully. "I'd like to think that Angel's soul is dancing somewhere."

"I'm sure it is," Susan soothed. Actually she wasn't so certain that Angel had had a soul and if she had just where it was at the moment. What she was certain of was that she was wrong and Adam Riley was right about Linda's death not being an accident. She was also certain that while Angel was telling Melissa about what she'd seen, she'd realized the enormity of it and hadn't wanted Melissa spilling the beans before she could make a profit. Fear for the child sitting in her porch swing swept through Susan. "It might be a good idea, for the sake of Angel's memory, not to mention this to anyone. You don't want people thinking she was a pothead."

"No. I wouldn't want that," Melissa agreed.

"And I think I should drive you home right now," Susan added, wanting to get the girl where she would be safe.

Melissa sighed. "I would like to go home."

Dropping Melissa off in front of her house, Susan waited until the girl was inside before driving away. But she didn't go immediately home. Instead she drove out of town to a spot by the river where she'd used to bicycle to as a teenager. Standing on the bank watching the water silvered by moonlight, she considered her options. Maybe what Angel had seen was simply a drug-induced hallucination, she argued. But she didn't buy that argument. The frown on her face deepened. She knew what she had to do. She had to tell Adam Riley what Melissa had told her. That was the only way to protect Melissa.

She drove to the police station but he wasn't there. Marsha Radcheck, the dispatcher on duty, had known Susan since grade school. When Susan explained it was important that she talk to the detective, Marsha gave her Adam's address. To her relief his car was parked in front of the boarding house.

Mable Mallery, the proprietress, was sitting on her front porch. She smiled with interest when Susan asked which room the detective was in and watched with curiosity while Susan continued inside and up the stairs. Susan knew that by tomorrow everyone would know she'd come to see the policeman.

Halfway down the hall on her way to his door, she hesitated. She could very easily be giving the detective the nail he would use to hammer down her coffin. Then she reminded herself that the sooner the authorities had heard Melissa's story, the safer the girl would be. Continuing to his door, she knocked before her courage threatened to fail her again.

Surprise registered on Adam's face when he answered the summons and found her there. For a moment, he wondered if he'd been wanting to see her so badly, he'd conjured her up. "I'm glad you came," he said, stepping aside to allow her to enter.

In spite of her anxiousness, the hint of huskiness in his voice caused a tingle of excitement. He'd discarded the suit he'd worn to the funeral in favor of a pair of jeans and a lightweight cotton pullover. Again she was impressed by his physique. But it was the welcome on his face that sent a curl of warmth through her. Her heart beat faster and she found herself thinking it had been a long time since she'd seen a man look so...appealing. *He's out to prove you're a murderess,* she reminded herself curtly. Again it occurred to her that she might be helping him, but she refused to have Melissa's blood on her hands. "This isn't a social call," she said, stepping into the room.

Trying not to think about him, she looked around at her surroundings. The place had obviously been furnished by Mable. There were doilies on the backs and arms of the two upholstered chairs by the window and on the tops of the occasional tables. The furniture itself was functional, not new but in good condition. In one corner, she saw a small portable refrigerator and a table holding a hot plate and coffeemaker. The couch which doubled as a bed had been unfolded and the television tuned to a murder drama. From the indent on the pillows, she guessed he'd been lying there watching it. A bowl of popcorn added confirmation.

The strain on her face told Adam that whatever had brought her to his doorstep had her badly shaken. Again the protective urge she inspired in him grew strong. "I'm still glad you came." Closing the door, he pressed the button on the remote turning off the television.

"I'm not so sure I will be after I say what I've come to say," she admitted stiffly.

Now it was Adam's turn to feel uneasy. Had she come to confess to having killed her husband? If so, he would stand beside her. The man, by everyone's reckoning, had been a brute. "I'm on your side. I told you that."

She wanted to believe the honesty in his voice, but she'd been fooled by a man before. "I really wish I could believe that."

"So, what did you come to tell me?" he coaxed, determined to prove to her that she could.

She drew a deep breath to calm her nerves. "I think you might be right about Linda having been murdered."

Adam hid his surprise. "What makes you think that?"

"I'm fairly certain Angel saw something the night Linda died." Fear that she was tightening the noose around her neck caused her voice to falter.

Worried that she might faint, Adam took her arm and guided her to the chair beside the couch. "You should sit down."

"You're going to think I did it," she blurted, sinking into the chair. "Ken made me look like a jealous shrew in front of his former wife. I was telling him what I thought of him for cheating on Linda with Barbara, but Ruth only caught enough to make her think I was throwing a jealous fit—and to make it worse, Ken made it seem like I have a violent temper. Neither of those is true. But she'll tell you they are if you question her. And who knows what others will say. I'm beginning to believe we have no clue how others see us."

Adam's gaze bore into her. "I know how I see you and it's not as some love-starved, crazed murderess."

She looked hard into his face. "You really mean that?"

He grinned crookedly. "I really mean that."

Looking into the brown depths of his eyes, Susan felt as if she were being enveloped in warmth. "I believe you do," she murmured, a curl of joy weaving through her.

"Now, tell me why you think Angel saw something the night Linda Kinter died," he said gently.

"It's because of something Melissa told me tonight. I was scared for her. I took her home and told her not to tell anyone else but she'll tell you if I tell her to."

Adam congratulated himself for his faith in the woman in front of him. If she had been the murderer he was looking for, she wouldn't be here. She'd be working out a plan to do Melissa in. "What did Melissa tell you?"

"She said Angel was sitting in her window around two in the morning the night Linda died. She was having a joint and looking out at the backyards when she saw Linda's soul come out the back door. Angel described it as a dark shadow and said it performed a kind of whirling dance, then hurried toward one of the neighbors' houses. She told Melissa she thought the soul was going to do a little voyeuristic peeking before heading off to wherever souls go.''

Adam could feel his murderer within his grasp. "Which house did the 'soul' head toward?"

Susan's expression became glum. "Melissa didn't know. Angel suddenly became wary and asked her not to tell anyone. She told Melissa she was afraid that if people heard this story they'd think she was hallucinating and put her in a drug rehab. I think when Angel got to talking about it, she realized what she'd really seen and wanted to make a profit from it." Susan's chin tightened. "The whirling dance…it made me think the shadowy form could have been the person Angel designated as The Dancer."

Adam nodded. "I'm certain you're right and now we know what Angel was holding over The Dancer's head. She saw whoever it was she gave that designation to coming out of Linda Kinter's back door the night the woman died. But who?"

He'd used the word *we*. He was talking as if he considered them a team. "I still find it hard to believe someone would murder Linda."

"Money is a very powerful motive. Ken Kinter's ex-wife is worth millions and with her father gone, she's free to marry whomever she wants," Adam stated.

Susan drew a shaky breath. "A week ago I would have sworn that Ken would rather take his own life than have one single hair on Linda's head injured. Now I don't know what to think. He was having an affair with Barbara Reynolds. And he was seeing his ex-wife and son behind Linda's back." She frowned. "But he couldn't have been who Angel saw. He was on the fishing trip."

"The most reasonable solution would be that he talked Barbara Reynolds into doing the job for him. He could have blackmailed her with threats of exposure. But that doesn't work because Angel's diary makes it clear that Juliet and Dancer are two different people. Besides, Barbara has an alibi for the night Linda was killed.''

Frustration swept thought Susan. "Who, then?"

"Maybe Kinter had something on one of your other neighbors and blackmailed them into doing the job. Or maybe he simply paid them or promised them a lot of money after the job was done and he'd remarried his ex.''

"I still find it hard to believe it could have been someone I know.'' A thought struck her. "Maybe it was Ken's ex. She's obviously still in love with him. Maybe she hired someone.''

"It would still have to have been one of your neighbors.'' Adam's expression turned grimmer. "There's something else we should consider.''

She liked his use of the word *we*. It had a comforting effect. She needed that to combat the discomforting thought that someone she knew was a murderer.

"If the drug was purchased directly from Zelda, then the purchase was made several months ago,'' he continued. "Maybe Linda did something back then that upset one of your neighbors enough they decided on revenge and simply bided their time until the perfect moment came.''

Susan stared at him in shock. "You think someone has been hating her for months while playing the part of a friend?''

"It's possible.''

Susan shook her head. "Linda worked hard at not offending people.''

"She hadn't endeared herself to Barbara Reynolds,'' Adam reminded her. "But she's ruled out. The Olivers were possibilities for Angel's death but they have a confirmable alibi for the night Linda died. The only people who have no confirmable alibi for either night, is you, Claire Kinter and Carol Hawkins.''

"I could swear Claire loved Linda like a daughter. Besides, with her arthritis she couldn't be The Dancer. If she'd twirled around, she would have fallen on her face.'' Susan drew a steadying breath. ''That leaves Carol. But I still find that hard to believe.''

''She was the one who spilled the beans about Ken's former marriage and set the scene for the murder,'' Adam noted.

''But Carol's always saying things she shouldn't,'' Susan argued back.

''You're not helping,'' Adam growled. ''So far, you're the only one I can build a solid case against and you keep shooting down the alternatives.''

''I didn't do it,'' she repeated, feeling like a broken record.

''So, help me find out who did.'' Rising, he held his hand out to her. ''Let's go talk to Melissa.''

She accepted his aid to help her to her feet, and the heat from his hand trailed up her arm. ''I'm scared,'' she admitted.

Unable to resist, he drew her into his embrace. ''We'll figure this out,'' he vowed.

Shocked by how secure she felt in his arms, she nodded into his shoulder.

Adam held her more tightly and desire flared to life within him.

She felt his maleness, and passions she hadn't experienced for years burned within her. Lifting her head, she looked up into his face and saw her own lust reflected in his eyes.

Adam knew at this moment he could have her. But he also knew that he would be taking advantage of her. Her fear was causing her to seek comfort where she could find it. He didn't want her under those conditions. ''We'd better get going,'' he said, forcing himself to release her.

Susan flushed with embarrassment. She knew he'd read the welcome in her eyes and rejected it. ''I wasn't trying to seduce you so that you would stay on my side.''

''I didn't suspect that you were.'' Tilting her chin upward with the tips of his fingers, he kissed her lightly. "But right now you're in a vulnerable state and I refuse to take advantage of you. When I do take you to bed, I want it to be under much more pleasant circumstances."

"Is that your way of asking for a rain check?" she asked, nervous anticipation winding through her.

"Yes."

The fire within her continued to rage. "Then you have it."

He grinned and reached for the door. "I've got to get you out of here, before my willpower crumbles."

Grinning back, she glanced down at his feet. "I'd suggest you put on some shoes."

"Wait in the hall," he ordered, letting his lust again show openly on his face.

Outside, Susan leaned against the wall. What was going to happen if they couldn't find another suspect? Fear threatened to overwhelm her. She was innocent. There had to be a way to prove it.

Joining her, Adam slipped a protective arm around her waist as they walked to his car. "Maybe Melissa will remember something more," he said encouragingly. "Something that will lead us to the killer's door."

"I hope so," Susan replied.

But Melissa didn't remember any more.

"Just to be on the safe side, I want you to keep a close eye on your daughter," Adam told Melissa's parents when he finished interviewing the girl. "And I'm going to ask the chief to put a man on her during the day while you're at work."

The father placed an arm around his daughter's shoulders, while the mother paled. "We'll keep a close watch over her," they promised in unison.

Melissa, Susan noted, seemed stunned to find herself the center of so much attention. "You do exactly what your parents and the police tell you," she said to the girl.

Melissa nodded.

Riding back to Adam's place to pick up her car, Susan studied the hard line of his jaw. "I'm still the most reasonable suspect, aren't I?"

"If I was to believe the gossip, yes."

"But you believe me, not the gossip?" she questioned, needing to hear him say it again.

"Yes." He continued to frown at the road ahead. "But my opinion may not hold much weight."

She knew what he meant. "The chief will want an arrest made and he believes the gossip."

Adam pulled up behind her car. "I'll find out who the real murderer is. I promise." He gently trailed his finger along the cord behind her ear. "I wouldn't want to have to forfeit that rain check."

Her skin tingled beneath his touch. "I wouldn't want that, either."

Knowing that his control was slipping, he quickly climbed out of his car, rounded it and opened her door. "Go home and get some rest," he ordered.

But later as she lay in bed, Susan wondered how he was going to prove her innocent. "How ironic," she muttered. She'd finally found a man who could make her forget the horror of her first marriage and want to move on and he was probably going to end up arresting her for murder.

Staring into the dark, she pictured Carol killing first Linda and then Angel. It just didn't seem possible. But who then? Maybe the Olivers' alibi for the night of Linda's death could be broken. Or maybe there were two murderers, both friends or husband and wife, one covering for the other. Pulling the covers up tightly around her, she fell into an exhausted sleep.

Chapter 13

"So, it looks like the Kinter woman was murdered and Angel knew who did it," Chief Byrne said. Even though it was Sunday, he'd summoned Adam to his office for an early morning meeting.

"And whoever killed Linda Kinter, most likely killed Angel," Adam finished for the chief.

"You got a suspect?"

Adam could tell from the chief's tone that Byrne had one.

"I'm still investigating."

"If I was to believe the gossip about Susan Hallston being sweet on Ken Kinter, I'd say she had motive and she has no alibi for either murder."

Adam had expected this. "True, but I'm not convinced she's guilty."

The chief eyed him speculatively. "Could it be that you're letting something other than your brain do your thinking for you?"

"No." Reading the skepticism in Byrne's eyes, Adam

new he didn't have much time left to prove Susan innocent before the chief demanded her arrest or turned the case over to someone who would see things Byrne's way. Rising, he headed to the door. "I'll let you know when I find out who the murderer is."

"People are going to demand an arrest soon," Byrne said as Adam's hand closed around the knob. "And I don't want any of my cops being accused of being so lovesick or lust-sick, they can't see the forest for the trees."

Adam turned back. "And I don't want to send an innocent person to death row."

"I'm on my way to church," Byrne returned, rising as well. "I'll say a prayer that neither of us makes a mistake."

Back in his office, Adam sat staring at the crime board he'd created. He'd reviewed the statements and the evidence he'd collected a hundred times. It was getting him nowhere.

Reaching for the phone, he dialed Susan's number. "Did I wake you?" he asked apologetically, picturing her in a cotton nightgown with her hair mussed and feeling his temperature rising.

"No. I was just on my way out to church." Her voice filled with hope. "Have you discovered something?"

"No." There was silence on the other end of the line and in his mind's eye he could see the fear in her eyes. "It's time to shake the tree and see what falls."

"And what exactly does that mean?" she asked nervously.

"It means that the going could get rough. I'm going to tell Angel's parents that I think she was murdered because she knew Linda Kinter was killed and who did it."

"And you think they'll suspect me because of the rumors about me and Ken?"

"Maybe. Or maybe they'll be able to lead me in the right direction."

"I'll keep my fingers crossed."

"One other thing. It'd be best for now if no one know
you and I are on the same side."

"Thanks for the warning." Susan's hands were shaking
as she hung up. Grabbing up her purse, she hurried out to
church, hoping that prayer would help.

Susan glanced at her watch. It was half past one. Hoping
to keep her mind occupied until she heard from Adam, she
was seated in the lounge chair on her back porch with a
stack of ungraded essays in her lap. She needed to have
them ready to return to the students by tomorrow but she'd
been staring down at the first one on the pile for the last
five minutes and not a single word of it had penetrated her
brain.

When she'd arrived home from church a while ago she'd
seen him waiting outside the Carter home for them to return from the Sunday morning service. He hadn't waved
or given any sign he'd seen her and she'd known that he
wanted her to keep her distance.

The banging of a door grabbed her attention. Looking
in the direction from which it had come, she saw Pauline
Carter leaving her house by the back porch door. The
woman strode across her yard, continuing through the Kinter properties, heading directly for Susan's place.

Feeling the world closing in on her, in robotic motion
Susan set the papers aside and rose.

"Pauline!" Ray yelled, following his wife out of the
house and jogging to catch up to her.

Adam followed a couple of paces behind.

Ray reached Pauline when she was still several feet from
Susan's porch door. "Calm down. You can't go throwing
accusations at people."

Pauline paid him no heed. She'd spotted Susan through
the wire screening that separated them. "Come out here
and face me! I want to know if you killed my daughter."

Susan's legs felt like jelly. It was clear from Pauline's
voice that she'd already made her mind up as to the an-

wer. Susan's gaze turned to Adam. His expression was shuttered. Had he changed his mind about her? Knowing she couldn't avoid a confrontation, she stepped outside. "I didn't kill Angel."

Pauline glared in disbelief. "Detective Riley just told us that Angel might have seen someone coming out of Linda's house the night she supposedly committed suicide. Her house wasn't broken into and she wouldn't have let a stranger in. You were the one she spent the day and evening with. And, you have no alibi." The hatred in her voice increased. "And you have a motive. I've always suspected that you wanted Ken for yourself. That's why you've never remarried. You knew Linda was distraught and you used the opportunity to do away with her and make it look like a suicide."

"No, I didn't. Linda was my friend and you're wrong about the way I feel about Ken." Susan looked to Ray for support but found none.

"We've been talking and Pauline's right," he said, his wife's accusation mirrored on his face. "You're the only one with a motive Linda would have allowed to get close enough to poison her."

Out of the corner of her eye, Susan caught sight of movement. Carol was coming across the lawns toward them. She looked back to Pauline to see Claire, Ken and Ruth coming from the other direction. Glancing toward the McFays, she saw Kay standing at her back door watching. She wondered where the Reynolds and Olivers were. Probably going out to buy the rope to string me up with, she thought dryly. The urge to laugh at this silent jest was strong. Realizing she was on the verge of hysteria, she took a calming breath. Again, she assured herself that because she was innocent, this would all pass. But deep inside, she was beginning to doubt that.

"What's going on?" Carol demanded, taking a position beside Susan, her manner protective. "You can't honestly believe Susan would harm Angel."

"They've never gotten along," Pauline spit out. "She gave Angel a C in history, just for spite."

"I gave her a C because she refused to do the work and did badly on every test. She should have had an even lower grade but I scrounged up a couple of extra points to bring her total up," Susan defended.

Pauline issued a disgusted snort. "She told me you had it in for her. She was prettier and smarter than you."

"I wouldn't say she was so smart. She got herself killed," Carol remarked dryly.

Pauline's cheeks reddened with rage. "How dare you make snide remarks about my daughter!"

"And how dare you go throwing accusations around," Carol returned.

It was ironic, Susan thought, that Adam's prime suspect was the one coming to her aid. She again glanced toward him. His expression continued to remain blank.

"Angel saw someone leaving Linda's house around two in the morning, the night Linda died," Pauline stormed. "Susan is the only logical choice."

"Angel saw someone leaving my house?" It was Ken, his face suddenly pale.

"She was smoking marijuana at the time. No one can be certain that what she saw wasn't a drug-induced hallucination," Susan blurted.

The others stared at her in stunned silence. It was Ken who found his voice first. "You knew about this?"

"Melissa told me last night after the funeral. I told Detective Riley." Her gaze traveled over these people she'd once called friends. "If it was me, why would I have gone to the police?"

"Because you'd be afraid that eventually they would find out anyway," Pauline retorted. "You've had us all fooled. I've always suspected you killed your husband but I was willing to overlook that. He deserved to die. But it looks to me as if you've decided that murder is a solution to all of your problems." She headed toward Susan, her hands outstretched. "But you're not going to get away with murdering my daughter."

"Mrs. Carter." Adam suddenly became mobile, capturing Pauline by the arm and holding her back. "I'd suggest you and your husband go home, now." His voice held the authority of command as he looked to Ray. "Take her back inside before I have to arrest her for assault."

Ray stood, regarding the detective with a belligerent expression. "I want the person responsible for my daughter's death punished."

"I want the same thing," Adam assured him.

Ray nodded, cast a final accusatory glare toward Susan, then took hold of his wife's arm. "Come on. We'll let the law take its course."

Tears flooding her eyes, Pauline continued to stare at Susan. "How could you? How could you?"

"I didn't," Susan repeated, knowing her words were falling on deaf ears.

"Those two gave birth to a rotten seed and made it worse by refusing to see her faults and trying to correct them. Now they're looking for someone to blame for her getting herself murdered," Carol grumbled under her breath.

"Is what Pauline said true?" Ken demanded, ignoring the Carters and concentrating on Adam. "Did Angel see someone leaving my house?"

"Maybe," Adam replied.

Ken turned to Susan. "My mother has always thought you were infatuated with me. I never believed it. But after yesterday and then this..."

Adam's gaze narrowed on him. "What happened yesterday?"

"She threw a jealous fit." It was Ruth who spoke. "I'm sure it was about me coming back into Ken's life."

"It was not a jealous fit. And, it was most certainly not about you," Susan returned curtly.

"I really don't think we should be carrying on like

this,'' Claire interjected before any more could be said. She reached over and took Susan's hand. ''I've known Susan all her life. I'm sure she's not capable of cold-blooded murder.''

''No, of course she's not,'' Carol echoed, but Susan heard the hint of uncertainty in the woman's voice.

''I'll want to speak to each of you again, individually.'' Adam's manner was coolly official as he took control. ''I'll start with Miss Hallston. The rest of you go home and wait for me there.''

The accusation on Ken's face had grown stronger. In Ruth's eyes Susan saw a glitter of satisfaction…a possible competitor for Ken was gone.

Tossing Susan a bitter, hostile glance, Ken took his mother by the arm. ''Come along,'' he ordered curtly.

''I'm sure this is all a mistake,'' Claire declared, allowing him to lead her away, but in spite of her earlier show of support, her voice lacked conviction.

Carol muttered something about this business being very unsettling and gave Susan a very weak smile of support as she turned to head toward her house.

Apparently, although I had a difficult time putting Carol in the murderer's shoes, she had no trouble putting me in them, Susan noted. Unless of course, Carol was the murderer. Then her initial show of support followed by it fading rapidly was a tremendously good ploy.

Shaken by how quickly those she'd considered friends had lost faith in her, she turned to Adam Riley. How many times did she have to be betrayed before she learned never to trust a man? ''You told me you thought I was innocent,'' she growled through clenched teeth. ''Every one of my neighbors thinks I'm a murderer and you did nothing to defend me!''

''We should talk inside.'' It was an order.

''You're the proverbial wolf in sheep's clothing. I've got nothing to say to you,'' she snapped. The realization of just how stupid she'd been suddenly struck her. ''You set me up. You wanted to see how strong a case you could build against me while I waited trustingly on the sidelines thinking you were on my side."

Considering her history, Adam couldn't blame her for what she was thinking. In stern tones, loud enough to be heard distinctly by anyone listening, he said, "This is a police investigation, Miss Hallston. You will talk to me in your own home or down at the station. You choose."

"There is nothing to talk about. I've told you everything I know."

Adam lowered his voice to barely above a whisper. "Stop being so difficult and invite me in. Right now, it's my guess that at least half a dozen ears are listening to us." In normal tones, he said, "I'd like to hear more about the argument you had with Mr. Kinter yesterday."

Susan tossed him a disgruntled glance, letting him know she wasn't ready to trust him again. But his mention of prying eyes had reminded her of how public they were and the desire to seek sanctuary won out. With a shrug of indifference, she preceded him into the house.

As soon as the door was closed behind them, she spun around to face him. "You probably set Pauline on me, didn't you?" Tears welled in her eyes. "I should have learned my lesson with Lyle. Men aren't to be trusted! You wanted to make certain that you could turn all of my neighbors against me so that I wouldn't have anyone to support me before you made your arrest. Well, I hope you rot in hell because I'm innocent."

"I know you are." Adam wanted to take her in his arms but he was afraid someone might see through the window.

Susan stood mutely for a moment, studying him. The warmth had returned to his eyes. "You do?" she asked shakily, still uncertain if she should believe him.

"Yes, I do." His voice held no compromise. "The problem is, as you well know, proving it."

Susan sank into one the chairs at the kitchen table.

"The good news is that the DA can't prove you did it,

either. All he can do is build a circumstantial case around opportunity and motive.''

''I had no motive!''

''Every one of your neighbors will testify that you did. However, there's no solid evidence against you. A good lawyer should be able to get you off.''

''Then, in addition to half or maybe the whole town thinking I killed my husband and got away with it, they'll think I killed Linda and Angel as well and beat out the law again.''

''If I could pinpoint who started the rumors about you and Kinter, I'd have a suspect but I can't. Everyone claims they've always heard it.''

Susan nodded. ''When we were kids, Claire was always talking about how I idolized Ken and how Ken thought I was so sweet. Our 'romance' was just one of those ideas that got planted in people's minds and never went away no matter how much either of us denied it. Claire, Carol, Pauline and Barbara all came over here to see if I was all right after Ken announced his engagement to Linda. Every one of them was worried that I'd be upset.''

''And, on the stand, at least a couple of them will claim that you were. Pauline told me that both she and Barbara Reynolds were convinced that you were hiding your true feelings.''

Susan felt her throat constricting. ''With friends like I've got, who needs enemies?''

''The way I see it, you've got two choices,'' Adam said grimly.

''From the sound of your voice, I'd say one was bad and the other was worse.''

''I don't like either one,'' Adam confessed, ''but we're caught between a rock and a hard place.''

Susan breathed a resigned sigh. ''So, what are they?''

''You can do nothing. In which case, Byrne is going to have me arrest you and you'll be tried on circumstantial

:vidence. Most likely you'll be acquitted, but that's never
a guarantee.''

"And even if I am, I'll still be guilty in the eyes of a
ot of the people in this town," she reiterated.

Adam nodded.

"So, what's my other option?"

Adam hesitated. "It's dangerous."

"What is it?" she demanded.

"We can try to set you up as a decoy...make it seem
worth the murderer's while to knock you off before you
:an be arrested. My guess is the killer will try to make it
ook like a suicide."

Susan held up her hands like trays on a balance scale.
Looking to one she said, "In other words, I can live out
he rest of my life with people thinking I'm a triple murderess..." she looked to the other "...or I can possibly
get myself killed trying to prove I'm innocent." She low-
:red the second hand, indicating increased weight on that
side of her "scale," thereby designating it the winner. "I'd
rather take my chances trying to catch the killer than spend
the rest of my life under a cloud."

"I'll be here to protect you," Adam vowed. From his
pocket, he extracted a small case. Inside was a tiny micro-
phone. "This is a bug. I'm going to put one in here and
one in the living room. Make sure that any guests you have
stay in either of those two rooms."

Susan followed him into the living room. "So, what do
I do?"

Finishing planting the bugs, Adam took her by the arm
and guided her into the hall and to a corner where no
prying eyes could see them. There he drew her into his
arms. "You follow my instructions to the letter. You sit
on your front porch in clear view until I finish talking to
your neighbors. When that's done, I'll get in my car and
drive away. Once I'm out of view, I'll park and call. When
I've determined that the bugs are both working properly,
then you wait. And, you stay in the living room or the

kitchen. If you have to go to the bathroom, say so and I'll time you. I don't want you out of my earshot unless I know the reason. And trust no one but me. Understand?''

His nearness gave her courage. ''Understood,'' she said.

Unable to resist, he kissed her. Her lips tasted even better than he remembered and he drew her to him until their bodies were molded together.

Susan trembled as desire raged within her. Wishing she could hold on to this moment forever, she added her own strength to the kiss. When he lifted his head from hers, the fact that they might never have a chance to kiss again swept through her. ''Maybe we shouldn't pass up this opportunity,'' she said, her voice holding an invitation.

For a moment Adam's resolve to wait until the case was solved weakened, then his jaw firmed with purpose. ''You don't know how hard it is for me to refuse that look in your eyes, but right now, I've got to keep my mind focused on finding the real killer. I refuse to have our wedding in jail.''

She frowned up at him. ''Wedding?''

''I guess I forgot to mention that I plan to marry you when this is over.'' He smiled at the stunned expression on her face, then his smile vanished and his manner became stern. ''Do exactly as I've said. Don't embellish,'' he ordered, then kissed her again and left.

Susan watched the front door closing behind him. She'd been certain she would never want to marry again. Now suddenly she was seeing herself with Adam and the image brought her pleasure. ''But first we have to trap a murderer and I'm the bait,'' she reminded herself. A cold chill ran through her.

Adam's first stop after leaving Susan was at Ken Kinter's house. Claire, Ruth and Ken were all there waiting for him on the porch.

''I thought it would be best for all of us to talk here,'' Ken explained, opening the door to allow the women to

recede him inside. "My son is next door and I'd rather
e be kept out of this as much as possible."

"Yes, of course," Adam replied. Claire had led the way
*i*to the living room. She seated herself in a straight-back
*h*air. Ruth started to sit on the sofa where Linda's body
*h*ad been found, paled, then chose a chair near Claire. Ken
*f*rowned at where his dead wife had lain, then seated him-
*s*elf in a chair across from his mother and ex-wife.

Tight little family group, Adam thought. "You said you
*h*eard Miss Hallston throwing a jealous fit?" he addressed
*R*uth.

She shifted uneasily, glanced at Ken as if seeking di-
*r*ection, then abruptly returned her attention to the detec-
*ti*ve, clearly having reached a decision on her own. "I
*k*now Ken has always thought of Susan as a sister and
*w*ants to protect her but if Linda was murdered, then I
*th*ink the truth needs to be spoken. Yesterday when I went
to find him, I heard what sounded like ranting but I
*c*ouldn't make out the words. When I got near enough, I
*h*eard Ken accusing Susan of being jealous. She denied it,
*b*ut I wouldn't have bought that denial for a wooden
*n*ickel. If you ask me, she's always been in love with Ken.
*A*nd the only way she was ever going to have him was to
*g*et rid of Linda."

Claire reached up and patted Ruth's hand. "I really
*th*ink we shouldn't speculate further."

Ruth suddenly looked very uncomfortable. "I'm so
*s*orry," she apologized to both Ken and Claire. "But I've
*a*lways felt it was best to speak the truth."

"And I've always admired that about you," Ken replied
*w*ith a reassuring smile. His expression sobered as he
*t*urned to Adam. "I suppose you will want my version of
*th*e conversation between myself and Susan?"

"That would be useful," Adam replied, wondering if
*th*e man was going to confess that it had been about his
*a*ffair with Barbara Reynolds.

Ken's manner became acutely protective. "My mother

has told you everything she knows and Ruth wasn't even here during the time of either murder. I see no reason for them to remain. I'm also concerned about my son. When we heard the shouting, I told him to stay inside, but I want to make certain he didn't hear what was being said and get frightened. I'd appreciate it if you'd allow them to go check on him.''

Obviously he was planning to tell the truth, Adam concluded. Equally obvious was that he didn't want to mention the affair in front of the women. "You're right, there is no need for them to stay," Adam agreed. As Ruth helped Claire to her feet, he rose also. "But I do feel I should warn all of you, that when this case goes to trial it could get messy. So far, all I have is circumstantial evidence. The defense will seek out any dirt they can on the prosecution's witnesses to make their testimony questionable.''

Tears glistened in Claire's eyes. "Will this horror never end?" The tears spilled out. "First Angel is murdered and then you lead us to believe that Linda was, too.''

"Come along. You need to rest," Ruth soothed, guiding Claire out of the room.

"I suppose that warning was more for me than for them," Ken said when they were alone.

Adam merely shrugged.

"I never meant to cause Barbara any harm. And I did love my wife. My affair with Barbara took the place of a night of poker with the boys. It was just fun and games.''

"So Mrs. Reynolds explained.''

"But Linda wouldn't have seen it that way and that was what Susan claimed she was so was upset about. Yesterday, when we had the confrontation I thought that since Linda was dead, Susan felt it was up to her to voice disapproval." Anger glistened in his eyes. "But I was surprised by her vehemence. You'd have thought I'd been unfaithful to her." His gaze leveled on Adam. Behind the haunted look in his eyes, Adam could see a morbid hint

f ego. "Do you really think she killed Linda to free me
r herself?"

Adam had to fight to keep his temper in check. "What
o you think?"

"I've always thought of her as a sister. And I could
ave sworn she was fond of Linda, but who knows what
oes on in a woman's mind." Revenge flashed in his eyes.
'If she did kill Linda, I want to see her hanged for it!"

Adam's next stop was the Carters'. There he didn't ask
ny questions. He simply told them that the trial could get
nessy. He pointed out that the defense would try to prove
nat there were others who would want Angel dead.

The Reynolds were just arriving home from having gone
ut to dinner after church when Adam reached their house.
fter informing them that it appeared that Linda Kinter's
eath and Angel's might be linked, he questioned them.
He was not surprised when the interview led to Susan with
oth Barbara and Ted declaring that although they didn't
or one moment believe she could be a murderess, she did
ave opportunity and motive.

Again he emphasized that information that might be un-
omfortable to others would have to come out at the trial.
Ted looked unshaken but Barbara paled.

Leaving the house, Adam's uneasiness grew. If this plan
o flush out the killer didn't work, Susan could easily end
p living out the rest of her days behind bars. Whoever
ad set out to frame her had done an excellent job. Even
hough the case would be based entirely on circumstantial
vidence, with so much testimony against her…testimony
rom people who were supposed to be her friends…a jury
night convict.

His last stop was Carol Hawkins' house.

"I can't tell you anything other than what I've already

told you,'' she said as soon as they were seated in her living room. ''I don't want to believe Susan is capable of cold-blooded murder. I've known her since she was a baby. She took care of Hattie as good as anyone could wish.'' She eyed him hopefully. ''Maybe that marriage of hers caused some sort of delayed stress syndrome like the one soldiers go through.''

''So, you think she committed the murders?'' Adam asked.

''I don't know what to think anymore. Are you certain Linda's death wasn't just an accident? Susan did say Angel had been smoking pot. Maybe she simply hallucinated seeing someone.''

''I have evidence that causes me to believe Angel did see someone that night and I'm convinced that the someone she saw, killed Mrs. Kinter.''

Carol shifted uneasily. ''Are you subtly letting me know that you intend to arrest Susan for murder?''

''If I do, it will be on circumstantial evidence. I should warn you that the defense will be digging up whatever they can on the rest of you to discredit any testimony you give against her.''

''They won't find anything they can use against me,'' Carol assured him.

Adam thanked her for her time and left.

Chapter 14

Susan watched Ken loading suitcases into the trunk of his car. His son looked unhappy. Ken ruffled the boy's hair and said something that brought a smile to the child's face. Toward Ruth, Ken was more reserved but Susan could easily envision him marrying the woman to be near his son. Or, maybe, Adam was right about money being the motive behind Linda's death. The fact that Ken had been having an affair was proof to Susan that he hadn't loved Linda as much as people thought. And he had to know how Ruth felt about him. She wasn't good at hiding her feelings. It could be that Ken had been involved somehow in Linda's death because he had hopes of reconciling with Ruth to gain control of her money.

Her gaze shifted to Claire. She was leaning heavily on her cane and beaming lovingly at her grandson from her porch. "That woman can get around just fine when she wants to," Hattie used to declare with impatience. "She uses that arthritis of hers to gain sympathy and keep Ken and Linda at her beck and call."

Susan looked down at Claire's swollen ankles. Her grandmother had been being overly critical, she decided.

Noticing Ken glance over his shoulder in her direction, she saw the anger and accusation on his face and her shoulders straightened with righteous indignation.

Seeing the direction of his gaze, Ruth pulled on his arm and said something that caused him to quickly finish loading the car, get Ruth and Jason inside, then climb in himself and drive away.

Claire waved until they were out of sight, then with only a glance in Susan's direction, she went inside.

The trees were moving slightly in the light summer breeze. A couple of kids went by on their bikes. In the distance Susan heard laughter and the smell of someone barbecuing wafted up to her. It was a typical scene. One she'd witnessed since the earliest days of her childhood. *But might never see again if this plan doesn't work,* she mused and a shiver trailed through her.

She looked down at the portable phone beside her. There was one last thing she needed to do before Adam finished his rounds. Picking it up, she dialed her parents. Her mother answered.

"Is something wrong? You sound worried," Lenore Hallston asked.

"I'm just a little tired. Linda's death and Angel's murder have been a shock."

"Have you changed your mind about my coming for a short visit? I can be on a plane by tomorrow," Lenore offered consolingly.

"No." That was too sharp, Susan scolded herself. "I wouldn't have any time to visit right now. Teaching summer school is keeping me busy. Besides, I'll be up to visit you as soon as the session is over." Her voice threatened to falter and she tightened her chin.

"You sound worried. Are you sure everything is all right?" Lenore asked again, the concern in her voice growing.

"I just wanted to tell you that I love you," Susan said softly.

"I love you, too. And, I'm looking forward to your visit."

"Me, too." The thought that this might be the last time she and her parents would have this kind of innocent, gentle conversation occurred to her. "Is Dad around?"

"He's out fishing, finding the best spots so you'll be certain to catch something this year. He felt terrible about you not having even a single strike last year."

"Nothing in this life is guaranteed."

"That's a very philosophical remark." The worry returned to Lenore's voice. "I should have flown home for Linda Kinter's funeral. Even though I didn't really know her, she was a good friend of yours. I know her death has been very hard on you."

Susan considered telling her mother the truth. Her parents still thought that Linda had committed suicide and Angel had been killed by her boyfriend or a drug dealer. Maybe this was the time to be frankly honest with them. If she was arrested and they knew nothing, it would be a tremendous shock to them. But the words refused to form. She still held out hope that Adam's plan would work.

"And then to have Angel Carter murdered in her own backyard, that's enough to set anyone's nerves on edge," Lenore was saying. Her voice took on purpose. "I'm making reservations tonight. Even if we don't have much time to visit, I'm sure you could use some good home cooking. You probably aren't eating properly."

"No." Again Susan chided herself for sounding too sharp. "Please, don't come. You'd be wasting money and I'd feel guilty about not having time to visit. I promise, I'm eating properly. I just wanted to hear your voice. Tell me what you and Dad have been up to."

For a long moment there was silence from the other end, then came a resigned sigh. "You always were stubborn. All right, I won't come." Lenore's voice filled with regret. "But I wish I had insisted you move to Alaska with your father and me. By staying in Bandits' Gorge, you've had more than your fair share of sorrow and misery."

It was too late to change the course of her life now, Susan thought. "I wanted to stay here. You were going to tell me what you and Dad have been up to," she prompted again.

Fifteen minutes later she saw Adam climbing into his car and leaving. Making an excuse, she cut her conversation with her mother short and hung up. A couple of minutes later, Adam called. He had her stay on the line while she went inside and he made certain he could hear her through the bugs. Once satisfied, he again cautioned her to stay in the living room or kitchen, then rang off.

Choosing the living room, she crossed to the bookshelf and pulled out a novel she'd always wanted to read but never had the time. Immediately she shoved it back. She didn't want to read. She wanted to scream…one long primeval, frustrated, fear-filled scream. Instead, she settled for pacing the floor.

Outside, darkness fell. An hour passed. Having given up on the pacing, she was seated on her couch surfing through the channels on the television, not giving any one more than a few seconds of her time, when a knock sounded on her front door.

Her nerves taut with anticipation, she practically bolted to her feet. Forcing herself to behave with calm decorum, she answered it to find Claire there.

"I want to apologize for showing any doubt about your innocence this afternoon," the woman said. "I know how much you liked Linda. It's foolish for anyone to think you would have harmed her."

Silently, Susan groaned. Claire being there could ruin everything. "I'm really not in the mood for company."

Claire's gaze flickered to the single-layer cake she was holding. "But I baked your very favorite…gingerbread with a thick coating of vanilla butter cream icing. I'm sure

is isn't as good as Hattie's but I thought you might enjoy
iving some."

Susan stared down at the cake, then her gaze lowered
Claire's swollen ankles. *It couldn't be her,* her rational
ind insisted. Claire was just being her usual mothering
lf and she was going to interfere with the real killer
owing up. "That's very sweet of you, but..."

"But nothing." Claire hobbled past her and headed into
e kitchen. "I refuse to allow you to think that all of us
ive turned against you."

Bowing to the inevitable, Susan followed. "This is very
nd of you."

"You've always been a sweet child." Reaching the
tchen, Claire placed the cake on the table, then seated
erself.

"Would you like some coffee?" Susan heard herself
fering, as she got out plates and forks. It was automatic
oliteness. The last thing she wanted was to prolong this
sit.

"No. It's a bit late for me to be having so much caf-
ine." Claire again smiled motheringly. "I'll just have
ome water. You could have milk the way you did when
ou were a girl."

"I saw Ken leaving with Ruth and Jason," Susan said
s she poured the drinks, choosing to follow Claire's su-
estion and have milk.

"Ken is driving them to Atlanta to catch a plane home.
e'll spend the night there and be back tomorrow. He
ought it would be best to get them away from here before
1 arrest was made and the media descended upon us."

Susan nodded. "He was probably smart to do that."

"I'm truly, truly sorry about all the trouble you're hav-
g," Claire said as Susan seated herself at the table.

Susan frowned at her. "Everyone seems to think I'm in
ve with Ken. I really wish you hadn't kept insisting that
e were childhood sweethearts. We never were."

"If you say so, dear. It's just that I've always pictured

Ken as being irresistible to any woman." Claire was near
purring with motherly pride. "Linda doted on him. A
Ruth never stopped loving him."

The insinuation in Claire's voice that Ken could ho
any woman under a spell, grated on Susan's nerves. "Ru
did divorce him."

"But she never stopped loving him. That business abo
her hating to live cheaply was all a fabrication. She woul
have done anything for Ken. But they had their son
consider. Ken wanted the boy to have all the advantage
money could buy." Claire's expression became sage. '
don't care what people say about money not being able
buy happiness. It's my opinion that it's only those peopl
who have it that say that. It should be obvious to any fo
that it can buy advantages."

"Are you saying that Ken married Ruth for he
money?" Susan asked.

"No, of course, he didn't. He's too much like his fathe
He believes in love. He cared for her. They would hav
stayed together and given up all her wealth if it hadn
been for me. I talked sense into them. I pointed out tha
they could see each other secretly and one day when he
father was gone, they and their son would have everything
The old man was sick. Who would have thought he woul
have lasted ten years."

Susan was growing uneasy. "Or that Ken would me
Linda, fall in love with her and marry her."

Claire's expression became petulant. "Ken like
women. A little too much for his own good. I thought tha
affair he was having with Barbara Reynolds would pacif
him."

"You knew about Barbara?"

"I had to cover for them a couple of times." Clair
frowned. "Then he met Linda and just had to have her."

All Susan could do was to stare at the woman in fro
of her. "I suppose Ruth didn't take his marriage ver
well."

"No. But I pointed out to her that she would always ave an advantage because she had his son and he could ever have any more children."

"Never have any more children?"

"Ruth had a very dangerous pregnancy. The doctor said at if she ever became pregnant again, she might die. Ken as so frightened for her, he had a vasectomy even before eir son was born." Claire shrugged. "In the end, it rned out for the best. He couldn't get either Barbara or inda pregnant."

Susan fought to keep her manner calm.

Claire nodded toward the cake. "You must try it."

"Aren't you going to have some?" Susan asked.

"I have to watch my weight," Claire replied.

Susan stared down at the confectionery. "I'm really not ery hungry, myself."

Claire sighed. "You've guessed the truth, haven't ou?" Before Susan could respond, she produced a small ut deadly-looking gun. "I ordered it from one of those oldier-of-fortune magazines," she said with childish glee. "And I'm rather good with it."

Susan continued to stare at her in disbelief. "But you ouldn't have been the one Angel saw coming out of inda's house. She said whoever it was did a little jig."

Claire smiled like the cat who'd eaten the canary. "I an get around just fine. I have a little touch of arthritis ut it's not nearly as bad as it looks. The swelling and edness is from my ointment. When I need to seem more rippled, I just rub it in. People are so much more considrate of fragile old ladies."

"It's all an act? You had Linda waiting on you hand nd foot for no real reason?"

"It's always nice to have someone else doing the work. Oh, and speaking of doing things for me, I have a little ote I'd like you to write." Claire motioned toward he notepad by the phone. "That should do nicely."

I hope Adam is hearing this loud and clear, Sus
thought as she pulled the notepad in front of her.

"Write, 'Dear Ken, I'm so sorry for everything. I love
you too much, Susan,'" Claire instructed. "And don
misspell anything or try to get cute."

Scribbling the note as instructed, Susan forced herse
to think. Claire had come very close to admitting she'
done in Linda but she hadn't actually said the words. An
she hadn't mentioned Angel. They needed her confessic
to both murders.

Claire smiled with satisfaction at the note. "Now pu
that aside and, really, you must try a bite of cake. I worke
hard on recreating Hattie's recipe."

Susan started to rise.

"Sit," Claire ordered.

"I need a knife to cut it," Susan insisted.

"No, dear." Claire's voice held a deadly warning. "N
reason for you to cut it. Remember, this is your last ac
You're despondent. You simply took a fork and bega
eating."

Susan settled back into her chair. "I suppose it has som
drug in it," she said. "Did you get it from Zelda like th
stuff you used on Linda?"

Claire's smile broadened. "Actually, the cake doesn
have anything in it. And what I'm going to use on yo
didn't come from Zelda. It's Hattie's digitalis." Claire pro
duced the prescription bottle, also in a plastic bag, and se
it on the table.

"You told me Dr. Miller had taken it away to dispos
of it," Susan muttered.

"I lied. Now, open the bottle and pour it into your mill
Then like a good girl, you're going to drink the entir
glass, fall asleep and never wake up. When they find yo
and this prescription bottle, it will be assumed you squir
reled it away for some reason, remembered it, and decide
to end it all."

With Claire watching, Susan opened the bottle and oured the contents into the milk.

Claire's expression became apologetic. "I do hope you elieve me when I say I am sorry about this. It's all An- el's fault. If she hadn't tried to blackmail me, I never ould have had to kill her and frame you." She sighed gain. "And I really did hate having to do away with inda. She was good to me. But she had to go. Ken was uch too smitten with her. He'd never have divorced her o marry Ruth. Now I'm sure the two of them will wed gain, if for no other reason than for their son's sake."

"I thought you didn't know about Ruth's father dying ntil after Linda's death," Susan said trying to make cer- in they got all the pieces of the puzzle together.

"I said Ken didn't tell me about the death until after inda was gone. Ruth and I have always kept in close ontact behind his back. It was our little secret. Now, rink!"

Susan lifted the glass toward her mouth, but stopped ith it hovering near her lips. "Why me?"

"You were the perfect scapegoat. You live alone, so ou had no alibi for the murders and it was easy to res- rrect that rumor about you and Ken. The stronger it grew, ie more it looked as if you had a motive. Drink."

"Was the drug you gave Linda in the fudge or the vine?" Susan persisted.

"The fudge, now drink."

"Carol's mentioning Ken's former marriage at a time vhen he was gone, was very convenient."

"Not convenient. It was well planned by me. I men- ioned it to her several times during the week preceding he fishing trip. And once Carol gets something on her nind, it generally comes out. If the conversation hadn't noved along as it had, I would have found some way to ause Carol to spill the beans."

Susan felt nauseous. The woman was actually bragging bout staging Linda's death. "Have you no conscience?"

Claire gave her a petulant look. "A mother has to d
what's best for her son. That's why you have to die befor
there can be a trial. We can't have Ken's affair with Bar
bara smeared all over the papers. Besides, you owe Ken
If it wasn't for him, you would have died a long time ag
at the hands of that husband of yours."

"Ken killed Lyle?"

"He didn't mean to. Lyle attacked him. It was self
defense. Ken called me. He was nearly hysterical.
brought a change of clothes for him, then left before he
called the police."

"All this time, you've let people think I killed Lyle."

"I'll admit I've hinted around at it through the years.
certainly didn't want anyone suddenly realizing that Ken
could have done it."

"You're very good at covering murders," Susan said
sarcastically.

"It just takes planning and never passing up an oppor
tunity." Claire nodded toward the cake. "You see, I even
kept the plate you brought to the last picnic, just in case
it should come in handy. This way, it looks as if you baked
the cake to have with your milk for one last nostalgic
moment." Claire motioned toward the cake with the gun
"Go ahead, try a bite or two. It's really rather good."

"I don't think so," Susan replied, not willing to trust
the woman not to have added a little something to the cake
as well.

"Suit yourself. People will simply think you made it
and then were too upset to eat it. In fact, leaving it uneaten
will make your suicide look even more realistic. It'll be
added proof of your despondency."

Susan frowned. "You won't get away with this."

"Of course, I will. Once you're gone, everyone will
breathe a relieved sigh to have this horrible business
ended. They won't look past the obvious. They'll want to
put it behind them as quickly as possible. Of course, both
Ken and I will be devastated. We both loved and trusted

ou. He will need to get away and what better place than Ruth's estate? As for me, he'll be concerned about my health and insist I join him. It will be lovely to have servants at my beck and call.''

''Detective Riley will catch you.''

''Don't be silly. He already thinks you're guilty. He'll happily believe that you took the easy way out.''

''You're insane.''

Claire scowled. ''No. I simply refuse to let other people interfere with the way I want my life to go. Ward, my dear hardheaded, departed husband, learned that the hard way.''

A chill ran along Susan's spine. ''What do you mean by that?''

''I kept telling him I didn't like dogs but he insisted on buying that puppy for Ken. Luckily, I'd planted that castor bean plant. It was easy to poison the stupid little thing. He'd eat anything. Anyway, Ward was determined to buy another puppy. Besides, he was getting on my nerves. I thought being a widow would be a nice change and I was right.''

''He didn't just hit his head on the side of the boat?'' Susan asked, already knowing the answer, but needing to hear it.

''I bopped him with an oar. It stunned him just enough, so that I could hold him under until he drowned.''

Susan was recalling what Hattie had told her about Claire's past. The woman's childhood had been very unhappy until her mother had passed away. Then it had improved greatly. ''Your mother died in a house fire.''

''You have your grandmother's memory.'' Claire nodded thoughtfully. ''My mother. Now there was a nasty bit of work. She never had a good word to say about anyone. She drove my father away from us. I wanted to go live with him but she wouldn't let me. One night after she'd taken a sleeping pill, I lit one of her cigarettes and laid it on her bed. I thought it'd never catch but finally the flames started. For a minute, I got scared then I looked at her.

She was lying there so peacefully. I knew then I was doing
the right thing. I breathed in enough smoke to make myself
sick so no one would suspect, then I ran for the phone and
called the fire department. Of course, no one would ever
have suspected a nine-year-old girl anyway.''

"No, they wouldn't," Susan agreed.

Claire's manner became self-righteous. "And I've never
killed unnecessarily. When Ken came home from college
and, instead of being satisfied with living with me, decided
he should have a place of his own, I simply scared old
Elsa Jamison off so he could have the house next door.''

"You put that rattlesnake on her back porch?"

"I did everyone a favor, including her. She was getting
too old to live alone and her sister wanted her to come
down to Florida and live with her. She spent her last years
down there just as happy as a cat in a field of catnip.''

"She could have died of a heart attack. Snakes were the
one thing she dreaded. Or the snake could have bitten her.
At her age and in her feeble condition, she would never
have survived.''

Claire shrugged. "Life is full of chances.''

"But you've been stacking the deck in your favor.
That's not playing fair.''

"Playing fair doesn't guarantee a win and I like to
win.'' Claire frowned impatiently. "Now, drink your
milk.''

"I think we've heard enough. Got it on tape, too,''
Adam said, striding into the room, his gun drawn.

"What?'' Claire let out a shriek of angry surprise.

Adam twisted her weapon from her hand before she
could react. In the next instant Claire was on her feet,
fighting him. If there was any doubt in either of their minds
about Claire being strong enough to strangle Angel, it vanished during the ensuing couple of minutes. Getting her
subdued and handcuffed took both of them. As Susan
placed a couple of calls, one to the chief to let him know
they had the killer and one to the station house for a squad

ar to pick up Claire, in the background she heard Adam
eciting Claire's rights to her while Claire spewed out a
tring of expletives that would have made a sailor blush.

"So, what happens now?" Susan asked Adam. She'd
ccompanied him to the police station and given her statement to the chief on tape while Claire was being booked.

"I'll write up my report tomorrow. It's time to call it a
day." Glancing at his watch, he corrected himself. "Or
ather a night. It's after one." Rising, he helped her to her
eet and, slipping an arm around her waist, guided her
utside and to his car.

"Do you think Claire will actually go to trial?" she
sked as they pulled out of the parking lot.

"Most likely not. A smart lawyer will plead her guilty
y reason of insanity and she'll be institutionalized for the
est of her life."

"What about Ken and Lyle?"

"There's no evidence to take him to trial. Claire's tes-
imony would, most likely, be declared hearsay by an in-
ompetent witness and thrown out. Besides, she said it was
elf-defense and I believe her."

"I do, too. I remember how shaken up he looked for
he next few weeks. I thought it was just because he wasn't
sed to seeing dead bodies."

They were at a stop sign. Tracing the line of her jaw
vith a sensuous caress, Adam said, "I am very tired of
murder and mayhem. I need a distraction. As I recall, I
aave a rain check due me."

A fire began to smolder within her. "Yes, you do."

Adam smiled and continued toward her place.

Susan told herself that she was ready for intimacy. Her
oody certainly was. But as she started to unlock her door,
aer hands were shaking so badly, she couldn't fit the key
nto the slot.

"Maybe tonight isn't such a good time," Adam said,
aking the key from her. "You've been through a lot. You

must be tired.'' More than he'd ever wanted anything in
his life, he wanted to stay with her, but considering her
past, he knew he shouldn't rush her.

''You're probably right,'' she conceded, as he opened
the door.

He kissed her lightly. ''I'll see you tomorrow.''

But as he started to walk away, an acute sense of emp-
tiness filled her. She caught his arm. ''Please, don't leave.
I don't want to be alone.'' She flushed self-consciously
then added, ''But I'm not ready for that rain check, either.''

Again slipping a protective arm around her waist, Adam
accompanied her inside. ''I won't make any demands on
you,'' he promised, more an order to himself than an as-
surance to her. ''I'll just provide a shoulder for you to lie
on.''

She smiled up at him gratefully as they continued to the
bedroom. ''I really appreciate you being so understanding.''

''I'm a very understanding guy,'' he returned, kicking
off his shoes and lying down on top of the bedspread.

Kicking off her shoes, she curled up beside him, resting
her head on his chest. ''This is so nice,'' she said, snug-
gling deeper into the crook of his arm.

What it was, was hard on his control. But, she needed
him and he liked that. He liked it a lot.

Susan had been worried that she would never feel truly
safe in a man's arms again. But lying there with Adam,
her taut nerves actually began to relax and the embers of
desire once again glowed. ''I've never had a pleasant intimate experience,'' she said.

''When the time comes, I'll do my best to prove to you
it can be very enjoyable,'' he vowed huskily.

As nervous as she was, her body seemed to be insisting
that now was the time. She straightened to allow a fuller
contact of their lengths and the heat within her increased.
''I'm not so tired as I am tense.''

Adam heard the hint of invitation in her voice. If he went slowly…didn't push her beyond where she was willing to go, a little foreplay couldn't hurt. *Just don't lose control*, he ordered himself. Shifting more onto his side, he trailed kisses from the hollow behind her ear down her neck.

"That has the most curious effect," she murmured, her voice near a purr. "It's both soothing and stimulating at the same time."

He wouldn't have used the word *soothing*, but she was right about it being stimulating, Adam thought. "I'm glad you like it," he said against her skin, continuing to explore her neck with his mouth while beginning to massage her back with slow but firm circular movements.

Her blood flowed hot and her body felt as if it wanted to melt beneath his touch. "You've obviously got the hands of a masseur."

Adam lifted her leg up over his, bringing her into more intimate contact. *Big mistake!* Fire raged through him. He eased her leg off, then began to work his way free. "Maybe this isn't such a good idea. I'm not so sure I have the control to stop if you ask. I'd better spend the night in your guest room."

A part of her continued to be afraid and argued that his suggestion might be for the best. But a stronger part hated the chill his desertion had left behind. It was as if she'd been in a secure, enjoyable place and was suddenly cast out into the cold. She wanted to return to that secure, enjoyable warmth. Again she caught his arm. "The only way I'm going to get past my fear of never enjoying intimacy is to try it again and see what happens."

Adam stopped his retreat. "You know our policeman's motto. We're here to serve," he said, again drawing her into his arms.

Fire raged through her. "I am definitely in need of your services."

Moving slowly, with caressing tenderness, he began to undress her.

Sensations...pleasureful, exciting sensations...coursed through her. "I never knew a man could make a woman feel the way you make me feel," she confessed.

"I've never known a woman who made me feel the way you make me feel," he returned, fighting to slow an arousal that was getting close to out of control.

"I'm glad." She was aware now only of his touch. It was as if they were in a universe all their own...a universe of pure enjoyment.

He kissed her stomach as he eased her shorts off and she giggled lightly as currents of delight flowed through her. Slipping off her panties, he nibbled her toes and she giggled again. "My turn," she said, feeling guilty because he was doing all the work.

Easing into a sitting position, she helped him out of his shirt, then out of the rest of his clothes. His hardened masculinity caused a curl of fear to dampen the fire within her.

Seeing the sudden anxiety on her face, he lifted her chin so that her gaze was held in his. "If I do anything that hurts you, you tell me and I'll stop." That promise would be hell to keep but he meant it.

She nodded, then his lips found hers and she let the soothing warmth of their touch fill her senses.

With tantalizing caresses, he stoked her passion until her body ached for his. Only then did he claim her.

For one brief moment, she was startled by the invasion, then as he began to move slowly in the age-old rhythm of bonding, pleasure washed through her, cleansing away any lingering fear. Lost in a paradise of exotic sensations, she added her own energies to the union until they were both lost in a world of enchantment and delight.

Susan woke nestled in the crook of Adam's arm. Outside, the sun was up. Stretching lazily, she lengthened her body along the line of his, rekindling the fire that still smoldered deep within.

His eyes still closed, Adam ran his hand along the curves of her upper torso and over her hip. "You do feel good in the morning," he said.

"You, too," she murmured against his shoulder, kissing it lightly. Then catching a glimpse of the clock, she let out a gasp. "I've got to get going. I've got a class to teach."

His arm tightened around her, refusing her her freedom. "Not until you agree to save my reputation by marrying me as soon as possible."

She frowned in confusion. "Save your reputation?"

"My car is parked outside your house and it's been there all night. It's my guess the neighbors are talking about us over their morning coffee."

She grinned back. "At least we gave them something other than murder and mayhem to discuss."

"Well? So, how about setting a date?" he asked, her answer meaning more to him than he'd ever thought possible.

She found herself wanting to be with him every moment, awake or asleep. "I suppose I'll have time to get a license this afternoon."

He kissed the tip of her nose. "I'll pick you up as soon as your class ends." Releasing her, he added, "You can take the first shower."

She considered inviting him to join her but knew she'd definitely be late if she did.

A little while later she was in the kitchen starting the coffee, when a knock sounded on her back door. It was Carol.

"Adam Riley's car has been parked in front of your house since I went out for my morning walk," she said. "What's going on?"

"He'd better be here with a search warrant, looking for evidence to use to arrest her," Pauline said, striding in behind Carol. Her gaze leveled hostilely on Susan. "I know you killed Angel. You're the only one with motive and the opportunity.''

"I told you to let the police do their work," Ray said, coming in behind his wife.

Adam and she had been wrong about what they thought the neighbors would be talking about over their morning coffee, Susan thought dryly. Murder and mayhem had continued to remain on their minds.

"What's going on in here?" Adam demanded entering at that moment.

"The lynching party has arrived." Susan's gaze traveled over the people she had once considered friends.

"That's a little harsh," Carol said.

Susan noted that although Carol looked uncomfortable with this description, she didn't declare any belief in her innocence. Susan also noted that neither Pauline nor Ray protested her description.

Adam scowled at the trio. "Claire killed Angel and Linda. And, she tried to kill Susan last night. She wanted her son free so that he could marry his wealthy ex-wife.''

For a long moment, they stared at Adam in stunned silence. It was Carol who finally spoke. "Her arthritis... She couldn't have done it.''

"She put her special ointment on her joints to make them look worse than they were," Susan said.

"Did Ken know?" Pauline demanded.

Susan pointed toward the door. "No. Now take your noose and go home.''

"I never really believed you did it," Carol spoke up her expression continuing to remain stunned as if she were still trying to absorb this turn of events. "But Claire...sweet, overly mothering Claire. It just doesn' seem possible.''

"If Claire has been arrested, what's Detective Riley doing here?" Pauline demanded, disbelief still lingering on her face.

"I'm here because I'm going to marry Susan." Adam

placed a protective arm around her shoulders. "Now go home and be grateful that an innocent woman wasn't railroaded by *friends* like you into the gas chamber for something she didn't do."

Susan smiled up at him. "My hero."

Guilt replaced the accusation on Pauline's face. "I'm so sorry. It was just that there didn't seem to be any other logical suspect."

"We're both sorry," Ray said, looking decidedly uncomfortable.

Concern suddenly spread over Pauline's face and she peered more closely at Susan. "Detective Riley said Claire tried to kill you. Are you all right? Did she hurt you?"

Susan couldn't deny that the woman's concern was genuine and her anger subsided some. Pauline had, after all, lost a daughter she adored. "No. She didn't hurt me. Adam was here to protect me."

"We should be on our way." Ray took hold of an arm each of his wife and Carol and began pulling them out the door. "We're real sorry about everything, Susan," he repeated.

"Yes." Pauline nodded, to give emphasis to the word.

"Guess it's time for me to go hide out for a while again," Carol muttered.

"I don't think I'll invite any of them to the wedding," Susan said when she and Adam were alone. "Eventually, I'll forgive them. Claire had devised a very good frame, planting ideas in everyone's head for quite a while. But for now, as my grandmother used to say, I think I'll walk my own path."

"As long as I can walk with you," Adam stipulated. He looked hard into her face. "I love you, Susan Hallston."

She traced the line of his jaw with her fingers. "I love you, too. From the first, there was a physical attraction but you've made it grow into so much more. You had faith in me when those I considered friends turned against me. And last night, you gave me back the dignity that Lyle had robbed me of and made me feel like a whole woman.' Her stomach growled. "A hungry whole woman."

Laughing, he drew her into his arms and kissed her soundly.

* * * * *

Take 2 bestselling love stories FREE

Plus get a FREE surprise gift!

Available October 1998
from Silhouette Books...

World's Most Eligible Bachelors

DETECTIVE DAD
by Marie Ferrarella

The World's Most Eligible Bachelor: Undercover agent Duncan MacNeill, a wealthy heir with a taut body...and an even harder heart.

Duncan MacNeill just got the toughest assignment of his life: deliver a beautiful stranger's baby in the back seat of her car! This tight-lipped loner never intended to share his name with anyone—especially a mystery woman who claimed to have a total memory loss. But how long could he hope to resist succumbing to the lure of daddyhood—and marriage?

Each month, Silhouette Books brings you a brand-new story about an absolutely irresistible bachelor. Find out how the sexiest, most sought-after men are finally caught.

Available at your favorite retail outlet.

Silhouette®

Look us up on-line at: http://www.romance.net   PSWMEB2

▼INTIMATE MOMENTS®
™ Silhouette®

COMING NEXT MONTH

#883 BRIDES OF THE NIGHT *Two outstanding stories in one irresistible volume

"TWILIGHT VOWS"—Maggie Shayne

Wings in the Night

Donovan O'Roark would do anything to keep another Sullivan woman from betraying the vampires of Dunkinny Castle. But when Rachel Sullivan filled the void in Donovan's soul, would he grant the beguiling virgin's request for eternal life—and love?

"MARRIED BY DAWN"—Marilyn Tracy

Vampire Gavin Deveroux *had* intended to eliminate vengeful Tara Michaels to safeguard his people. Then Gavin and Tara found themselves racing against time to be married by dawn. Were they destined to discover the greatest love of all?

#884 HARVARD'S EDUCATION—Suzanne Brockmann

Tall, Dark and Dangerous

Navy SEAL Harvard Becker was aghast when he was forced to work alongside alluring *female* agent PJ Rogers. To Harvard's amazement, his no-nonsense partner taught him a thing or two—on and off the field. Could it be that Harvard had finally met his match?

#885 HER COUNTERFEIT HUSBAND—Carla Cassidy

Mustang, Montana

Even before her heartless husband disappeared, Elena Richards knew their marriage was over. But now a decidedly different "Travis" was back—with amnesia!—and Elena was carrying his child. Could this marriage be saved?

#886 FOR THE CHILDREN—Margaret Watson

Cameron, Utah

FBI agent Damien Kane had pledged to protect Abby Markham and her twin nieces. But could he risk heartbreak again? Even if it meant offering the woman he loved a family of her very own?

#887 HIDING OUT AT THE CIRCLE C—Jill Shalvis

Way Out West

Frightened for her life, Haley Whitfield sought refuge on Cameron Reeves's ranch. Despite her tight-lipped secrecy, the laid-back, warmhearted cowboy offered her solace in his tender embrace. Could Cam convince Haley to trust him with her uncertain future?

#888 MOTIVE, MEANS...AND MARRIAGE?—Hilary Byrnes

Women To Watch

When Helen Stewart was assigned to prosecute her former lover for murder, she vowed not to succumb to her smouldering attraction for the sexy Irish cop. Yet when Patrick Monaghan swore his innocence, Helen knew she couldn't turn her back on the man she still desperately wanted.